P9-DEY-274

wallflower
in bloom

CLAIRE COOK

A TOUCHSTONE BOOK
Published by Simon & Schuster
New York   London   Toronto   Sydney   New Delhi

★ Touchstone
A Division of Simon & Schuster, Inc.
1230 Avenue of the Americas
New York, NY 10020

First Touchstone hardcover edition June 2012

TOUCHSTONE and colophon are registered trademarks of Simon & Schuster, Inc.

For information about special discounts for bulk purchases, please contact Simon & Schuster Special Sales at 1-866-506-1949 or business@simonandschuster.com.

The Simon & Schuster Speakers Bureau can bring authors to your live event. For more information or to book an event contact the Simon & Schuster Speakers Bureau at 1-866-248-3049 or visit our website at www.simonspeakers.com.

Designed by Renata Di Biase

Manufactured in the United States of America

10 9 8 7 6 5 4 3 2 1

Library of Congress Cataloging-in-Publication Data

Cook, Claire, 1955–
   Wallflower in bloom: a novel / Claire Cook.
      p. cm.
   "A Touchstone Book."
1. Self-realization in women—Fiction. 2. Reality television programs—Fiction.
I. Title.
   PS3553.O55317W35 2012
   813'.54—dc23   2011044716

ISBN 978-1-4516-7276-3
ISBN 978-1-4516-7278-7 (ebook)

For late bloomers everywhere.

wallflower
in bloom

Who will buy the cow if you give away the milk for free, yet once you get a taste of the milk, who can resist coming back to the cow?

My brother was dazzling, as usual. "Do. You. Have. Passion?" he roared. His white teeth gleamed. His elegant hands beckoned. His bedroom eyes twinkled. The sold-out mostly female audience drooled.

My brother's eyes were a big part of his It Thing. You couldn't look away. They were blue. Endless blue. Deep, glittery blue, like the ocean when the setting sun hits it just the right way.

Of course, luck of the gene pool and all that, my own eyes were wallflower brown.

I watched my famous brother scan the room, somehow appearing to make contact with each and every set of seeking eyes in the audience. "The Ancient Greeks asked only one question at a person's funeral: *Did. He. Or she. Have. Passion?*"

When he lifted his palms to the heavens, his crisp white tunic exposed just the right amount of muscular forearm. "Find yours. See it clearly in your mind's eye. Design the life your passion desires. And remember, passion doesn't sleep. It is always there, waiting for you."

Everywhere I looked, people were scribbling in notebooks. Some of them were surreptitiously videotaping with cell phones and tiny flip cameras, even though they weren't supposed to. The whole point was to get them to buy the videos. But the world was changing at lightning speed, and now we were even posting our own video clips on YouTube and Facebook in the hopes they'd go viral. I mean, on one hand, who will buy the cow if you give away the milk for free, yet once you get a taste of the milk, who can resist coming back to the cow?

Ohmigod, I was starting to sound like my freakin' brother.

He was really getting into it now. "The voice of passion. Is. Not. A book. It's not a feature film. It's short and direct, like a haiku straight to your heart."

You could hear a cliché drop. Some people were nodding, but most were leaning forward in their seats, waiting for The Answer.

"But if you start from a place of self-criticism, of self-rejection, you'll never hear what it's saying to you. Accept yourself. Start where you are. And the voice of passion will speak to you. It will come like a bolt of lightning. And you'll know. Your. Life's. True. Purpose."

When I stood up and dimmed the fluorescent lights from the back of the room, preselected audience members rose to light candles circling the front lip of the stage.

My brother reached behind the curtains at the back of the stage and pulled out a battered acoustic guitar. He plugged it into the amplifier, straddled a high wooden stool, crossed one distressed jean–clad leg over the other.

And then he actually sang "O-o-h Child," that old '70s song by the Five Stairsteps, the one about how things are going to get easier. And brighter.

Mine were the only dry eyes in the house.

"Hold the fort," my father had said before he and my mother left me to babysit the concession table while they took their usual place in the front row. My parents stood up now, flicked on matching Bic lighters, and waved their arms high while they rocked side to side in time to the music. From the back, in their tie-dyed T-shirts that proclaimed TAG! in fluorescent green, they could have been twins, except that my father's gray curls dead-ended just over his ears, while my mother's continued up to the top of her head.

My brother getting famous was the best thing that had ever happened to them. They'd been recreational Deadheads since the '60s, and once my sisters and brother and I were born, they just threw us into the car whenever there was an outdoor Grateful Dead concert anywhere within striking distance. I grew up thinking summer vacation meant standing in a field somewhere, jumping up and down to "Sugar Magnolia."

My parents took it hard when Jerry Garcia died. They'd been counting on becoming full-time Deadheads in their retirement. For a few years they followed tribute bands like Dark Star Orchestra half-heartedly, then they took up bowling. No one was happier than they were when my brother became the family rock star a few years ago.

Like everything else in his life, the whole guru thing had pretty much landed in my brother's lap. One minute he was just another guy playing his guitar, with a gift for inspirational gab between sets. Then a fan put a snippet of one of his over-the-top motivational orations up on YouTube, and a week later a producer from *The Ellen DeGeneres Show* was on the phone booking him. And of course, my brother being my brother, he was a big hit. And the rest is history.

I yawned and stretched and got ready for the onslaught. Once my brother did his thing, his followers would buy anything that wasn't nailed down. My parents handled this end of things, both online and at events like this one, and earned a retirement-friendly commission on every item sold. I straightened a pile of T-shirts packaged in little boxes shaped like guitars. I moved the CDs and DVDs a little closer to the books because they were blocking the energy beads.

A short group meditation was followed by deafening, mountain-moving applause. My parents hurried back and slid next to me behind the table.

My mother adjusted the No. 2 pencil behind her ear and gave me a quick kiss on the cheek. "I think that was his best job ever," she said, like she did every time.

"That's my boy," my father said. He alternated this with "way to go."

"How'd I do on the lights?" I asked.

My father laughed. "What a card," he said, as he swung his arm over my shoulder. I noticed we were almost the same height now. Either he was shrinking, or I was having a vertical growth spurt to match my horizontal one.

I kissed my father on the cheek and ducked out from under his arm. I had to make my way up to the front fast so I could herd my brother to the signing table before his rabid fans waylaid him.

"Single file," my mother was saying to the people already approaching the table as I walked away, "and no pushing. We'll start when you're ready." There was no mistaking my mother's former profession. She still had that fifth-grade teacher's vibe going on, and everybody always obeyed her and funneled right into a single line. Two security guys from the hotel crossed their arms over their chests for reinforcement.

I entertained myself by turning sideways and chasséing through the crowd, homing in on Tag by the booming, melodious sound of his laugh. "Excuse me," I said when someone wouldn't get out of my way, and when that didn't work, I used a discreet elbow.

"Unbelievable," I heard my brother say. "What a blast from the past! What are you doing in Austin?"

I worked my way up to him, fully expecting to see some woman he'd once slept with and whose name he was frantically trying to remember. I knew the drill. I'd stick out my hand and introduce myself so she'd have to tell me her name. And then my brother would pretend he'd known it all along.

"Dee," my brother said, turning to me. "You'll never guess who showed up. Steve Moretti. I went to UMass with him."

I swallowed back another yawn. The more famous my brother became, the more old friends came out of the woodwork.

"Steve," my brother said, "this is my sister Deirdre."

And then the Austin crowd parted to reveal the guy who'd last seen my underpants.

2

*Failure is a brief and necessary layover on the way to success,
but you'll never reach success if you check your bags at failure.*

Okay, so let me back up for a moment. I was my brother's keeper. Literally. As in his gatekeeper. If you wanted to get to him, you had to come through me. The setup made perfect sense. He knew I had his back with the fierce loyalty that comes with family. I knew if I screwed up, he'd hire one of our sisters.

If you haven't heard of my brother yet, you will. He's well on his way to becoming the next big thing, coming soon to a town near you. His name is Tag, as in *you're it.* He's kind of a cross between a guru and a rock star. Think Deepak Chopra meets Bono.

Think Tag, he's It.

Being gatekeeper to the family star was a pretty good gig, if you didn't mind not having much of a life of your own. And the more brightly my brother's light seemed to shine, the less I had. Basically, I worked 24/7, and if Tag could find a way to jam some more hours or days into the week, I'd be working those, too.

Yesterday, I'd flown from San Diego to Detroit, then on to Des Moines. Tag liked me to check out potential venues in person before we booked events, so whenever I could make it work, I set out a few days early and crammed some extra stops into my already overloaded schedule, then rendezvoused with Tag and my parents at the next gig. Which meant my brother was still at home eating bonbons when I crawled out of bed in Des Moines at the crack of dawn this morning to fly to the Austin event.

As I walked across the empty hotel lobby, I stopped in front of a long fish tank to take a sip of my room-brewed coffee. A kaleidoscope of fish were nibbling on flakes of food scattered across the surface of the water. I was riveted. I'd once read an article about the calming and meditative effects of watching marine life. Maybe I'd get some fish of my own someday. Or at least start visiting the aquarium on a regular basis.

The woman behind the front desk was whispering sweet nothings to someone on the phone when I walked over to check out. A sweat suit–clad couple holding hands passed me as they headed out for some morning exercise.

When I climbed into a cab, I stared past the driver's head to a picture of his wife and kids clipped to the visor. The day had barely started, and the universe couldn't wait to point out that perhaps there should be more to my life than work, work, and more work.

My cell phone released a tinny instrumental version of "She Works Hard for the Money" the second we pulled away from the curb.

"What?" I said.

"Failure is a brief and necessary layover on the way to success," my brother said, "but you'll never reach success if you check your bags at failure."

"Can it," I said. "It's way too early."

"It's good, though, right?"

I could picture it at tomorrow's Austin event. Tag spouting this mumbo jumbo, his bleached white teeth gleaming, his scruffy pre-beard beckoning, his fans hyperventilating.

I yawned. "Genius," I said. I checked my watch. "Don't forget your ten o'clock interview. Your notes are in the red folder on the upper right-hand corner of your desk."

When it comes to Des Moines and Austin, you can't get there from here, so I had to switch planes in Milwaukee. Except that once I got to Milwaukee, the plane to Austin had been canceled. So I had to fly to Dallas–Fort Worth and then take a new plane to Austin. By that point, I was ready to drive, or maybe even walk, the final leg. Until I pulled up the MapQuest app on my cell phone and saw that it was two hundred and eleven miles.

I'm not that ambitious.

When I eventually landed at the Austin airport, I was seriously late. I yanked my carry-on out of the overhead bin, then pulled my yoga pants up to meet my baggy white T-shirt. I raced through the terminal so quickly my carry-on kept twisting off its wheels. After the third time I gave up and just dragged it.

The smell of Texas barbeque called out from the Salt Lick at the edge of the airport food court and reminded me I'd barely eaten all day. I didn't have time to wait in line, so I grabbed a packaged turkey sandwich from Java Airport Coffee House instead, plus some peanut M&M's to hold me over until I got to the sandwich. I stopped to check out a live band playing next to the overlook near the top of the airport's central escalator. If Tag were with me, he'd have insisted on stopping long enough to play a song or two with them. I settled for wiggling my hips in time to the music while I inhaled the rest of my M&M's.

I rode the escalator down to the ground level, checking out the cool guitars on display over the luggage carousels as I headed out for a taxi. Apparently Austin took its reputation as live music capital of the world seriously.

Outside, a wall of heat hit me like a sauna. I dove for a taxi. I guzzled half a bottle of lukewarm water and turned on my cell phone. Five zillion new messages for my brother popped into my in-box. I ignored them.

I unwrapped my turkey sandwich, trying not to think about how germy the backseat of the taxi was. My phone rang again.

"What?" I said through a mouthful of turkey.

"Have you seen my green golf pants?" my brother asked.

"Have you tried the closet?"

"Which one?"

I rolled my eyes. "The master bedroom walk-in. Halfway down the left side, with your other golf pants."

"Hmm, I didn't know I had a golf section. Hang on . . . Okay, got 'em."

"Whew. What a relief." I covered the phone and took another bite of barbeque-less turkey.

"So, how'd I do?"

I swallowed. "Finding your golf pants?"

He laughed his million-dollar laugh. "The interview."

"I didn't listen."

"Why not?"

"Uh, because I was up in the air? Don't worry, they're e-mailing me an MP3. I'll give you notes as soon as I listen to it. And don't forget, your car for the airport will be there at seven fifteen tomorrow, a.m. Your carry-on is packed and waiting by the front door."

"Seven fifteen? Seriously?"

I rolled my eyes again. "There's exactly one nonstop flight a day from Boston to Austin, so buck up, bro."

By the time my taxi turned onto University Avenue and pulled up in front of the massive conference center, I had exactly seven minutes.

"Deirdre Griffin," I said to the guy at the desk as I reached for my company credit card. "I'm checking in. And I'm supposed to be meeting your events manager in the main restaurant at four thirty. Can you please let her know I'll be a few minutes late?"

He handed me back the credit card and ran a room key card through the coder machine. "The main restaurant is on the mezzanine level, between the gift shop and the business center," he said without looking up.

I weighed the energy expenditure of convincing this idiot to pick up the phone and call the restaurant for me.

Decision made, I turned and bumped my carry-on in the direction of the elevator.

When I got off on the fourteenth floor, I followed the little signs with the arrows to room 1423. I scanned my key card. The light flashed red. I tried it again. Red again.

I dug for the little cardboard key folder and saw that my room number was really 1432.

I sighed, but couldn't resist taking a moment to extend my non-suitcase-pulling arm and pirouette on my toe while I wheeled my suitcase around in a perfectly executed 180-degree turn. Maybe it was a combination of the anonymity and the long hallways, but hotels always made me feel like dancing.

After double-checking that I had the hallway all to myself, I did a few chorus kicks as I rolled my way back down the hall and around the corner. Maybe someday I'd make my own dance exercise video: The *Hot Hot Hot*el Workout for Solo Travelers.

I found my real room, scanned my key card, and actually managed to get a beep accompanied by a green light this time. I jerked the door open and hurled my stuff on top of the king-size bed. I unzipped the front zipper of my carry-on and pulled out my regulation-size travel Baggie.

I sent my flip-flops flying with two final chorus kicks, circled my hips while I peeled off my yoga pants, then pulled my T-shirt over my head as the grand finale. I switched dances and pony-stepped to the bathroom with the Baggie and peed as quickly as I could. Then I rolled fresh deodorant on not-so-fresh armpits, squeezed some toothpaste onto my toothbrush, and ponied my way back to the carry-on.

It's not like I'd never kept an events person waiting before, but I was pretty sure I remembered this one saying I was her last appointment and I didn't want to miss her. I brushed my teeth with one hand while I rummaged for something to wear with the other. I pulled out some overpriced black stretchy travel wear. I found a scarf I hoped was funky enough that maybe the wrinkles would look like they were supposed to be there.

My clean undergarments seemed to have disappeared, so I settled for twisting my bra back to center and gave a tug to the baggy old underpants I'd chosen for flying comfort rather than flair. My fingers tore a hole through the worn cotton fabric. When I opened my mouth to swear, toothpaste drizzled from one corner.

My door beeped.

The handle turned.

A man walked in.

I heard a loud scream and realized it was coming from me. Toothpaste mixed with saliva was pouring down my chin like a waterfall.

The man put up his hand like a stop sign.

I screamed some more.

He scrunched his eyes closed and reached behind him for the doorknob.

"My bad," he said as he backed out of the room.

3

You don't have to be a winner to start,
but you have to start to be a winner.

A s soon as I'd chained the door and spit the toothpaste I hadn't managed to swallow into the sink, I dialed the front desk.

"A man just walked into my room," I yelled.

"Probably maintenance," a voice said.

"He had a suitcase!" I screamed. "A hunter green suitcase. On rollers." My throat was really starting to hurt from all this screaming.

"Oh." It sounded like the jerk who'd checked me in.

I waited.

"Oh?" I finally said. "A man walks into my room and all you're going to say is *oh*?"

"The computer must have messed up. It does that sometimes."

I had a lot of respect for computers and I hated it when people blamed them for their own personal shortcomings. I shook my head. The movement cleared my brain enough to remember my appointment with the events person. I stretched the cord as far as it would go and pulled on my stretchy black travel outfit with the hand not holding the phone.

When I brushed my hand over my hip, the flesh freed by the rip in my underpants bumped out like a tumor. I swallowed back another scream. I decided to dump out my suitcase in order to find underpants, and when I finally did, I began to undress and dress my lower half again.

"You're both going to have to come down and get new key cards," the voice in my ear continued.

"Why do *I* have to get a new key?" I held the phone in the crook of my neck while I finished pulling up my pants. "I was here first."

"Hotel policy."

"Ohmigod. You have a policy for this? What kind of place *is* this?"

"And one of you is going to have to switch rooms."

"Well, it's not going to be me," I said. And then I hung up as hard as I could.

If this stupid hotel gave that guy my room, I'd move my brother's event. Or I'd sue. Or I'd move my brother's event *and* sue. I'd only packed and unpacked my suitcase about a zillion times this week. There was no way in hell I was going to pack up twice in one hotel, especially since everything I'd brought with me was now strewn all over the bed and floor.

The elevator took forever getting down to the lobby. I tapped one foot impatiently while I checked my phone to see if I had a direct number for the events person.

The elevator beeped.

When the door opened, I was looking right at a hunter green carry-on.

"We have to stop meeting like this," the guy attached to it said.

The elevator door started to close between us. The guy reached out and caught it with one hand.

"Ha," I said. I looked past him to the lobby, not wanting to make eye contact.

"They'll offer you a coupon for a free breakfast for the inconvenience."

"Inconvenience," I repeated. The guy and the carry-on were blocking my exit, which seemed to me to be the current inconvenience. Not to mention awkward. And embarrassing.

"If you hold out, you can bump them up to dinner." I could hear the smile in his voice. "I'm just saying."

Even without quite looking at him, he was actually kind of good-looking. Dark hair, wide-set eyes. Strong jaw. Lean torso. No wedding ring.

Great. The man who had seen my peanut-M&M's-and-turkey-sandwich-bloated body in ancient ripped underwear and with toothpaste spewing out of my mouth was Just. My. Type.

I couldn't seem to move. It was like humiliation had rooted me in place. Even my ankles felt heavy. I glanced down. Something was peeking out from under one pant leg and resting on the inside edge of my shoe.

I did a double take and glanced down again. Yep, it was the corner of my recently removed ripped underpants. I'd been known to leave the house with the occasional T-shirt on inside out, and decades ago I'd gone to high school one day with a sock stuck inside one leg of my jeans, but this was a new low.

"Hey, I'm really sorry," the guy said, still holding the door.

I took a tiny step toward the elevator door, dragging the leg with the underpants attached to it as carefully as possible.

The guy was still staring at me. I wondered if I could get away with pointing over his shoulder and yelling, *Look!* And as soon as he turned and looked, I'd reach down, grab my underpants, and run.

He shook his head. "You must have been terrified. Listen, I'm sure nothing like this will ever happen again, but just to be on the safe side? You should always make sure you put the chain on as soon as you get in the room, okay?"

I took another ministep. I glanced down again as casually as I could. The underpants were about three-quarters of the way out now.

If I'd been giving birth to a baby from the bottom of my pant leg, one more push would do it.

"Anyway, rest assured that I'm on a completely different floor now." He ran a hand through his hair as I stayed frozen like a really bad statue. "Okay, well, again, I apologize for the scare."

I didn't dare move.

He finally stepped into the elevator with me. "Hey, are you okay? Do you want me to call someone for you?"

I took a deep breath.

I held my head high.

Then I walked away from my torn, stretched-out, decrepit underpants as if they could have belonged to anyone.

The elevator doors hissed closed behind me.

I crossed the lobby and got my new key card. I talked the idiot at the desk into upgrading the free breakfast for the inconvenience into not just a free dinner but a free room-service dinner.

I caught the events person on her way out the door. As we sat in the lobby going over the details for the next day—sound system, security, table and chair placement—I could almost forget about my public underwear humiliation.

It all came back as soon as I was alone again in my hotel room. So I ordered a turkey club complete with bacon, chipotle mayo, Swiss cheese, avocado, and chips. I swallowed it all down along with my embarrassment—and an Ultimate Austin Frozen Margarita.

As what was left of my margarita melted, my cell phone rang. Twice. I ignored it. My room phone rang. I ignored that, too.

A text beeped in. I finally picked up my cell.

You don't have to be a winner to start, but you have to start to be a winner.

"Shut up," I screamed at my phone. At my brother. At my life.

Then I turned on the TV and scrolled through a zillion stupid channels so I wouldn't feel so alone. I paused long enough to watch a man in tight jeans teaching the Boot Scootin' Boogie to a group of laughing line dancers on some country channel. I got up and tried a few steps with them, but being on the opposite side of the screen only made me feel left out, so I clicked the TV off.

I thought about taking a walk. Maybe I'd even go underwear shopping while I was out. I'd read in the in-flight magazine about a cool lingerie store in Austin called Petticoat Fair. Maybe I'd stroll right in like I owned the place and buy a whole wardrobe. So the next time a guy walked in on me, he'd stop and say, *Whoa, baby.*

Pathetic. Absolutely pathetic. I'd sunk to a point in my life that my only hope for a good time was to be better prepared in case another hotel accidentally gave somebody a key to my room.

I shoved my suitcase and its splayed contents over to one side of the vast, unnecessary expanse of bed. When I slurped the remnants of my margarita through the straw, the sound it made was so loud I could almost imagine I had company.

"Say, 'Excuse me,'" I said out loud.

"Excuse me," I answered in a deep, sexy male voice.

"There's no excuse for you," I said.

Then I crawled between the sheets on the other side of the bed and pulled the covers up over my head. Screw the walk.

4

Morning, noon, and night, my brother is pretty much a chiasmus machine, and a chiasmus machine is pretty much my brother, morning, noon, and night.

So, my life being my life, fast-forward to the next day and there I was at my brother's Austin gig.

Steve Moretti held out his hand.

I ignored it.

"I thought you looked familiar," he said.

"Cute," I said. I tried to will the heat that was creeping into my cheeks back down to wherever it was that it was coming from.

I grabbed my brother's tunic-clad forearm. "Come on. You should be at the signing table by now."

Two women with long blond hair pushed their way in front of Steve. "Tag?" one of them said. "Do you remember me?"

A brunette wearing jeans and a T-shirt that read I BRAKE FOR AN-GELS cut in front of the two blondes. She stood next to my brother and held out her cell phone with one hand to take a picture.

I inserted myself between them and held out my hand to block the shot. "Pictures at the signing table only."

"Wow, I like your earrings," she said to me.

I kept my hand up. "Nice try," I said. People had been kissing up to me to get to Tag my whole life. I hadn't fallen for *nice earrings* since the Beatles were still together.

My brother smiled at the woman apologetically, good cop to my bad cop.

I yanked his arm. "Come on."

Tag yanked back. "Where are you staying?" he called out to Steve.

I pretended I was invisible.

"Right here," Steve called back.

Tag dragged me a few steps toward him so he didn't have to keep bellowing. "How about a late dinner? As long as you don't mind hanging out with my family."

I gazed off in the opposite direction.

"Wouldn't miss it," I heard Captain Underpants say.

The thing about my brother was that he had only two speeds. He was either completely on, or he was asleep. And he couldn't stand to be alone. Not even for a minute. He collected people, and once he had them, he never let them go.

All by way of saying that I knew there was no way in hell I could get away with skipping dinner with my family and the guy who'd last seen my underpants, so I didn't even try.

"Ma'am?" the waiter said.

I glanced up from my menu. "The ChocoVine looks good."

"*The taste of Dutch chocolate and fine red wine,*" Tag read. He shook his head. "It's like Yoo-hoo with fourteen percent alcohol, Dee."

I shrugged. "That's what I'm counting on."

"So," my father said once everyone else had ordered a chocolate-free drink, "tell us about yourself, Steve. Always a big treat to meet one of Tag's old friends."

"Actually, I think I've met some of you before," my brother's old friend said.

I looked around for the nearest exit. I didn't think he'd actually tell our story, but you never really knew what people might do for a laugh.

Steve smiled. "We'd stopped at your house on the way to a party on the Cape one weekend freshman year. Remember, Tag?"

"Hey, that's right." Tag laughed like they were still back in college. "I think I remember something like eight of us piled into somebody's beat-up Ford Falcon?"

The waiter put a glass of wine on the table in front of my mother. She thanked him, then took a moment to center the glass on the cocktail napkin. "As I remember, you dropped off a duffel bag filled with laundry and expected to pick it up fully folded on your way back."

Tag laughed and picked up his glass. "What can I say? I was out of clean clothes."

"Spoiled," I said.

"I know you are, but what am I?" my famous brother said.

"Now, now, children," my mother said.

"All I remember," Steve said, "is that you told us all to keep our hands off your three gorgeous sisters."

"Ha," Tag said. "Those days are gone. Now this one pays me to try to fix her up."

"Shut up," I said.

Tag grinned. "No, you shut up."

My father leaned across the table toward Steve. "It's not that she can't attract them. It's just that she has a hard time closing the deal."

"Dad!"

My mother put her hand on my father's forearm. "That's enough, honey." She lifted her wineglass. "Now who wants to go first? Deirdre?"

The sooner we got this part over with, the sooner I could chug my ChocoVine. I lifted my glass. "You can take Salem out of the country, but you can't take the country out of Salem."

My brother shook his head. "Nice. Nothing like starting off a meal with an old cigarette commercial."

My mother leaned into my father. "It's not the men in my life, it's the life in my men."

My father kissed her on top of her head. "Mae West. Who I believe also said, 'I'd rather be looked over than overlooked.'"

"Which might actually be true when you're Mae West," I said. "Can we drink now?"

We all clinked our glasses over the center of the round, white-tablecloth-covered table.

Steve took a sip and put his wineglass down. "Great ritual. Growing up, my family just waited for the meal and said 'rub-a-dub-dub, thanks for the grub.'"

My mother clicked into teacher mode. "A chiasmus is when the second half of an expression is balanced against the first half, but with the parts reversed. It's essentially an inverted kind of parallelism. We started encouraging them at the dinner table when the children were quite young."

"And look how I turned out," I said. I took another gulp of Choco-Vine.

"We're a very chiastic family," my father said. He wiggled his eyebrows. "Sounds almost sexy, doesn't it?"

"Actually," Tag said, "they're pretty much the method to my mojo. They're amazingly powerful. And totally addicting—once you start coming up with them, you just can't stop."

"And don't think he's kidding," I said. "Trust me, I have to write them all down. Morning, noon, and night, my brother is pretty much a chiasmus machine, and a chiasmus machine is pretty much my brother, morning, noon, and night."

"That reminds me," my father said. "We've got a new product on order for Tag." When he grinned, his whole face lit up. With his button nose and curly gray hair and eyebrows, he looked like a trimmer, off-season Santa Claus. "And let me tell you, it's a humdinger."

My mother shook her head.

My father grinned some more. "Okay, you know the guy who invented the Jesus Toaster? The one that toasts the likeness of Jesus onto the bread like a holy vision?"

My mother let out a puff of air.

"What?" my father said. "It's tastefully done." He did his eyebrow thing again. "Get it? Tastefully?"

"Is this in any way related to the likeness of the Virgin Mary that recently appeared on the potato chip?" I asked.

"That's my girl," my father said. It was hard to tell if he meant me or Mary.

"I always wanted one of those see-through glass toasters," Tag said. "You know, so you can get the toast exactly the way you like it?"

"Oh, please," I said. "When was the last time you made your own toast?"

My father slapped both hands down on the table to get our attention. "Anyway, we're not going for the Jesus Toaster because"—he held up one hand to block my mother's view and pointed at her with the other—"you-know-who wouldn't go for it. But we ordered the peace sign toaster, and the pièce de résistance, the one that toasts a custom imprint of—"

"No," I said.

"Seriously?" Tag grinned. "Awesome. I'm going to be toasted the world over. Which photo are we using?"

I rolled my eyes. Across the table, Steve smiled. His square teeth were still the color they were meant to be, as opposed to the fake white of my brother's, and he had a slightly off-kilter smile that gave him kind of a childlike quality. In a good way. If only I could stop thinking of him as Captain Underpants. If only I'd started working out about six weeks ago.

If only I'd worn better underwear.

I drained the rest of my ChocoVine. "Now where do you think that waiter went?"

My brother blinked his baby blues, conjuring up the waiter, who brought us another round of drinks. Then we ordered dinner. If I ate any more turkey, I was going to start to gobble, so I went with the broiled salmon. What I actually wanted was the blue-cheese burger and sweet potato fries my brother ordered, but there was no way in hell I was going to eat anything high calorie in front of somebody who'd recently seen me practically naked. I mean, let him think I had metabolism issues.

"So what brings you to Austin, Steve?" my father asked.

Steve smiled his crooked smile. "I'm an urban landscape designer. I pitched a design to the university today."

"I'm sure it went over brilliantly," my mother said.

He shrugged. "Time will tell. And I also want to check out the gardens at Lake Austin Spa Resort while I'm here."

I reached for one of my brother's fries. "Ooh, I hear that place is amazing."

My brother slapped my hand. I handed him a lettuce leaf by way of trade.

Steve tilted his head and looked in my direction. "I'm planning to head over there tonight to see it all lit up, if you want to take a ride over."

"Sounds like a plan," Tag said.

Okay, so maybe he hadn't been looking in my direction. Whatever. I'd head up to my room, try to catch a decent rerun.

"Deirdre?" Steve said.

Two women in sundresses and great Texas boots stepped up to the table. "Tag?" one of them said.

Tag smiled his dazzling smile. He also kicked me under the table.

I held out my hand to the woman who'd spoken. "Hi," I said. "I'm Tag's sister Deirdre."

"Wow," she said. "Lucky you."

5

*What a long strange trip it's been, and what
a stranger longer trip it's becoming.*

I was decades too old to be sitting in the backseat of a rented
minivan driven by my parents. It didn't help that I was wedged in
between the two blondes from the restaurant, Cindy and Tracy.
Or maybe it was Kimmy and Stacy.

"Great boots," I said once we were all buckled in.

In the impossibly small space, Tracy/Stacy managed to cross one
leg until her cowboy boot was resting on the ruffled hem of her sundress. "Allens," she said as she wiggled her toe.

I was pretty sure I'd read about Allens Boots. "The place with the
antler chandeliers and the stuffed armadillo holding a beer bottle?"

They looked across me at each other.

"Maybe," Cindy/Kimmy said. "I only noticed the boots."

"Gee," I said. "Give me a stuffed armadillo holding a beer bottle
any day."

My human bookends laughed uncertainly, and Tag turned around
in the middle seat to give me his knock-it-off look. I crossed my eyes
at him, then went back to trying to yank the left side of my pashmina
out from under Tracy/Stacy. I was wearing a black bohemian skirt and
a black tank top. I figured any parts of me that didn't disappear into

the darkness would be camouflaged by the pashmina's yard and a half of deep teal fabric. Silver and turquoise glittered from my sandals and added what I hoped was just enough bling to keep me from looking like a total loser.

Tracy/Stacy reached forward and twirled a lock of Tag's hair around her finger. I was pretty sure he was only pretending to remember her, but it didn't seem to be bothering either of them. If they'd been sitting next to each other, they'd probably be making out by now.

There's a Dentyne commercial that says the average person has twenty-eight first kisses. When I first saw it, I thought it was meant ironically, as if we're all in such denial that we pretend every kiss is our first one, over and over again, until one day that magical twenty-ninth kiss wakes us up to the reality that we're not kissing virgins anymore.

When it finally hit me that the commercial meant that most people actually kiss twenty-eight separate people during the span of their lives, I was depressed for days.

I mean, if that stupid commercial was true, I still had at least ten more strangers to kiss. To date. To maybe move in with. To probably move out on. To have to get over.

Steve Moretti turned around in his seat next to Tag. "Piece of gum?"

He seemed to be looking at me, so I took one. Since he was Tag's wingman, I figured it was just a matter of time before Cindy/Kimmy put the moves on him. I mean, really, in the bubble of this minivan, it was like we'd flashed back a couple of decades and my parents were driving us all to a junior high dance.

Sure enough, Cindy/Kimmy flipped her hair, giggled, and reached for a piece of gum. "I like your shirt, Steve," she said. Then she giggled some more. Maybe I should pass her a note or something. *Do u* ❤ *Stevie?*

I'd always hated not having a window seat, especially in a situation like this one, but I finally managed to twist around enough to get a partial view of the passing scenery. In my geographically impaired brain, probably inspired by the wooden puzzle of the United States

I'd had as a kid, I'd pictured all of Texas flat, but Austin was surprisingly hilly. Big, Spanish-style terra-cotta-colored McMansions looked down on us from above.

The Very Best of the Grateful Dead was blasting from all four corners of the minivan. This was for our benefit. My parents were so inseparable they even shared an iPod. Wherever they went, even when they drove, a pair of twin earbuds forking out from a single wire connected them to each other like a plastic umbilical cord. To be good minivan hosts, tonight they'd plugged in an adapter. It was impossible not to sing along, so we were all butchering the lyrics as we rode. Even I had a hard time being depressed listening to the Grateful Dead. When "Truckin'" came on for the second time, I was almost ready to hang it up and see what tomorrow brings.

"Uh-ooh-ooh," my seatmates sang on either side of me, like human stereo speakers. As they clapped their hands and played air tambourine, my mood began to plummet. The more I thought about it, the more I knew what tomorrow would bring: more of today.

I had to admit I was sooooooo over it. I mean, how did a perfectly intelligent, attractive, at least relatively, woman like me get here? At this stage of my life I should either be chauffeuring my own kids to middle-school dances, or jetting around the world doing something so fascinating and all-encompassing and important that I'd made the conscious choice not to have said children because it wouldn't be fair for them to play second fiddle to my incredible, possibly world-impacting career. I mean, it's not that I had to be famous, but I thought by this point I should at least be *significant*.

Back—okay, *way* back—in high school, I was named "the girl most likely to leave this honky-tonk school for the big time." Granted, my friends and I were on the yearbook committee, but still. How could I have fallen so short of my goals? My hopes. My dreams. The truth, the sad, sad truth, was that I couldn't even remember what my dreams had been anymore.

Was there a cutoff age for late bloomers, or could I still squeeze in for last call? Sitting there, in the back of the minivan, I had to believe there was still time.

I mean, if Texas could turn out to be hilly, why couldn't I turn into someone who razzled and dazzled, who wore sundresses and cowboy boots? I'd knock off the ChocoVine and switch to seltzer. I'd eat only fish and fruits and veggies. I'd use all the extra time I gained by not eating to walk, then run, then run some more. I'd have my plain brown curls dyed platinum, and then I'd get somebody to teach me how to flat-iron my hair without losing a finger. Then, when I was a whole new me, I'd buy my own damn ruffled-hem sundress and some kick-ass cowboy boots.

The minivan dipped like a seat on a roller coaster as we headed down a steep hill. I clawed the vinyl seat in front of me to brace myself. To our right, a lake appeared, house lights glowing along its shore as far as the eye could see.

"Wow," I said. "So beautiful." Even I knew that Austin was landlocked, but I said it anyway: "It looks like it could be the ocean."

Kimmy/Cindy leaned in front of me to see. "Maybe the Pacific?"

Tag turned around and laughed like she'd said something witty. My brother has a penchant for women like Kimmy/Cindy. In fact, I was pretty sure one of his ex-wives had still believed in the tooth fairy until their daughter lost a tooth and Tag apprised her of their parental responsibility. So if Tag ended up with Kimmy/Cindy, instead of Tracy/Stacy, the old flame he didn't seem to remember anyway, would his wingman go along with the switch? Ooh, the plot inside the minivan might be thickening.

Wait, I was losing my focus. It didn't really matter who ended up with who, or even whom. What mattered was keeping my eyes on the distant prize. I made a promise to myself: As soon as I got my act together, I would never be a wallflower wedged into the third seat of a minivan with my parents, my brother, and my brother's posse du jour again.

Steve turned around. "That's actually Lake Travis."

"Really?" I said brilliantly. Maybe as soon as I was all blond and thin and interesting, I'd work on becoming a scintillating conversationalist.

He smiled. "Really. It's almost sixty-four miles long, and about four and a half miles at its widest point. It was created with the construction of the Mansfield Dam, which impounded the Colorado River—"

Kimmy/Cindy leaned across me and poked Steve's shoulder with a fingernail. "See, I knew you were interesting."

She had a nice manicure—rosy at the base and tipped in crisp white. Maybe after I worked on my conversation, I'd move on to my nails. In the meantime I settled for gnawing off the jagged edge of a thumbnail.

My mother caught my eye in the rearview mirror and shook her head. I squinted at her. She mimed taking my thumbnail out of my mouth. Seriously. It had come to this. My AARP card was practically right around the corner and my mother was still telling me to get my thumb out of my mouth.

"Truckin'" played for the third time and we all joined in on the chorus. Either my parents' iPod was having shuffle issues, or they'd programmed "Truckin'" to play every fifth song. Maybe it was their theme song. Or maybe just the featured song of their Driving in a Minivan with the Kids mix.

"Uh-ooh-ooh," Tracy/Stacy and Kimmy/Cindy sang. They were starting to show real potential on those air tambourines.

Steve looked up from the GPS on his cell phone. "Take the next left."

My father turned onto North Quinlan Park Road and we passed a big sign for Steiner Ranch. We drove along a beautifully landscaped road with nice wide walking trails on either side and clusters of newer-looking homes until the neighborhood changed to something more rustic.

Out of nowhere another lake appeared. We took a sharp left just before we drove into it. A gray metal gate stopped us. Under the minivan headlights it looked like a modern sculpture. My father lowered his window to address the small rectangular box beside the gate.

"Welcome to Lake Austin Spa Resort. How can I help you?" a disembodied voice said from the box.

Steve leaned forward and called out from his seat. "Hi. Steve Moretti. I should be on your list. And I hope you don't mind, but I brought a few friends with me."

"Enjoy your visit, Mr. Moretti."

The huge gray gate swung open soundlessly.

We drove through and parked along the edge of a cobblestone drive. My father pushed a button and the child-safe side door of the minivan opened on its own. Maybe if we sat there long enough, he'd come around and let us out of our car seats.

Tag jumped out and reached two hands back to the Tambourine Twins. Tracy/Stacy ground the heel of one cowboy boot into my instep on her way past me.

"Excuse you," I said, but she didn't seem to notice.

My guru brother draped an arm around each of his groupies' shoulders, and the threesome sauntered off toward the twinkling lights.

I turned sideways in my seat and tried to lift my foot up high enough to inspect it for damages. "What a long strange trip it's been," I said, mostly to myself, "and what a stranger longer trip it's becoming."

"Ha," Steve said. He jumped out of the van and leaned back in so he could make eye contact. "Need a hand?"

"Sure," I said. "Unless you happen to have an extra pair of crutches."

6

When you dig in the earth, the earth digs you.

Lake Austin Spa Resort was spectacular. Vine-covered arbors dotted the property and framed a meandering promenade that shaded a long row of connecting cottages. I recognized wisteria climbing up one arbor, and Steve identified bright orange trumpet creeper swirling around and around another. The guy knew his greenery.

Soft, inconspicuous lighting illuminated trees, bushes, and garden after garden after garden. I knew somebody must have put them there, but the plants looked so natural it was as if they'd all just sprouted up spontaneously one day.

"Wow," I said. "Everything looks so happy here."

"When you dig in the earth, the earth digs you," Steve said.

My mother clapped her hands. "Good job, honey. Your first chiasmus."

Steve bowed, his right hand in front of his waist and the left one behind, then he switched hands and did it again. He had a nice, easygoing way about him. Back at the conference center garage, when we'd gotten into the whole who-rides-with-whom thing, I liked the way he'd left his own rental car behind and jumped in the minivan so we could all ride together. Maybe I could ask him for a spontaneity lesson.

"Hey, Dee," Tag said. "Write that down. I might be able to use it."

I ignored him.

He gave me his I'm-not-kidding look.

I sighed and took out a purple marker from my purse and started writing Steve's chiasmus on the palm of one hand.

"Oh, grow up," Tag said.

"You grow up," I said.

The Tambourine Twins giggled. "I used to do that for math tests," one of them said. "I could get all the multiplication tables on my hand without writing on any fingers."

"Impressive," I said.

I'd expected the resort to be one of those stuffy, relentlessly upscale places, but it wasn't like that at all. It was laid-back in the way a truly beautiful woman can throw on jeans and a T-shirt and some pink lip gloss, and look stunning.

On that thought, I hiked up my pashmina for a little more upper arm coverage, then bent down to fish out a pebble that had wedged its way between my sandal and my instep.

Guests strolled the gently lit walking paths, many in white bathrobes and flip-flops. A black-and-white cat stretched out decadently across the steps leading up to some guest rooms as if waiting for the delivery of a bedtime snack to cap off a perfect evening. The day's sweltering heat had mellowed, and the air carried the peaty scent of garden soil and hints of sweet flowers. I couldn't remember the last time I'd taken a moment to notice the night air, let alone to breathe it in.

We checked in at the reception desk, and then our group headed out to the patio where a duo was performing some kind of jazz/folk fusion. I stood for a minute listening to a woman with a haunting voice sing, "I Could Get Used to You." Then the male half of the duo began to play the saxophone, rich and sexy. My parents started to dance off in a corner of the patio, and I knew it was only a matter of time until everyone else in our group began to couple off.

I wandered down to the lake, midnight blue under a big Texas moon and a sky full of stars. I stepped out onto a softly lit dock edged with kayaks and hydrocycles. How much fun would it be to come back here one day and stay for a week, maybe two. Tai chi in the morning, then breakfast and a hike up into hill country, and then maybe a paddle around the lake. After that, a perfectly prepared spa lunch, followed by some water aerobics and a massage.

Maybe I'd come here solo, all self-sufficient and serene. Or I'd finally call the old friends I never got around to calling anymore and plan a girlfriend getaway. Or, wonder of wonders, maybe I'd even come here with a guy someday. We'd burn off the calories from our spa meals by making mad, passionate love. We'd pool-hop our way around the resort, taking leisurely swims in each one before dripping our way to the next. We'd curl up side by side on lounge chairs, sharing the shade of a big thatched umbrella, and read for hours on end. When we needed a break, we'd head up to the spa in our matching white robes for a Swedish couple's massage.

A text message triple-beeped as it landed, interrupting my little fantasy. I fished my cell out of my purse.

Hey, where r u?

"*Aaahhh!*" I yelled. I dialed down my personal volume to what my mother would have called my inside voice. "You are driving me *crazy.*"

"Already?" a voice said behind me.

I jumped, then whipped my head around. The sole of one of my sandals caught in the space between two deck planks, and I pitched forward.

Steve Moretti caught my shoulders just before I went over the edge and splashed into the lake. It didn't come off as a particularly romantic gesture, like catching me in his arms or anything. It was more the way you might use a dolly to tilt a refrigerator until it was upright again.

"Thank you," I said. I pulled in my stomach as if that might retroactively make the body he'd just lifted a few pounds lighter.

"You're welcome."

I adjusted my pashmina, which had managed to slide through my fingers until it stretched out behind me like a jump rope. Several boatloads of people were drifting in the center of the lake, listening to the music. A couple in a canoe waved. Steve and I waved back at the same time, as if we were the official Lake Austin greeters.

The sax player launched into a solo.

"Great music," I said.

"Who's driving you crazy?" Steve said at the exact same time.

Neither of us said anything.

"Nothing like the sax," Steve said.

"My brother," I said at the same time.

"You first," we both said.

We laughed.

The deck started to rock, maybe from the wake of a passing boat, maybe from our hilarity. Steve touched my elbow. "Come on," he said. "Let's go check out some gardens."

We followed a path up a hill and peeked in the windows of a building that looked like a little book-filled parlor. Huge sunflower faces nodded at us as we walked by. Birdhouse gourds, just like the ones we used to grow as kids every summer, dangled from a white arbor that was mostly hidden by a canopy of foliage. Prickly pear cactuses flanked the path like spiked sentries.

"Wow," I said as I looked around, trying to take it all in.

"Nineteen acres. Over a thousand species of Texas plants, vegetables, herbs, spices, and wildflowers." Steve bent down to get a closer look at something. "Including much of the food for the resort and spa restaurants as well as the ingredients for the spa treatments. It's a terrific example of organic, sustainable gardening."

I could imagine him lecturing to an auditorium full of plant people, or pitching his design to a university committee as he clicked away at a PowerPoint presentation. He didn't have Tag's It thing, but he had an earnest enthusiasm that seemed like a quieter kind of magic. I found myself wanting to feel that kind of energy. About something. Anything.

We followed a path into the herb and vegetable garden, each variety marked by a rectangular metal sign stuck into the ground.

Steve whistled a long *woo-hoo*. "Will you look at those eggplants."

I started to laugh, but then I turned to follow his gaze. Rows of sexy, curvy eggplants peeked out from under lush green leaves. "Wow. Who knew eggplants could be so gorgeous."

Steve checked the label in front of a purple-and-cream-striped eggplant. "Pinstripe. Hmm, if I were an eggplant, I think I'd be Pinstripe."

"How debonair," I said. I scanned the row and chose my favorite, a gleaming magenta.

I read the label. "Dancer."

"A beauty," Steve said.

"Thank you," I said.

We strolled on to the herbs. "Patchouli," I read. "My parents will be beside themselves."

"Can you believe all these varieties of basil?" Steve pinched off two leaves and held the first one and then the other close to my nose. "Which do you like better, lemon or Thai?"

"Lemon."

I pinched my own leaves and held them up to him. "Cilantro or oregano?"

Steve laughed. "That one's coconut thyme."

I shrugged. "Okay, so it was a trick question."

We followed a path along the water's edge, passing a smaller dock that looked like it was designed for meditation or even tai chi. Maybe I could dump Tag and get a job here, so I could start and end every day out on that dock. I'd be an all new me in no time.

"Pizza or sushi?" Steve said.

"Pizza. Anchovies or not?"

"Not."

I wiped a hand across my forehead. "Whew, that's a relief." I turned to look at him. "So, you love your work, huh?"

"Sometimes the politics get to me. Makes me wish I was still back in my landscaping days. Rake up some leaves, throw in a few azaleas, call it a day. But most days I still feel lucky to do what I do."

"Must be nice."

We passed a hammock tucked beside the lake, then the path led us to an open expanse that felt almost like a college quad or a New England town common. We stopped when we came to a crossroads in the center. I counted six separate paths in front of us.

"Sure looks like a metaphor to me," I said.

Steve nodded. "I think we've got the high road and the low road here . . ."

I pointed. "That one's the road less traveled and that's the path of least resistance. I'll let you decide—all these choices are making me nervous."

Steve made a quarter turn right, and I followed. "So, what about you? Do you actually work for Tag, or does he just like to boss you around?"

"Ha." I blew out a puff of air, my lips inadvertently vibrating like a horse angling for a carrot. "That would be both. But yes, I work for him. I'm sort of his glorified personal assistant. A little bit of PR and marketing, but mostly making his tour arrangements, doing his social networking, answering five gazillion e-mails and phone calls a day—most of them from him, I might add. Helping him find his golf pants. Most days I feel like it sucks."

"So why do you do it?"

The long cement slab walkway in front of us circled its way up a hill like a loosely coiled snake. Big stone steps sliced through the center, providing a shortcut to the top of the hill. I stepped up on the first one. "Because every time I quit, he offers me more money?"

I climbed to the next step. "Because his business owns the house I live in?"

I jogged up two more steps and noticed a waterfall ahead, which meant the crashing sound I heard only felt like it was coming from inside my head. "Because my family is like a giant soul-sucking octopus, and once they get their tentacles on you, there's nothing you can do to get away?"

I trudged through some ground cover, then put my feet together and jumped up to the next step. "Because I'm lazy?" I whispered.

I sat down hard on the edge of the stone slab. It was still warm from the heat of the day. Steve caught up and sat down beside me.

"Is that ginger I smell?" I said, mostly to change the subject.

He pointed at a plant with fuzzy leaves and pretty salmon-colored flowers. "*Costus guanaiensis*. Spiral ginger."

"Gee, what don't you know?"

He laughed. "A lot. But I do know that life's way too short to spend it doing something you're not that into."

I shrugged.

"Summer or winter?" Steve said.

"Summer," I said. "Spring or fall?"

"Toss-up."

"I agree," I said. "That one was kind of a trick question."

When he grinned, the crinkles around his shiny brown eyes got deeper. Our eyes met and held. I started to look away, but then I didn't.

He tilted his head. "Ask first or just kiss?"

He smelled like soap and tasted like dinner, but in a good way. He kept his hands on my shoulders as we kissed, as if I might start to keel over again at any moment and he wasn't taking any chances.

"Hey, hey, hey, what's all this?" my brother's voice said out of nowhere.

Change is hard, so people hardly ever change.

We were lined up on the long curved cement walkway, facing each other like opposing teams about to play Red Rover. Cindy/Kimmy and Stacy/Tracy stood on either side of Tag, giggling. Tag and I were glaring at each other. I wasn't sure what Steve was doing, because I was afraid to look. In my mind's eye, I could picture him backing away slowly until he could safely turn and run.

"Get a life," I said.

"You get a life," Tag said. "Keep your hands off my friends."

"What?" I said. "Are you freakin' kidding me? How old are you?"

"Hey, buddy," Steve said. "Come on."

"*You* stay out of it," Tag said.

"What. Is. Your. *Problem?*" I said.

"You know the rules," Tag said.

"Unbelievable," I said. "Okay, I'll tell you what your problem is, besides a bad case of arrested development. You actually believe your own press clippings." I hiked up my pashmina. "You're not *my* guru, Tag, so get over yourself."

The Tambourine Twins stopped giggling.

Blood was pounding in my ears, and oddly I could really smell the ginger now. "Just because you run the rest of the family doesn't mean you can tell me who the hell I can and cannot freakin' kiss." I could feel resentment bubbling up and up inside of me like heartburn. I fought to find the right words. "You're not the boss of me," I yelled.

Tag smiled. "Uh, technically I am."

I wanted to wipe that stupid smile right off his face. I wanted to punch his lights out.

"Not anymore," I said. "I quit. I quit. I quit. And just in case you missed it, I. Freakin'. Quit."

We glared at each other.

"I hate you," I said.

"I hate you more," he said.

I turned to the Tambourine Twins. "He doesn't actually remember either of you. And just so you know, cowboy boots look really stupid with sundresses." I took a wobbly breath. "Even when you're blond and skinny."

Tag turned to Steve. "And here I thought you wanted to talk business with me. So, what, were you thinking it might pay better if you hit on my sister first?"

"Stop," I said, but it came out almost like a sob. I tried to breathe, but I couldn't seem to remember how. I put a hand on my forehead to shield my face as I looked around for an escape route. I could continue up the hill, but I didn't know where I'd end up. To go back the way we'd come, I'd have to push past my brother and his groupies.

Steve reached for my arm.

I shook him off and turned to take the high road.

"Wait," he said. "This is ridiculous."

Maybe I'd take the low road after all. I turned around and pushed past him. "And just so *you* know, I have better underwear. Much better underwear. Which you will never see."

Running in strappy sandals with hot tears streaming down your face and a pashmina flowing out behind you like a sad twist on a superhero cape isn't easy, but I did the best I could. I saw a group of women in white bathrobes heading in my direction, so I jumped off the path before they could ask me what was wrong.

Tag was an idiot, but I was an idiot, too. What was I *thinking*? Of course Steve Moretti only wanted to use me to get to Tag. Maybe he'd developed some new kind of plant and he wanted Tag to endorse it. They'd plaster Tag's face all over the label, just like that stupid Jesus Toaster. Maybe it was even named after him. Ha. It was probably an eggplant. An eggplant named Tag. It would be shiny and perfect.

By dodging the bathrobe-clad women, I'd stumbled on a shortcut back to the reception area. And in the first stroke of luck I'd had since birth, a black town car was just dropping off a guest. I asked the driver if he had time to take me back to the hotel.

He held the door to the backseat open, and I climbed in.

I handed him my brother's credit card.

The good news was that I had only nine more first kisses left.

What goes unsaid in some families could fill the deep blue sea.

Unfortunately that has never been the case in ours.

When we were growing up, my friends' mothers had watched enough episodes of *Bewitched* to know that at the end of the day you put on some lipstick and change into something sexy, but not too. You kiss your husband at the door and take his briefcase with one hand while mixing an aluminum shaker of martinis with the other.

My friends would magically disappear during this interlude, perhaps locked in the basement playroom with their siblings. If they were lucky, the bar was located in the playroom and every once in a while they'd have their own happy hour. They'd take turns mixing a splash of gin with a splash of rum with a splash of crème de cacao, keeping the quantities tiny enough that their parents wouldn't miss them at the next party, and backfilling with water when necessary. Eventually the playroom door would open and the whole family would sit down boozily at the dining room table to some crisp potatoes and an unidentifiable roast cooked to shoe-leather consistency.

I loved eating over at my friends' houses.

My parents were politically opposed to martinis. Instead, they tucked a few marijuana plants in between the beefsteak tomatoes in our garden. On weekends after the harvest, when they thought we were all sleeping, they brought out their bong. It was an enormous red Lucite thing, at least three feet high. They stored it in the attic, next to the Christmas decorations, and told us it was a telescope. When the bong came out, the Grateful Dead sang nonstop from speakers the size of small continents and the sweet smell of pot wafted its way under the closed family room doors and up to us. We used to tiptoe out of our bedrooms and halfway down the stairs and just sit there, breathing it in.

The bong was the only thing we never talked about. Maybe my parents just couldn't connect the dots between their own need to take another walk on the wild side and their desire for us to stay out of trouble.

But everything else we discussed at family meetings. By the time my father walked through the front door after a hard day's work in the Sears appliance center, my mother had her fifth graders' papers corrected for the next day and a tuna-noodle casserole baking in the oven, whole wheat breadcrumbs sprinkled on top instead of the Ritz crackers dotted with butter my friends would get. My father would take off his suit and tie and slip into a flannel shirt and his old dungarees with the peace sign embroidered on one back pocket.

My sister Colleen would set the table while my sister Joanie poured milk into a pitcher, since we weren't allowed to put containers on the table. I'd set out the bread and the margarine dish, the salt and pepper shakers. Tag would waltz in when dinner was ready.

"Why doesn't Tag ever have to do anything?" one of us girls would say.

"I washed the car last weekend," Tag would say.

His words would be muffled, since nine times out of ten he'd be speaking through the cut-off leg of a discarded pair of panty hose. Long, straight hair was the rage back then, and we'd all been born with thick wavy locks. So the girls took turns ironing one another's hair, or dousing it in Dippity-do and rolling it around empty orange juice cans. Tag stuck his head under the kitchen faucet to wet down his hair twice a day and pulled a stocking over his head to flatten it into submission until he had to go out in public again. He looked like a wannabe bank robber.

My mother drew the line at cutting a hole in the part of the stocking covering Tag's mouth so he could eat, which meant he had to remove the contraption at dinnertime. Which in our family was a synonym for meeting time.

"Change is hard, so people hardly ever change," my father might say by way of grace.

"Oh, Timmy," my mother would say as she spooned a big gob of casserole onto a dinner plate and passed it to him. "How about something a bit more optimistic?"

"You spend nine hours hawking refrigerators at Sears, Eileen, and see how optimistic you are," my father would say. My father dreamed of owning his own surf shop one day. When I struck it rich, the first thing I was going to do was buy him one, right across the street from the beach. The storefront would be fluorescent green with hot pink trim and daisies in the window boxes, and it might also rent bicycles built for two.

My mother passed a plate to Tag.

Colleen sighed dreamily. "All you need is love, and love is all you need."

Tag pounded the end of his fork on the scarred wooden table. He looked like a judge about to proclaim, "Order in the court."

"Keep your mitts off Bruce O'Dell," he said instead.

"Mind your own beeswax." Colleen glared at him and blushed at the same time.

"Which one is Bruce O'Dell?" I asked.

Everybody ignored me. It was pretty much the story of my life. Tag was the oldest, and Colleen was a year younger, the oldest girl. They crashed through boundaries and pushed the limits. I was a year younger than Colleen, never the oldest or youngest anything, just the middle child, which by definition meant not special. By the time it was my turn, the battles had all been won or lost, and I had my marching orders. Then Joanie Baloney, a year younger still, came along and somehow it was all adorable. She danced her way through the same borders that fenced me in, doing exactly what she wanted.

Tag leaned across the table. "You might think he's a nice guy, Coll, but he's my friend. I know what he's really like. Trust me, he's a bad motorcycle."

"Define your terms," my mother said.

"A bad scene," Tag said. "The worst."

Colleen leaned across the table, too. "Bag it, Tag. You say exactly the same thing about every guy who asks me out."

"Well, am I right, or am I right?" Tag held his palms up to the heavens in what would become one of his quintessential It gestures.

"What's the big deal?" Colleen said. "I mean, they're good enough to hang around with you, and you think you're God's gift to the world."

"Coll, face it. There's a big difference between being good enough to hang out with and good enough to date my sister."

"He has a point," my father said. "I used to be one of those boys. They only want one thing."

"Guys talk," Tag said.

"Chicks talk, too," Colleen said.

"Don't degrade yourself," my mother said. "I did not give birth to poultry."

"Sure, girls talk," Tag said. "They talk about did he take you to a nice restaurant and did he remember to pull out your chair. Guys only have one question."

"Did you get laid," my father said.

"Language," my mother said. "And just to be clear, as long as you are living under this roof, the aforesaid will not be an option for any of you."

Colleen poured another glass of milk, and the rest of us went back to our tuna-noodle casserole. I extracted the peas carefully and piled them up on one side of my plate. I hated peas. I hated the way my stupid family never paid any attention to me.

"And of course," my mother said, "if we were to make it a rule, it would have to work both ways. There are no double standards in this family."

"Yeah, right," I said. "Tag never lifts a finger around here."

Tag put his elbow on the table and scratched his cheek with his middle finger. Joanie giggled.

I slammed my glass down, and a wave of milk splashed over the edge. "I saw that, Tag. Mom, Tag just gave me the finger."

"That's enough, Deirdre," my mother said.

"But I didn't *do* anything," I said. "Why doesn't Tag ever get in trouble?"

Nobody bothered to answer. They just went back to discussing their stupid dating rules, and since I'd probably never even get asked out on a real date anyway, it's not like they applied to me.

So I ignored my stupid family and stared across the table at the avocado green vines that twisted and crawled their way up the wallpaper all the way to the ceiling. Harvest gold flowers sprouted randomly among the vines. I imagined slipping unnoticed from my chair and climbing up those vines and taking my place with the sad-faced flowers.

Because I was the family wallflower.

8

Better to run over than to be overrun.

Even though I'd quit and might never speak to him again, I had the cabdriver drop me off at Tag's house when I got home from Austin. I'd just let myself in when my sister Colleen's red Honda CRV rolled down the long tree-lined driveway and parked. The car door opened and Colleen jumped out. Her hair was pulled back into a curly, messy ponytail, and she was wearing sneakers and walking shorts. I considered a quick exit through the back door, but if she'd already seen me, she might follow me down the road to *my* house, which would be worse.

She pulled out two large canvases from the back of the CRV and managed to walk them to Tag's front door.

I swung open the door and greeted her with a "What's up?"

She looked down at my suitcase. "Why aren't you in Texas with Tag?"

"Cramps," I said.

She looked at me.

"Bad ones."

She shook her head.

"Mom and Dad are with him," I said. "I was there for Austin, so all that's left is Houston. His Guruness will be fine. What are you doing here?"

Colleen pushed past me into the house. "Nice to see you, too. I just have to change out some art. I've got a buyer for two of the pieces in Tag's bedroom. And we've got nothing for dinner."

I followed her down the hallway and into Tag's room. "Does Tag know?"

"About dinner?" Colleen placed the canvases on Tag's bed. They were multimedia things—huge images of Tag in sepia collaged with actual print newspaper clippings about him and then painted over in graffitilike Sanskrit and Asian symbols along with Tag's signature tagline over and over in fiery red: DO YOU HAVE PASSION? Then the whole mess was covered with thick layers of decoupage goop to protect it for all eternity.

"About the paintings," I said.

Colleen lifted one off the wall. "He can't tell them apart. As long as he's in them, he loves them."

I decided not to mention that Tag wasn't the only one who couldn't tell them apart. To my eyes, the paintings Colleen had just taken off the wall looked pretty much like the ones she'd brought with her.

Colleen was an artist and her husband an antiques dealer. They were the only family members who didn't live in the town we'd grown up in; they had a house a couple of towns away. But Tag had still managed to outsmart them. He'd bought a historic schoolhouse a block from the ocean and saved it from condo conversion. As if that wasn't enough to make him a hometown hero, he turned it into gallery and classroom space for the Marshbury Arts Association. My sister and her husband managed it in exchange for prime storefront space in the building. Tag had a great tax write-off, the perfect place to host his own local gigs, and another family member under his control.

Just to get her out of my hair faster, I helped Colleen switch the paintings. I'd checked out of the hotel as soon as I got back from

Lake Austin Spa Resort last night, then grabbed the final flight out of Austin, which just so happened to be going in the wrong direction. As soon as we landed, I'd scarfed down two slices of pizza and a beer in the Milwaukee terminal and tossed and turned in yet another hotel until morning. Then I'd jumped on the morning's first flight to Logan. To say that I was tired and grouchy was an understatement.

Colleen rested the paintings she was taking with her against the front door and headed for the kitchen. Tag's home was an old red farmhouse with a fieldstone foundation that sat up on a knoll, king of the hill. He'd left the front of the house largely unchanged, but as soon as you got to the kitchen, the whole thing opened up. Black soapstone counters and an old-fashioned white porcelain sink balanced the shiny professional-grade stainless steel appliances and huge dining island. The view past the massive fieldstone fireplace and walls of glass to the pool and cabana and out to the rolling hills beyond was breathtaking. If you knew where to look, you could even see a trail down to a dock on the North River, which wound its way through spectacular marshes until it spilled into the ocean.

My parents lived in the converted carriage house out back. My sister Joanie and her kids and her husband lived in a renovated Cape on the other side. Tag's first ex-wife and their kids lived in the converted barn; he'd bought and renovated a midcentury ranch abutting the opposite end of the property for his second ex-wife and their kids. The way I looked at it, if my brother kept getting married, eventually he'd own the whole town.

I lived on the property, too, in a converted sheep shed. It was lovely, but sometimes all I could think was *Baa*.

Colleen opened the refrigerator wide so I could see inside, too. "Ooh, pasta primavera," she said. "I'm all over that." She reached for the large bowl, its contents labeled on the plastic-wrapped cover in a swirl of red marker with a big red heart around it.

Tag's two ex-wives had started a catering business together a few years ago. It was called Afterwife. Seriously. I seemed to be the only one who didn't find the name hilarious, but even I had to admit that a little bit of notoriety turned out to be great for business. That and Tag's standing daily order, no matter where in the world he was traveling, kept them squarely in the black. My sister Joanie, who cleaned house for Tag twice a week and did his shopping for extra money, wrapped up anything we didn't eat right away and put it in Tag's industrial-size freezer. When Tag was around, he usually dined out so he could commune with his local fans. I couldn't remember the last time I'd gone farther than my brother's kitchen to graze when I wasn't traveling.

Colleen looked up from the pasta primavera. "Unless you want to split it? Doug and I will never eat all this."

"Nah," I said. "I'll probably just have that salad in there after I finish working out."

I could feel Colleen giving me her *yeah, right* look. I ignored it. Colleen was the thinnest girl in the family and completely superior about it. She'd been trying to get me to walk with her for years. I had a vague plan that I'd start training secretly first, then once I was sure I could kick her butt I'd ask her if she wanted to run a road race with me.

As soon as she left, I locked the front door, as if everyone in a half-mile radius didn't have a key to Tag's house. In one of the lower cabinets, I found a pile of the unbleached cotton bags with Tag's logo printed on them that Joanie used for grocery shopping. I filled them with enough provisions from the kitchen to last at least a few days, maybe more, and then I lugged everything out to the garage, along with my suitcase, and loaded up Tag's golf cart.

He always left the key in the ignition, so I just fired up the cart, opened the garage door, and started putt-putting my way toward my place: home sweet sheep shed.

Just before I turned onto a dirt path that was a shortcut, a car pulled down the long driveway heading in my direction. For a quick crazy second I thought it might be Steve Moretti. As if he'd changed his own plans, booked a flight, rented a car, and knew where to find me. As if Tag might have given him the address. As if Steve might ever want to see me again.

Then I recognized the car. It was Mitchell.

He pulled over and climbed out. When I rode slowly up to him, he pretended to jump out of the way of the golf cart. Until then, I hadn't even considered bothering to run him over, which was probably a sign of my growing maturity about our situation.

I put the golf cart into park but kept the engine running. "No, I don't want to give it another try."

Mitchell grinned. When I met him, he had limp, stringy blondish hair that he wore long enough to make it look limper and stringier. He played the drums in a band on weekends, which was his justification for the fact that he also had it dyed every four weeks. Once he began going bald, he'd started shaving his head, as if he could make it look like he was doing it on purpose. Somehow he couldn't quite pull it off; it made him look like a just-hatched Tweety Bird.

"Hey," he said.

For ten years, this is how it went with Mitchell and me: We'd go out, he'd treat me like gold, I'd fall in love, he'd move in, he'd get lazy, I'd want more, he wouldn't, I'd kick him out, we'd take a break and see other people. Then we'd do it all over again. And again. And again.

After a while the breakups started to blur, and at this moment I couldn't even remember why we'd called things off the last time. As Mitchell stood in front of me, I did a quick calculation and realized we'd been apart for six months. This was the danger zone, when enough time had passed that all the bad stuff started to slip away and a kind of wistful longing crept in to take its place. I mean, we had so many shared memories. Did it really matter that Mitchell didn't believe in marriage, that he didn't want kids, that he'd always held on to his apartment even when we were living together at my place?

"Leave," I said. "Now."

Mitchell rubbed one hand back and forth across the stubble on his scalp, as if he were his own lucky charm. "I'm glad I caught you. I kind of wanted to talk to you for a minute. Just so, you know, you didn't hear it from someone else."

My heart did a funny thing that made me think of a flounder flopping around on a fishing dock.

Mitchell glanced over at his car and then turned back to me.

"I met someone," he said. "She's pregnant. We're getting married."

We looked at each other. A decade flashed before my eyes.

"Liar," I said.

The golf cart engine revved. My foot must have made it happen, but I felt totally disconnected from the movement. I wished Tag had left some golf clubs in it. I could pretend I was Tiger Woods's wife, Elin, and whack the shit out of Mitchell, the closest thing I'd ever had to a husband. At least Elin got alimony. At least Tiger had an Ambien prescription.

"I can understand how it might take a little time to get used to the idea. But we're actually really happy about it." Mitchell rubbed his head again. "You'll like her."

"Go away," I said.

"Is Tag around?"

It was my turn to look at Mitchell's car. The front of it was pointed at Tag's house. If Mitchell had been on his way to see me, he would have taken the next turn off the main road, into my driveway, and not this one.

"Ohmigod," I said. "You didn't come here to tell *me*. You came to tell Tag."

Mitchell's hand was still on his scalp. "I want him to marry us, Dee. I mean, I know it might be a little awkward for you, but Tag's like a brother to me."

I put the golf cart into gear.

Then I pushed the pedal as far as it would go and aimed right for the man who had wasted the most valuable years of my life.

Just before impact, a chiasmus flashed before my eyes like a vision: *Better to run over than to be overrun.*

9

When people show you their true colors,
color yourself convinced the first time.

The first time I met Mitchell I was sitting at a little round table having a glass of wine with someone named Belinda. Belinda and I had gone to high school together. We'd chosen the Marshbury Tavern because it was the only place for miles around that had entertainment on Tuesday nights.

Belinda was in town for the week to visit her parents. She lived in North Carolina but kept closer tabs than I did on what was happening on the hometown front. Belinda was one of those people who sent you a birthday and a Christmas card with a chatty little note every year, year in and year out, whether or not you ever sent them a card back, whether or not you'd ever really known each other in the first place.

"So," she said, "whatever happened to Marla Embrey?"

"Marla Embrey," I repeated. "Which one was she again?"

Belinda sighed and reached for her wineglass. Clearly she was starting to wish she'd tracked down Marla Embrey instead of me. I wasn't intentionally trying to disappoint Belinda. High school just hadn't appealed to me much the first time around. Trying to give it a second incarnation by reliving it did even less for me. I'd also noticed that people who no longer lived in the town they'd grown up in automatically assumed those who did knew everything that was going on. The truth was that the way to handle still living there was to let go of the past.

Belinda regrouped and tried a new direction. "By the way, I was so sorry to read about Tag and his wife splitting up."

I shrugged. "Split happens."

Tag's star was rising fast back then and this was our family's first major run-in with the tabloids. Shortly after the breakup, my father had made the mistake of talking to someone at the town landfill. That someone had in turn sold the story for big bucks.

The headline in the *National Enquirer* screamed, "Tag Tells Wife of Seven Years: You're No Longer It." And the first paragraph of the story contained this little gem: "The New Age phenomenon's own father told a close family friend requesting anonymity, 'That boy never could manage to keep it in his pants.'"

It was a wake-up call for the whole family. We closed ranks. For the first time, we were careful whom we talked to and what we said.

I didn't know it then, but it was the first step toward my isolated, family-only claustrophobia of today.

I took a sip of my wine while I rooted around for some safe conversational ground. "I can't believe they're playing 'There's a Kind of Hush (All Over the World)'" I said. "I mean, how retro can you get?"

Belinda looked over at the band. "The drummer even looks a little bit like Herman of Herman's Hermits."

"Peter Noone," I said.

"You know him?"

I laughed. "No. Peter Noone was Herman of Herman's Hermits. I had a huge crush on him. After Sajid Khan and before Micky Dolenz."

Belinda leaned forward as if she were about to get a tabloid-worthy scoop. "Okay, Micky Dolenz was one of the Monkees, but who was Sajid Khan?"

I shrugged. "He rode an elephant on a TV show called *Maya* with the guy who played Dennis the Menace. I was madly in love with him. I was probably only five or six, but my mother helped me write him a fan letter, and he sent me a signed postcard of himself. And the elephant. I lived off the high for an entire year."

Belinda picked up her wineglass and suddenly froze. "Don't look," she said without moving her lips, "but he's coming over."

I looked. "Sajid Khan?"

It was the drummer. He walked almost to our table, made eye contact, ran a hand through his straight, stringy hair, and then kept going in the direction of the men's room.

"Ohmigod," Belinda said. "The drummer totally likes you."

I rolled my eyes.

"Holy déjà vu," Belinda said. "It's like we just flashed back to high school. Or maybe we just time-traveled to a John Hughes movie. *Sixteen Candles. The Breakfast Club. Making It in Marshbury.*"

I rolled my eyes again.

When the drummer came back from the men's room, he stopped at our table.

"Hey, Herman," I said.

He ran a hand through his hair and smiled. "Do you really think I look like him?"

It would take me the next decade to learn that when people show you their true colors, color yourself convinced the first time.

When he asked me out, I said yes.

"Would you keep it down?" I said. "I barely even hit you."

Mitchell was lying on his back. His eyes were closed and he was holding one thigh and rolling back and forth. "Oww," he kept saying. "Oww, wow, wow, wow, oww." It was almost like one of Tag's group chants.

I wondered if I could get away with leaving, or if, in this crazy, crazy world, tapping the man who'd completely wasted the most marketable years of your life on the leg with a golf cart that barely did fifteen miles an hour and not hanging around could possibly be considered a hit-and-run.

He interrupted his chanting to whisper, "Call. An. Ambulance."

"Oh, puh-lease. You call an ambulance."

"I can't believe you *hit* me," he said. I'd almost forgotten how whiny his voice was.

"You should be thanking me for missing your hands," I said. "At least you'll live to drum again."

Mitchell groaned. He mumbled something about the pedals.

When I didn't say anything, he went back to his chanting.

"Listen," I said. "I barely slept last night. I'm going to get going now."

He opened his eyes. "You're just going to leave me?"

"What a coincidence," I said. "I was about to say the exact same thing to you."

I found his cell phone in his car and threw it at him so he could call his pregnant bride-to-be. It was the best I could do.

I took off before I had to listen to his phone call. I didn't even want Mitchell, at least I was pretty sure I didn't, but it still stung. More than stung. In fact, it felt a little bit like a golf cart had hit me, too, right in the gut. A few tears escaped, and I blinked them away as I drove. By the time I pulled up to my front steps, a sheep shed had never looked so good.

Tag's architect and his team had indeed done an incredible job on it. They'd kept most of the shed's original rough interior barn board, which made it feel warm and cozy and also meant that I could hammer a nail in a wall pretty much anywhere without making a mess. The kitchen was just the right size for someone who didn't cook, and it was open to a cute little dining nook and a mini–great room beyond. The guest bath even had a pocket door to save space. They'd tucked a narrow staircase up against the wall when you first walked in, which you had to climb hand over hand like a ladder. The second-story addition created a surprisingly big master bedroom with south-facing windows and a French door leading out to a tiny balcony. It had a spacious walk-in closet and a master bath with a garden tub and a separate shower.

The sheep shed was a sunny, happy space for one person—two if you were *really* getting along. It would have been perfect, if only it had been mine.

"For all intents and purposes, it *is* yours," Tag would say whenever I offered to buy him out. "It's just a business thing."

"It's not a business thing," I'd say. "It's a control thing. You're a total control freak."

"I know you are, but what am I?" my stupid brother would say.

I put everything I'd pilfered from Tag's house in the fridge and bumped my suitcase up the stairs in front of me. I had a stacked washer and dryer tucked into a corner of the walk-in, so I dumped out my dirty clothes on the floor in front of them. A pair of stretched-out dingy underpants rose to the surface, and for a minute I thought my ripped underpants had mysteriously reappeared after I had abandoned them in the hotel elevator. Then I remembered that, minus the rip, I owned a wardrobe full of clones.

I opened my underwear drawer and started throwing underpants on the floor, one after another after another. Big fat ugly underpants I'd fallen into wearing after Mitchell moved out the last time. Because they were comfortable. Because no one was going to see them anyway. Because I really didn't give a shit. About anything. Anymore.

I turned my head, but before I could close my eyes in self-defense, the way I usually did, I caught myself in the closet's full-length mirror. I tried to look at myself as if I were assessing a stranger. My eyes had raccoon circles under them from yesterday's mascara. My hair was flattened on one side and sticking out on the other. I was wearing baggy sweats and a baggier T-shirt and I looked lumpy and bumpy and frumpy. It was as if my shrunken insides had donated their weight, their bulk, to my outside.

I closed my eyes and rolled the top of my sweats down over my hips. I rolled the bottom of my T-shirt up as high as it could go. Then I counted to three and made myself open my eyes and face the mirror again.

I tried leaning forward. I angled to the right and then to the left. I pulled in my stomach and held my breath. I squinted my eyes in case I'd lucked out and Steve was nearsighted. But even if I factored out the toothpaste drool cascading from my mouth, the man who had walked into my hotel room had seen, up close and personal, the disaster I'd become.

If only I could turn back the clock. I'd be in killer shape when I met Steve Moretti. I'd be wearing dazzling underwear when he walked in on me. By the time he figured out I was Tag's sister, he'd have already fallen head over heels for *me*. He wouldn't want to use me to get to Tag. He'd only want to get to me. When Tag found out about us and got all territorial, we'd already be a couple. We could both tell Tag to get over himself. Together.

My head was starting to pound. Really pound. I was old enough to know my Austin meltdown wasn't only about Steve. He was just one more person in a long, long line of people trying to use me to get to the rest of my family. If only I'd hightailed it out of town as soon as I graduated from college. I would have called my family once a week and sent presents on holidays. Visited for a week in the summer, or maybe early fall, when it was still beach weather but the tourists were gone.

I'd drifted through high school, mostly marking time. Tag played in a band and Colleen was an artist, so those worlds were taken. If I joined a club or tried out for a play, the minute I turned around

Joanie would be right behind me. Until I could get out from under the shadow of my siblings, it didn't seem possible to carve out a space of my own.

Even my friends seemed more interested in my family than in me. *Do you think Tag will be home?* they'd ask as we got out of the car or walked up the brick path that led to my house. *Is he seeing anyone?*

Anyone and everyone, I'd say. *Take a number.*

Will Colleen be home? I want to ask her where she got that miniskirt she had on today.

In junior high, I went steady twice, which didn't involve much more than a few pause-laden phone calls, a couple of dances, and spin the bottle in somebody's rec room while the parents were upstairs. I didn't date much in high school, and when I did, it was usually one half of a double date. *You're perfect for each other,* one of my friends would say, fixing me up with her boyfriend's friend.

Of course this was never true, but by then it would be too late. I'd have to sit in the front seat and listen to some guy with knobby elbows and a wannabe mustache go on and on about himself while my friend and her boyfriend groped each other in the backseat.

I whiled away the time with crushes on movie stars and a moderately cute guy named Chad Gibson who, by virtue of his last name, was sentenced to four years sitting in front of me in homeroom. Freshman year we ignored each other. Sophomore year he turned around and asked to borrow a pen one day. The next day he gave it back.

Junior year he walked me home. We talked about books and movies and teachers we hated, and when I stopped to switch my shoulder bag to the other side, he reached for it and carried it the rest of the way.

When we got to my house, I invited him in. My mother was baking chocolate chip cookies. Then Joanie wandered into the kitchen and never left.

By that weekend, she had a date with him. *Don't look at me,* she said when I threatened to kill her. *He told me you were just friends.*

Freshman year in college, I stood in line on Sundays to call my parents collect from one of three dorm phones. I drifted, rudderless, not sure who I was without being wedged in between my siblings. I switched majors twice. The next year I switched dorms. I made friends and had boyfriends, lovers even. When we graduated, two friends and I landed jobs in Denver. I had a boyfriend named Ethan, and we hiked and climbed and went river rafting together. Still, my home-sickness was like a low-grade fever. Maybe a childhood spent being a conduit for my siblings had left me without the ability to thrive when I pulled the plug.

After a year, I moved home and barely left the beach for a month. Being near the ocean was soothing. The rhythm of the sea felt like home. It was as close to climbing back into the womb as I could get without completely humiliating myself.

I stayed in the area and worked a series of dead-end local jobs and dated a series of dead-end local guys while Tag's star began its me-teoric rise. When he hired me to be his PA, it actually worked for a while. It was fast-paced and every day was different. I was good at it, and even reflected glory can be intoxicating. Nothing was ever enough for Tag, though. Before long my job had swallowed most of my life, and what was left I'd squandered away on Mitchell, whom I'd just begun to date.

I loved denial—it was warm and cuddly like a favorite childhood blankie—but standing here now, sweats rolled down over my hips, I forced myself to push it away and look at the facts. I'd spent the last decade in and out of a dead-end relationship as I worked seven days a week, twenty-four hours a day at a job that made me disappear bit by bit on the inside, as I bulked up inch by inch on the outside.

I shook my head to clear away the past and turned to take in the depths of my walk-in closet. Some women arrange their clothes by season: winter-spring-summer-fall or spring-summer-fall-winter. Others do it by color: lightest to darkest or darkest to lightest or even whites here, blacks here, and colors over there. Some just cram everything in wherever it will fit.

I had a system, too, though I was pretty sure I'd never acknowledged it before, even to myself. My closet was arranged by size: Now, Not That Long Ago, Once Upon a Time, Never Again, and In Your Dreams. I didn't even have to check the tags to verify the humiliating range of ever-increasing numerals displayed on them.

I wondered what size I'd be when I'd finally had enough.

10

Let go of the past and go let the future in.

Okay, so mixing a drink was probably not the best next move. It was definitely five-thirsty somewhere in the world, but we still had a few hours to go in this neck of the woods. And I wasn't really even that much of a drinker. If I were to get all Dr. Phil, the truth was that food was my drug of choice. I ate to self-medicate, to soothe and calm myself, to distract me from my troubles.

Then I drank to give the food something to absorb. Or possibly because I got tired of all that chewing. Or maybe to me alcohol was like a fork-free version of dessert.

I had to admit that boozewise, I leaned toward the sweet stuff. Baileys Irish Cream, frozen strawberry daiquiris, Kahlúa sombreros, piña coladas. And I also had to admit that right now I could have killed for a bottle of ChocoVine.

Killed made me think of golf carts and Mitchell and marriage and some other woman having my baby. I tried to conjure up an image of an ugly little Tweety Bird–headed infant in smelly diapers to make myself feel better, but it didn't help all that much.

And then I started thinking about Steve Moretti again. Which made me realize I hadn't checked my cell phone since I'd turned it off when I climbed into the town car at Lake Austin Spa Resort. There might actually be a message on it from Steve. Wasn't there an old saying about how letting go of one thing made room in your life for something better? If there wasn't an old saying like that, there really should be. *Let go of the past and go let the future in.* It wasn't the most brilliant chiasmus I'd ever come up with, but I could work with it.

But then again, there might not be a message on my cell from Steve, and even if there was, it might not necessarily be something I'd actually want to hear. And there sure as hell would be lots of angry text messages and voice mails from Tag, and possibly from my parents, as well as about a zillion Tag-related messages I'd have to decide whether or not to deal with. I mean, I'd quit, but had I really *quit?*

So basically what it came down to was that I was simply too tired and beaten down to handle turning on my phone without a little fortification. And for the first time in my life I could remember, I was too wiped out to feel like eating.

So that left liquid reinforcement. I clomped back down the steep stairs to the lower level of my sheep shed, turning sideways because the treads were so narrow you couldn't get your whole foot on them. I opened my tiny refrigerator to inspect the contents. I'd grabbed a few bottles of wine from Tag's wine fridge, and also a bottle of some fancy shmancy Russian vodka he kept in his freezer. I usually made it a point to stay away from the triple-digit-proof stuff, but it looked so cold and refreshing I'd snagged it anyway. I'd also taken some chocolate soy milk that Afterwife had started carrying, mostly because I liked the old-fashioned glass milk bottle it came in. I'd had a vague idea that after I drank the milk I'd use the bottle for a vase to hold the flowers I was going to pick from one of my brother's gardens to make myself feel better.

I leaned my head against the refrigerator door as a new revelation hit me. If I'd really quit, I couldn't even ask my ex-sisters-in-law if they'd let me in on Afterwife, maybe take over the marketing end of the business. *Because I'd never been a wife.* If Mitchell somehow managed to die from his golf cart injuries, I wouldn't even get the street cred of being his widow. His pregnant bride-to-be would be his almost-widow.

I'd be nothing.

I dug out my blender and slammed it down on the counter. I shoveled in some big scoops of the Ben & Jerry's Triple Caramel Chunk ice cream I'd grabbed at Tag's, then buried it in chocolate soy milk. I opened the bottle of pretentious vodka and filled the blender right to the tipitty top. I knew the proportions were off, but at the moment, I didn't really give a triple caramel shit.

"Let the pity party begin," I said.

I curled up on my loveless love seat in my tiny great room. I thought about starting a fire in the little fireplace and burning my pitiful underpants one by one, but I was afraid all that scorched elastic might set off the smoke alarms. So I turned on the TV instead.

I lucked out and found a *Mary Tyler Moore Show* rerun. Growing up, I'd watched the show religiously with my family on Saturday nights, long before I understood what it meant to be a single woman who knew she needed to move away when a long-term relationship ended.

It wasn't just any episode I'd stumbled upon, but Season 1, Episode 1, "Love Is All Around." Mary has just moved to Minneapolis when her neighbor Phyllis butts in and invites Mary's old boyfriend Bill to visit. Bill is a doctor and such a jerk that he even brings Mary flowers he stole from a patient's hospital bedside. Finally, *finally* Mary gets up the courage to tell him good-bye for good. When he leaves, she tears up and tells herself how lucky she is to be rid of him.

I wiped my eyes as the credits rolled. "I'm really lucky, too, Mary," I said. "I'm so lucky."

I took a long drink from my tall glass. It was like the world's most incredible milk shake. The vodka had completely disappeared into the rich, sweet chocolate-covered caramel of the ice cream. Boyohboy,

Ben and Jerry sure knew their stuff. I wondered if one of them was single.

I drained my glass and shivered as the Russian vodka hit my brain. American men could mail-order Russian brides—who knew, maybe if I placed an ad, a Russian man would order me. Totally cracking myself up, I took a moment to laugh, then clicked off the TV. I picked up the glass again and tucked my cell under my armpit on the same side. I took the handful of steps required to get to the kitchen and grabbed the blender off the counter with my other hand. Then I worked my way back up the steep stairs, occasionally putting the blender down and leaning on it for balance. I decided my next house would be a single story ranch in the south of France. And I was a poet and I didn't even know it.

I threw my phone on the comforter I'd been meaning to replace for at least two years and put the blender down carefully on the table at my side of the bed. Wait a minute. I didn't even like this side of the bed. Ten years ago Mitchell had claimed the other side. And I'd let him. But they were both my sides of the bed now.

I moved the blender over to the table on Mitchell's former side, just because I could, and poured myself another glass of frosty heaven. I wondered if Ben and Jerry would be open to expanding with a line of soy-and-vodka-based ice-cream drinks. Frosty the Snowsoyshake? Shake, Rattle, and Drink? As soon as I had a good night's sleep, maybe I'd pitch them. I mean, my time working for Tag certainly qualified as product development, so I had plenty of experience.

I took a long rejuvenating drink. And another. Those Russians sure knew their vodka. Then I decided I'd cruise the Internet for a little while, catch up on the state of the world, and work up to the messages on my cell phone. My laptop was all the way over on the little desk on the other side of the room, which was starting to feel like a long, long way to go just to catch up on the state of the world, but its larger screen seemed like a good thing right about now, and I had to pee anyway, so if I made it all part of one loop, then it made sense.

I should have gone to the bathroom before I picked up the laptop, but I didn't think of that until I got to the bathroom. But no worries, I just put the laptop on the floor. When I bent down to pick it up again, I got a little bit wobbly. Lack of sleep and those damn time zone changes will do it to you.

As soon as I got back to my bed, I was okay again. It was like my bed was this great big soft fluffy life raft, and I was just floating around in the middle of the ocean. The water could be teeming with sharks and stingrays and idiot boyfriends and guru brothers who could suck the life out of you, but as long as I stayed right here, nothing could touch me.

I fired up my laptop and opened a news site. I clicked past a bunch of burglaries and shootings and wars and cheating politicians and rising this and shortages of that, looking for a ray of sunshine. I mean, what a world.

A headline jumped out at me: "Celebrity Dancer-to-Be Checks Into Rehab, *Dancing With the Stars* Viewers to Choose Last-Minute Replacement." A producer from *DWTS* had been trying to get Tag on the show for at least three seasons now. Tag was pretty athletic, but he danced a lot like Elaine on *Seinfeld*, so it had become kind of a family joke. Maybe I didn't get the pick of the gene pool when it came to some things, but I'd been the best dancer in the family by a long shot.

Oh, how I'd loved to dance when we were kids. And I was good. Everybody said so. Even in my crib, according to my parents, as soon as I'd hear music I'd pull myself up by the rails and start bouncing away in perfect time to it.

I started dance classes at five. I was a fluffy ducky in my first recital. When it was over I refused to take off my scratchy yellow tutu. I even slept in it until it fell apart. By third grade I was so good I was ready for a double promotion. The teacher moved me into Colleen's ballet, tap, and modern jazz combo class. I pointed, I tapped, I made jazz hands. I practiced all week on the linoleum floor in the kitchen so I could keep up with the big girls on Saturday mornings.

And then my mother, *my own mother*, talked the teacher into letting Joanie into the same class. Just so she wouldn't have to spend the whole morning chauffeuring us around to different activities.

"Oh, she's adorable," everybody said. And then suddenly Joanie was the family dancer.

The whole thing was so traumatic that after the session was over, I dropped out, never to dance again. At least in public. The truth was that I turned into a closet dancer. Instead of singing in the shower, I danced. Even now, when I checked into a hotel room on business and *All That Jazz* or *Footloose* or *Dirty Dancing* just happened to be playing, I'd pull the curtains closed and dance my ass off.

I clicked on the link.

> Actress Kelly Genelavive checked into rehab this week after being arrested for allegedly stealing an Oscar belonging to her former boyfriend, actor Kent Lazer, and putting it up for sale on eBay.

I liked her spirit. If she wasn't in rehab, I'd call her up right now and tell her about Mitchell and the golf cart so we could commiserate. I took another sip, smaller this time, and went back to reading.

> The mandatory thirty-day inpatient internment resulted in the cancellation of Genelavive's earlier commitment to this season's *Dancing With the Stars*, slated to begin rehearsals next week. The show has left the choice of her replacement to its viewers, and a

Facebook page has been set up for voting purposes. The female candidate with the most votes by midnight EST tonight will join this season's *DWTS* celebrity and professional dancers in Los Angeles on Monday.

The voting link followed, along with the proclamation, "IT COULD BE YOU."

Wow. It could be me. I mean, it really could be me. I was just one step away from Tag, who was guru to thousands upon thousands. He'd maxed out his Facebook friend list, and his Facebook fan list was enormous. His Twitter followers more than tripled his combined Facebook numbers. And his e-list, the one that we'd been building for the last ten years by collecting e-mails with event registrations and with every online order placed, was huge. I mean, staggeringly huge. I knew. I was the one who was in charge of them all. I was the one who wrote the newsletters and e-blasts, who posted on Tag's behalf on Facebook, who tweeted his twinkling tweets on Twitter till my fingers practically bled. I mean, you could look at it that they were essentially my lists. Didn't I deserve to benefit from my own hard work?

He might not realize it right away, but Tag would even want this for me. He'd want me to be happy. He'd want me to spread my wings and soar. He'd want me to dance again. And it would be great PR for Tag, right? Plus this way no one would have to see how he danced. And by the time the next Steve Moretti walked in on me, I'd not only be fit and fabulous. I'd. Be. Famous.

I emptied the blender into my glass. In the end, it wasn't all that different from all the other messages I wrote for him:

Galactic greetings and the sunniest of salutations, my friends.
Allow me to introduce you to my dearest sister Deirdre.

Almost from birth, we knew she was the family dancer. Such grace. Such talent. Such soul. But for years, far too many years, she put it all aside to support me in my dream. Our dream, my friends. And now an opportunity presents itself for all of us to join together and bestow our own gift on this most deserving recipient. Please use the link below to cast your vote for my sister Deirdre and make her lifelong Dancing With the Stars *dream come true. And our message to her and to ourselves will be: Let go of the past and go let the future in.*

Peace in, peace out,

Tag

By the time I pushed Send I knew I was at the perfectly perfect beginning of the rosiest chapter of my life. I was so freakin' happy I was practically floating. I closed one eye so I could pick up the remote on my bedside table. I clicked around on it until I managed to find the right button to turn on my iPod player.

Bonnie Raitt broke into a bluesy "Let's give them something to talk about."

"I hear you, Bonnie," I said, my voice in my ears sounding like an old forty-five played at 33 rpm. "And I'm pretty sure we just did it."

11

It's not the size of the dog in the fight,
but the size of the fight in the dog.

—MARK TWAIN

Two miniature Russian guys were lodged in my head, doing that famous Russian squat dance with tiny steel-toe boots against the back of my eyeballs. My mouth was as dry as the Sahara Desert, and my stomach completely understood how Mount Vesuvius felt just before it erupted.

I opened one eye carefully. The little bedside clock read 6:03. Judging by the sunshine pouring in through the floor-to-ceiling window and the French doors, that would be a.m. If only I had a remote control for the curtains I hadn't bothered to close. This daylight thing was killing me.

I'd woken up around midnight. I'd practically crawled my way into the bathroom to pee and then wash down either four or five Advil with as much water as I could swallow. After all that exertion, I found myself craving a snack. I made it halfway down the stairs, then pictured myself falling to the bottom only to be found when the smell of my mangled and decomposed body alerted Tag's lawn guys. I bumped the rest of the way down the stairs on my butt like a drunken toddler.

When I got to the kitchen I poured a glass of cow's milk and went right for the Devil Dogs. Tag ordered them by the caseload: sixteen Devil Dogs to the economy box, twelve boxes to the case. They'd been his favorite since we were kids.

Growing up, Saturday was allowance day, and the four of us would walk the mile to Marshbury Center and stock up at the A&P. I'd preferred the round shape and crisp chocolate shell of Ring Dings. Joanie Baloney always went for the cellophane-wrapped three-packs of Sarah Lawton Chocolate Chip cookies at the register. Colleen would save most of her money for magazines like *Tiger Beat* and buy one paltry roll of Necco Wafers and ration it so it lasted all week. Every once in a while after I finished my stash, I'd sneak into the top drawer of her shiny white bureau and steal a single powdery gray licorice-flavored wafer just to see if I could get away with it.

The year Tag moved up to Marshbury Junior High, he left the rest of us stranded like babies at Harborside Elementary, one of four elementary schools scattered across town. Suddenly he had friends from all over the place, four times as many as we did, three-quarters of them strangers to the rest of us. But Colleen had managed to beat him to a growth spurt. Almost overnight she was skinnier than ever and almost a head taller than Tag. She scrubbed her face three times a day and tried every shade of Clearasil in an attempt to discover the magic one that would make her pimples disappear.

"Catch ya later," Tag said one day as soon as we got to Main Street. "I'm gonna do my own thing."

It was too late. Some boys had seen him with us. "What's happenin', Tag," one of them said. "Takin' a walk with the *girls*?"

Tag smiled, all confidence. Then he turned and pointed at Colleen's Clearasil-dotted face. "Just tryin' to help zitface pop a few whiteheads."

The boys burst out laughing. Colleen ducked her head and kept walking, Joanie in her wake. I froze, just long enough.

Tag turned toward me, a junior high comedian looking for some new material to impress his fans. "Yeah," he said. He pointed a thumb in my direction. "And after that I'm gonna put fatso here on a diet."

I went numb. I couldn't seem to move. The boys were on our side of the street now. The biggest one threw an arm across my shoulders and pinched my cheek with the other hand. "Whoa," he said in Tag's direction. "Where'd you find this porker?"

He was on his back before he knew what hit him, Tag sitting on his chest and punching him in the face.

The night before at dinner, my father's chiasmus had been a quote from Mark Twain: *It's not the size of the dog in the fight, but the size of the fight in the dog.*

"Don't. You. Ever," my brother finally said, "trash-talk one of my sisters again."

I ran the whole way home, my chest burning, hot tears streaming down my face. When Tag got home, he even offered me a Devil Dog, but I'd already decided I wasn't going to speak to him for the rest of my life. Just because he'd defended me didn't mean he hadn't started the whole thing.

It was the last time I ever walked to Marshbury Center on allowance day. I stayed home and read a book instead, and gave my Ring Ding money to Joanie Baloney, who was the only one I could count on to bring me back the change.

I opened both eyes. Dread was sitting on my chest as if it were an animal. I mean, dread so real it had physical presence, like a Labrador retriever I could teach tricks to. *Here, Dread. Sit, Dread. Roll over, Dread. Play dead, Dread.*

My hand found a hard object and I realized I'd slept with my laptop. I slid it over to my lap and pressed a key. No power. Good. Who knew how long it would take to charge up again. I patted my bed with both hands, but it was my right toe that came in contact with my cell phone under the sheets. I caught it with my heel and slid it toward me until I could reach down and grab it with one hand.

I closed my eyes and thought for a minute. My cell had been turned off, so chances were it still held a charge. If I turned it on I'd have to face whatever messages it held. But since I had to charge my laptop anyway, I might as well charge both devices at the same time, so that when I finally faced whatever was in store for me, I'd get it all over with at once.

It made sense. I flopped over sideways, then slowly wiggled my way to the edge of the bed like an inchworm. I turned onto my stomach and slid off the bed till my feet touched the floor. I carried my laptop and phone over to my little desk and plugged them into the surge protector. I thought for another minute, then unplugged the surge protector and plugged both chargers directly into the outlet. I mean, maybe I'd get lucky and the house would be struck by lightning and fry them both. It would probably take me at least a week or two to replace them. Maybe longer.

I walked slowly and carefully into my bathroom and washed down another four Advil with tap water. I considered throwing up, but I didn't want to lose the Advil and I didn't really have the energy anyway, so I just peed again. I looked at the shower for a long, spacey minute, maybe more, and thought about how good it would feel to finally get out of my T-shirt and sweats and feel clean again.

"Later," I said. My voice was low and raspy, as if I'd been out all night, laughing and talking with friends.

When I finally made it to my kitchen, my first thought was that I'd been robbed. There were Devil Dog wrappers everywhere. I picked up the clear cellophane wrappers as fast as I could, trying not to count them as I threw them away. *I can't believe I ate the whole thing* flashed through my head from an old commercial I could no longer attach a product to.

I opened the tiny refrigerator. I stared at the eggs for a while but couldn't quite picture getting them from the shell into a pan and onto a plate. I shut the refrigerator door and opened the freezer. A plastic container filled with frozen Afterwife chicken-and-Gorgonzola pasta called out to me. I plopped the whole thing onto a plate. Liquid fat sputtered and spattered all over the walls of my little microwave as I nuked it, but I didn't have the wherewithal to do anything about it. I poured a glass of ginger ale to settle my stomach and carried the whole thing back to my bedroom.

I ate every single bite, then put the plate on my bedside table. I thought about closing the blinds, but it seemed a lot more efficient to pull the covers over my head. Alka-Seltzer, I thought, *I can't believe I ate the whole thing* was a commercial for Alka-Seltzer.

I fell asleep again like a ton of bricks, maybe two tons. I dreamed about Ethan, my boyfriend from my postcollege stint in Denver, who'd ruined everything by inviting me to Sunday dinner with his family, because it made me realize that if I stayed, Sunday dinner would never be with my family. "Why?" Dream Ethan said. He was standing on the corner in the threadbare flannel shirt he always used to wear, but his eyebrows were gray and a baby was peering over his shoulder from his backpack. "These could have been your eyebrows."

I turned away and suddenly I was walking down Main Street in Marshbury and Mitchell was on the same sidewalk, riding a golf cart in my direction. His drum set was somehow slung over his shoulders, and he had long, limp, stringy hair again, just like when we first met.

I didn't like the way he was looking at me, so I turned and started heading in the opposite direction. A group of junior high boys came out of nowhere and surrounded me.

"What a porker," one of them said.

"Whoa," another one said. "She's a tusker, a real tusker."

Maybe the second boy was sticking up for me. "What's a tusker?" I asked.

Sajid Khan came out of nowhere. "Silly girl. A tusker is an elephant."

"Really?"

He nodded. A pretty girl came out of nowhere, too, and powdered his nose. "And now you have to dance or I want my postcard back," Sajid Khan said.

"I don't want to dance," I said.

"Dance, dance, dance," they all started to chant, even Ethan and the baby, even Mitchell, who was flooring the golf cart and heading straight for me.

The chant turned into a knock on the door. A loud knock. A knock that just wouldn't go away.

"What?" I said. I opened my eyes. Downstairs, someone was knocking like crazy on my door.

I tiptoed halfway down the stairs and sat down. My front door had a glass insert, and if I turned my head just right, I could see who was out there without being seen.

The top of a head covered with short curly hair appeared. The knocking started again.

"Open up," a voice yelled. "Come on, I know you're in there, Deirdre."

12

*She who hesitates is lost, but she who doesn't
hesitate might end up even loster.*

"W*hat* were you thinking?" Joanie Baloney said when I
opened the door.

"Nice to see you, too," I said. Tag's golf cart was directly
behind her, tilted at a funny angle. I remembered hitting Mitchell,
and for a minute I wondered if he'd damaged it. Then I realized I'd
managed to drive one wheel onto the bottom step when I parked the
cart as close as I could get to make it easier to unload the groceries. I
squinted. Mitchell hadn't even left a dent. What a crybaby.

Crybaby made me think of baby baby—Ethan's dream baby,
Mitchell's baby-to-be. Sadness flooded over me like sleeping sickness,
and all I wanted to do was find my bed again.

"Nice parking job," my younger sister said.

"Boo!" My six-year-old niece, Jenna, jumped out from behind the
golf cart.

"Boo!" My two-year-old nephew, Johnny, jumped out, too.

Joanie and Jenna were wearing matching little purple cotton
dresses that were perfect for a six-year-old, and the purple of Johnny's
golf shirt was exactly the same shade. I just knew Joanie's husband,
Jack, was sitting at home in a bigger version of the same golf shirt.

Maybe I'd never had kids, but at least I'd never humiliated any either. Joanie said they all loved to dress alike, but I could only hope they were humoring her.

Jenna and Johnny threw themselves at me, a cross between a hug and a tackle. They both had curly dark hair and shiny brown eyes, and when I looked at them, all I could think was that these apples hadn't fallen far from the family tree. They could have been us when we were kids.

I squatted down to hug them back. "Hey," I said. "What's up, munchkins?"

"Brush you teeth," Johnny said.

I turned my head. "Sorry. I've been working up to that."

"Can I come watch you be on TV?" Jenna said. "I'm a good dancer." She pushed away from our group hug and started twirling around on the front yard.

I wasn't quite following her. I looked at Joanie.

"Okay, kids," she yelled. "Give Auntie Dee another hug and go tell Daddy Mommy said to push you on the swings."

"I don't need a push," Jenna said.

"Me want a push," Johnny said.

Maybe all that dressing alike had caused some kind of extrasensory family perception, because a purple-shirted Jack magically appeared at the end of the path that led from their house to mine. He waved. Joanie waved back.

Then she crossed her arms over her chest and walked past me and into the sheep shed.

I followed her inside. "What were you thinking?" she said again.

I started to walk by her in the direction of the refrigerator. "What?" I said. "Tag's fine. Mom and Dad are with him."

She grabbed me by the arm. "You look like shit. And it's all over the news."

I aimed my breath away from her. "That I look like shit?"

"I can't believe you took advantage of Tag like that."

"Like what?" I said. "By quitting?" Fuzziness surrounded my head like a helmet, but just beyond that something was lurking. And it wasn't a good thing.

Joanie tilted her head. "Uh, Tag beseeches fans to vote his favorite sister onto *Dancing With the Stars*?"

"What are you talking about?" I said.

"Nice try, Dee," my little sister said.

I closed my eyes as it all came back. I kept them closed as I tried to come up with a believable story, but my pickled brain cells just didn't have it in them.

"Of course I didn't take advantage of Tag," I said, fighting to concoct a good story as the dread enveloped me. "I just thought it would be great publicity. And, come on, you've seen him dance. It's not like we could send *him*."

Joanie looked at me. We were a family built on the scaffolding of meetings. A family held together by the glue of conversation. A family of rules. And I'd just broken pretty much every single one of them.

My eyes teared up. "Mitchell's getting married." My lower lip started to quiver. "She's pregnant."

"I know," Joanie said. "He stopped by to ask Jack to be one of his groomsmen."

I couldn't believe it. "That little shit. What did Jack say?"

"That he'd have to ask me first?"

"Good answer. Do you think we could clone Jack for me?"

"Don't try to change the subject," Joanie said. "Listen, Tag is going ballistic. Mom and Dad are trying to keep him under control. The way I look at it, you've got two choices."

I couldn't even think of one.

Joanie dug her fingers into my arm, as if I might try to make a run for it.

"What are they?" I asked eventually.

"Okay, one, you can check yourself into rehab."

"Right," I said. "Maybe Kelly Genelavive needs a roommate."

"I'm not kidding. Rehab gets you out of practically everything these days. You can write a statement from Tag before I drop you off. He'll look great when he pretends to forgive you." Joanie let go of my arm and took a step back. "I have to tell you, the way you look right now, a month in rehab couldn't hurt."

"Oh, puh-lease. I got drunk one night. And it wasn't even my vodka."

"You're a mess," Joanie said. "You really need to get your act together."

"That's my other choice?" I said.

"No. Your other choice is to do it. To get on a plane and get the hell out of here before Mom and Dad and Tag get home. Have an adventure. Make the most of it. Enjoy your fifteen minutes of fame."

I tried to imagine waltzing into a dance studio in Los Angeles, razzling and dazzling everyone with my charming personality, putting on my nonexistent dance shoes and actually dancing. I mean, it's not like I had to win or anything. I just had to not be the first dancer voted off. Okay, maybe not the second either. But the third would be respectable. I mean, how hard could *that* be?

I snapped out of the fantasy and my eyes teared up again. "The truth is I can't even make myself check my messages."

Joanie put her arm around me. "You're pathetic. I don't know how Tag puts up with you. Come on, we'll do it together."

We started with the voice mails. Actually, Joanie did. She sat at my desk, and I found her a piece of paper and a pen in case there was anything important to write down. Then I crawled back into bed and pulled the covers over my head again.

Joanie came over and pulled the covers off. "Shower. Now."

Since I didn't seem to have much of a choice, I took my baby sister's advice. Once I brushed my teeth and peeled off my grungy clothes and let the hot water wash over me for a while, I started to feel almost human again. I mean, any movement felt better than no movement at all, right? Maybe that was my signal, the universe sending me its version of the Nike slogan: *Just. Do. It.*

But wait. She who hesitates is lost, but she who doesn't hesitate might end up even loster.

I really needed to think things through, but my brain felt like it had been exchanged with the Tin Man's in *The Wizard of Oz.* Maybe "If I Only Had a Brain" could be my first dance. The costume designers could create a silver metallic ballroom gown for me, which would give the illusion of being some kind of glamorous twist on tin cans. It would be long and flowing, and if I didn't eat between now and the first show, maybe I'd even look reasonably okay in it. Wait, it wasn't the Tin Man who didn't have a brain. The Scarecrow was the brainless one. And right now, I could totally relate.

The knocking started up again, this time on my bathroom door.

"Hurry up," Joanie yelled. I flashed back to the little three-bedroom ranch we'd grown up in, all three girls sharing one bedroom, Colleen with her own twin bed, and Joanie making the springs creak on the top bunk over my head every time she rolled over. Tag in his tiny solo kingdom across the hall, and my parents sharing the shoe box of a room next to his.

But it was the single bathroom that presented our biggest family challenge, especially once all four kids hit our teenage years one after another like dominoes. My mother attacked it as she did everything, with a family meeting followed by a big paper chart that she attached with magnets to the refrigerator in what my father referred to as our one-bum kitchen. Our scheduled showers were each ten minutes long, with a ten-minute break between each one to let the cranky old water heater fire up again. An egg timer sat on the ledge of the chipped salmon-colored porcelain sink, and we were supposed to set it before we stepped into the tepid water.

Every so often, in my 6:20 a.m. school day grogginess, I'd forget and before I knew it, Joanie, whose turn always came after mine, would be pounding away on the bathroom door.

All these years later, on a hungover Saturday afternoon, her pounding had the same distinctive style. *Tap. Tap-tap-tap. Tap-tap-tap-tap. Bang. Bang. BANG.*

My reaction hadn't changed either.

"Hold your horses!" I yelled.

13

*Beware of wolves in sheep's clothing, especially
in a sheep shed with your sister.*

I wrapped a towel around my head like a turban and pulled on my old terry cloth robe. The white, or at least whitish, robe made me think of Lake Austin Spa Resort, which made me think of Steve Moretti. Why was it again that I'd run away instead of just telling Tag to buzz off and leave us alone?

Joanie was waiting right outside the bathroom door, ready to huff and puff and blow it down if she had to.

"Geez Loo-eez," I said. "You're so impatient. Hey, you didn't think to start the coffeemaker, did you?"

Joanie looked as if she'd like to start knocking on my head.

I shrugged. "That's a no, huh? Okay, I'll be right back. Can I get you anything? Chocolate soy milk? Russian vodka?" I was trying to be funny, but at the mention of last night's poison my stomach turned over.

"Stop." Joanie held up one hand, palm out like a crossing guard. "You have three e-mails and four voice mails from a *Dancing With the Stars* producer named Karen. She said she's talked to you a couple of times about Tag."

"Ha," I said. "Who hasn't?" I mean, really, everyone from *American*

Idol to *Desperate Housewives* had tried to get Tag to participate in some capacity, any capacity.

"Just say no, Dee," Tag would always say. "It's like dating in high school—the more the girl says no, the more the guy wants her."

"So what do I do?" I asked Joanie.

"Uh, call her back?"

I flipped my head forward and started towel-drying my hair, just for something to do. When I flipped my head back up again, I hadn't solved a thing, and now I was dizzy.

"Listen," I said. "I really need some caffeine. And a snack."

"Listen," Joanie said, "I'm trying to be a good sister, but I haven't got all day."

"Got it. Okay, what do you think I should do?"

Joanie shrugged. "I think you should do what your gut is telling you."

"My gut is telling me to eat."

Joanie let out a puff of air.

"Sorry," I said. "Okay, let's just assume that being on *Dancing With the Stars* would be less painful than facing Tag. What do I say to this producer?"

"You pretend you're negotiating for Tag and get everything you can out of her."

"Wow," I said. "You're right. I completely forgot that I know how to do this."

Joanie scrolled through the call log and handed me my phone. I tapped Call and counted the rings until it went to voice mail. "Hi," I said. "This is Tag's sister Deirdre." I almost gave her my last name, but then I thought, if Tag didn't have to use a last name, why should I? Maybe it would even be cooler if I shortened my name from Deirdre to D. *The phenomenon known as Tag's even more phenomenal sister, who goes only by the letter D*, the headlines would read.

I remembered I was on the phone. I cleared my throat. "So, well, how exciting is this? I'm sure Tag's agent can handle the deal, but if you'd like to move this along, I'd be just delighted to have a first-class ticket leaving from Logan Airport as early as possible tomorrow morning, and if I could pick up a rental car at LAX, that would be fabulous. I'm assuming you put the out-of-town dancers in temporary executive apartments. I'd like a two-bedroom, please, so I have room for guests. Would that work from your end? Let me know. Thanks so much, and have a nice day, Karen."

I tapped the screen to end the call and handed my phone to Joanie. "Now can I go make coffee? Oh, and can you delete all the messages from Tag and Mom and Dad, so I don't have to deal with them?"

Joanie smiled and nodded as if I were one of her kids and she had everything under control. "I already did. Boyohboy, is Tag ready to kill you. Anyway, I just left some business stuff." She handed me a piece of paper with a phone number. "Oh, and some guy named Steve something or other wants you to have breakfast."

"Breakfast," I repeated, as if breakfast with Steve Moretti were a planet, in another universe so far away I couldn't even picture it. What day was this breakfast? What time zone was it in? What would my life be like now if I'd gone to this breakfast place instead of running home to crash and burn?

Joanie was still smiling. "Okay, and now I think we should take you shopping for some new clothes. Unless you want to borrow some of mine?"

I looked at her little purple cotton dress. Everything about it screamed: *Even though I am an adult woman, I'm going to keep wearing junior sizes for the rest of my life just to prove I can.* I mean, I might be a mess, but Joanie had her own case of arrested development. Being the youngest had clearly screwed her up. If she wasn't adorable, she didn't know who she was.

My heart swelled with compassion. It's amazing that any of us made it through our childhoods. My parents were loving, intelligent people, and yet none of us had survived unscathed. Tag had somehow received the message that the whole world revolved around him, and even though it fueled his rise to fame, it also made him so needy for attention that he eventually exhausted even the most diligent wife. Colleen always had to one-up Tag, and even though she'd become successful in her own right, I knew it probably killed her that the most lucrative art pieces she created starred none other than her nemesis, Tag.

And Joanie, the sweet, adorable little family pet, had carved a career out of cuteness, first for herself, and now for her all-dressed-alike family. Imagine spending the week trudging through stores to locate clothes that came in the same color and were also available in men's large and boys' extrasmall, girls' small, and junior way-too-small. Then to have to do not only your own grocery shopping and cleaning but your big brother's, too, because even though you were still cute as a button, you needed his money to make ends meet?

I mean, in some ways I was the most normal one in the family. Of all four kids, I'd turned out the best. I might work for Tag, too, but at least I could put it on my résumé. If Tag couldn't get past the whole *Dancing With the Stars* thing, I realized I could just walk down the street in L.A. and probably get a zillion job offers. Everyone knew that personal assistants basically ran Hollywood. Even though I was overqualified, I had no problem with the PA title as long as it paid enough. But I could also present myself as a social media strategist, a public relations maven, a manager. The world beyond Tag was my oyster.

"You're not hearing a single word I'm saying to you, are you?" Joanie said.

"Of course I am." I paused. "What?"

Joanie rolled her eyes. "Shopping?"

"Oh. Right." I took a breath while I considered. "You know, I think I'd rather just rest up. If the producer calls back, I can always shop when I get out there."

Joanie's chocolate eyes were wide open now, like little round Ring Dings. "So that means you're going?"

Her eager look was unmistakable. "What, are you trying to get rid of me?" I said with a laugh.

"Of course not. But I think we need to sit down, so you can walk me through everything. What needs to happen, what's the order of priority. Tour schedules and pending issues. Form letters for the fan mail. How often to post on Facebook and Twitter. And I want to make sure I have all the passwords, so I don't have to bother you. Maybe you should just leave me your iPhone and take my Android."

A chill ran across the back of my neck. When I looked down, goose bumps were prickling my forearms.

I'd almost forgotten why we called our youngest sibling Joanie Baloney. It wasn't just that it rhymed. From the time she could walk, Joanie was full of it, full of baloney. Even though she was as cute as the day was long with those Shirley Temple curls and that dimply smile, you couldn't trust her for a minute. She'd even scammed me on those Ring Dings she used to buy for me on allowance day.

"So," I said during family meeting one night, "how much do Ring Dings cost, Joanie?"

I'd just come from the A&P with my mother, where I was stunned to find that Ring Dings had dropped in price from my walking-to–Marshbury Center days.

Joanie named the price she charged me every week.

"Liah, liah, pants on fiah," I said, my Boston accent intensifying with my rage. "Mom and I saw the price stickers right on them today."

Joanie smiled like a little angel. I mean, you could practically watch her wings sprout. "Well, that's because the sticker doesn't include the walking charge."

Decades later, Joanie Baloney still had the same angelic smile.

"You little brat," I said. "You want me to go to L.A. so you can steal my job."

"I wouldn't really be stealing it," she said. "I'd just be babysitting it while you were too busy for it."

I shook my head. "Right. And then when I came back I could clean Tag's house and catch up on his grocery shopping."

Joanie opened her eyes wide. "No, I think we'd hire out for that so it didn't build up. When you finally came back we'd all sit down and work out the details. I mean, face it, Deirdre, this isn't about you. It has to be about what's best for Tag."

Beware, I thought, of wolves in sheep's clothing, especially in a sheep shed with your sister.

"Leave," I said. "Now."

"Just wait"—Joanie put her hands on her hips—"until Tag gets home."

It knew it was immature, but I put my hands on my hips anyway. "Just wait," I said, my voice all cute and adorable, "until Tag gets home."

My baby sister stomped down the stairs dramatically and slammed the sheep shed door on her way out. I watched her from the window just to make sure she was really gone and not planning to circle back and steal my passwords. It took every ounce of willpower I had not to go after her and mow her down with Tag's golf cart, too.

14

It's not what you're telling your heart,
but what your heart is telling you.

I brewed only enough coffee for one cup, because I figured it didn't make sense to wake up completely if I just had to turn around and go back to sleep again in a few hours. Then I carried my mug out to Tag's golf cart. Tag didn't mind sharing most of his possessions, but his guitars and his golf cart were strictly off-limits, so returning the cart would give him one less thing to be pissed at me about. Unless, of course, that little tattletale Joanie Baloney ratted me out.

Or, maybe worse, Mitchell might start whining to Tag about me hitting him with the golf cart I wasn't allowed to drive. I flashed on an image of Tag standing on a beach somewhere wearing one of his long white organic cotton tunics with jeans and bare feet, marrying a shaved-headed Mitchell and his seriously pregnant girlfriend. In a way, I'd have only myself to blame since I'd been the one to suggest Tag become a justice of the peace, because weddings made such good photo ops. And of course I also had to admit I'd been the one who was stupid enough to choose a sensitivity-impaired boyfriend in the first place.

I started up the golf cart. Apparently I'd missed most of a beautiful day. The air was cool, but the sun was warm, that perfect New

England blend. I could smell just a hint of the ocean, and I could almost imagine wandering the path down to the water and dangling my bare feet from the dock as if I didn't have a care in the world. Or picking a bouquet of black-eyed Susans and arranging them artfully in the emptied-out chocolate soy milk bottle.

At that, my stomach remembered last night and did a backflip.

"Okay," I said. "Never mind. We'll save the flower arranging for another time."

I followed the path from my driveway through the woods and over to Tag's house. Now that Joanie was gone, I could almost pretend that nothing had happened last night. As soon as I returned the golf cart, maybe I'd throw the dirty clothes from my last trip into the washing machine. Not because I was necessarily ever going anywhere again, but just because they'd eventually have to be washed anyway. I had this hazy dazy feeling that if I could keep everything in slow motion, maybe I could just drift along until my life somehow slipped back to normal again.

I put the golf cart into neutral and let myself into Tag's house so I could open the garage from the inside. Once the cart was safely parked in its rightful spot, next to Tag's Porsche and behind his motorcycle, I headed for the kitchen.

"Well, look who's here." Tag's first ex-wife, Wendy, met me in the hallway and gave me a hug. She was blond and delicate with wrists so thin they made me think of seabird legs.

The other half of Afterwife, Tag's second ex-wife, Blythe, poked her head out from behind the refrigerator door. She looked a lot like Wendy, except she was younger and had thicker wrists.

"There she is," Blythe said. "The family dancer."

"Uh-oh," I said. "Word's out." I crossed over to Blythe and gave her a hug, while I peeked over her shoulder into the fridge at the same time.

"That's an understatement," Wendy said. "You're all over the Internet."

"Are you hungry?" Blythe asked, as if being all over the Internet was nothing so unusual, which was true, I supposed, if you'd been married to Tag. The only thing that made this situation the least bit remarkable was that it revolved not around Tag but around same-old-boring-no-life-of-her-own me.

"Starved," I said. I simply had to play it cool, and before I knew it the whole *Dancing With the Stars* thing would just blow over the way these Internet things always did. The next time I was sitting in my brother's kitchen with his two ex-wives, none of us would even remember it.

Wendy reached for a plate and some silverware. Blythe pulled a rectangular pan out of the fridge and started cutting me a big square of Afterwife's famous spinach-and-portobello lasagna.

Since they seemed to have things under control, I climbed up on a stool at the kitchen island and drained the last drops of my coffee.

"It should still be warm," Blythe said as she placed the lasagna in front of me. "But let me know if you'd like it heated."

"Something else to drink?" Wendy asked.

"No thanks," I said. "I don't want to put you to any trouble." I put my napkin on my lap, since I wasn't alone, and started to eat. My brother's two ex-wives stood there and watched.

"Delish," I said between bites.

They both smiled and kept watching. I didn't get it: two skinny blond women cooking all day and not eating anything. Maybe there was a vicarious thrill in there somewhere, the way I might scroll through page after page of shoes on the Zappos website without ordering and somehow feel satisfied enough when I was finished to just slide on my same old flip-flops again.

"So," Wendy said. "Just do it. Tag will get over it."

"He always does," Blythe said.

"Exactly," Wendy said.

I looked up. "We're not talking about eating his lasagna, right?"

They both laughed. They even laughed alike. I loved them like sisters, and liked them even more sometimes, but the nagging possibility that Tag might clone his wives still creeped me out from time to time.

"Oh," I said. "You mean *Dancing With the Stars*. Yeah, well, I'm waiting to hear back from the producer. I still don't know anything officially yet."

Blythe sighed. "Oh, no. You don't think they—"

"Went with someone else?" Wendy finished.

"Why?" I said, surprising myself by feeling a twinge of disappointment. "Did you hear something I didn't?"

They looked at each other.

"No," Blythe said.

"We thought *you* did," Wendy said.

It was like hearing double. My headache was coming back. And my lasagna was almost gone.

"No," I said. I thought for a moment. "And I guess I'm not waiting that hard to hear back. The truth is I can't decide whether or not to go. No. Actually the truth is I can't even make myself think about whether or not I want to go. And my head hurts."

Wendy opened Tag's kitchen drawer and pulled out a pad of paper and a pen. "We'll make a list—"

"Of the pros and cons," Blythe said.

Wendy drew a line down the center of a page. Blythe and I watched her write *Pros* on one side and *Cons* on the other.

They looked at me.

"Okay," I said. "Pros. One: I have no life. Two: I have no life. Three: Tag is coming home to kill me. Cons. One: I have nothing to wear.

Two: I haven't danced since third grade. Three: If I do go through with it, Tag might kill me more."

Wendy looked up from scribbling. "Those aren't the things that matter."

"It's what's in your heart that matters," Blythe said.

I shook my head. "Do you two rehearse, or do you just naturally finish each other's sentences?"

They looked at me. Neither of them said a thing.

"Sorry," I said. "Okay, I think maybe I should do it. But I'm terrified. And it's probably not going to happen anyway."

Wendy looked at the paper in front of her as if it were a Magic 8 Ball. "All signs point to—"

"It's looking like it will," Blythe said, "so you need to deal with it."

The lasagna was kicking in. "What I really need to deal with is a nap."

"Who knows what doors it might open," Wendy said. "Maybe it's time to get excited—"

"About your life," Blythe said.

I yawned. "I think I just want to lay low and hope that it all blows over by the time Tag gets home."

"No," Wendy said. "You're telling yourself what you *should* want."

"What you *should* be feeling," Blythe said.

Wendy clasped her fingers together and stretched her seabird wrists up over her head. "When Tag and I split up, my whole family told me to pack up the kids and come back home. It's crazy to stay, they said. Demeaning. Demoralizing. And I kept trying to convince myself that they were right, to persuade myself that's what I wanted, but the truth is that Tag is a terrific ex-husband. And a wonderful father. He goes out of his way to get along with anyone I date. So I have a great life here, with or without him, but especially with."

"Ditto," Blythe said.

"So what it comes down to," Wendy said, "is this: It's not what you're telling your heart—"

Blythe put one hand at the base of her throat, like a necklace. "But what your heart is telling you."

I closed my eyes and listened. Then I turned and gazed out through the wall of windows, past the pool and across the vast fields beyond. I didn't start to whine or try to fill the silence with a flip comment. I actually tried to hear what my heart was telling me.

Some of the leaves on the trees were just starting to change color. Birds and squirrels converged at the bird feeder, all focus and energy as they stocked up for the coming season. The setting sun was hitting the pool in such a way that half of it was in shadow and the other half sparkled with possibility.

I gazed into my brother's ex-wives' kind, open faces. Even the Afterwives had taken a bad situation and turned it into an opportunity. Maybe, just maybe, I could, too.

They smiled at me encouragingly.

"I think my heart is telling me to dance," I said.

15

Nobody can go back and start a new beginning,
but anyone can start today and make a new ending.

—MARIA ROBINSON

Karen, the *Dancing With the Stars* producer, was fast. By the time I'd finished my lasagna and pep talk and gotten back to the sheep shed, she'd e-mailed me my e-ticket, as well as the confirmation for my rental car and directions to my temporary apartment.

My heart changed its mind immediately. I clicked Reply and attempted to wiggle my way out with a quick e-mail: *Sorry to last-minute you, but I'm afraid I won't be able to participate after all. A sudden emergency has come up.*

Karen e-mailed back within seconds: *It's called stage fright. You'll be fine.*

I seriously doubted it, but I did what I had to do: I threw my dirty clothes into the washing machine.

I sat on my bed and gazed at nothing. Then I found the little piece of paper Joanie had given me with Steve Moretti's phone number on it. I stared at it until my clothes finished the spin cycle. *So,* his message probably said, *how about breakfast? I'd like to pick your brain about the best way to present my business proposition to Tag.*

Or maybe it went like this: *Listen, I'm really sorry about that kiss. Let's just have a nice breakfast and pretend it never happened, okay? Hey, by the way, what's Tag's cell number? I forgot to ask him for it and I really need to get in touch with him to follow up on something.*

Maybe it was better not to know what Steve's message said. But then again, the sooner I found out how bad it was, the sooner I could get over it.

I took everything out of the washer and put it into the dryer. Joanie had said she'd erased all the angry voice mails from Tag and my parents, but by now another stream of them had landed to take their place. I deleted them as quickly as I could but still caught my father's "Now, honey," and my mother's "Deirdre Marie Griffin, what were you—" Tag's bombardment was relentless as usual and all about how pissed off he was and how ungrateful I was and how I'd better be on top of damage control. I hit Delete, Delete, Delete.

Finally, I found Steve's message.

Hey, this is Steve. The guy you just kissed and ran away from? Anyway, just in case you're wondering how I got your number, your father slipped it to me on a folded piece of paper right after your brother told me he'd break my face if I went near you again. So, family dynamics aside, what about breakfast tomorrow? I have an early meeting, so I'm thinking we get up at the crack of dawn and sneak out and find a real authentic Texas Starbucks. How about six thirty in the lobby?

I sat on my bed and played it three more times. The last time I said all the words out loud right along with him, like a duet. At best, it was inconclusive. Maybe he was actually interested in me and not Tag, but maybe he was just smart enough to wait till we got to breakfast to tell me what he really wanted.

I did the math. At 6:30 that next morning Steve was referring to I was in another lobby in another state. I'd finished a sleepless night at the Sheraton near the Milwaukee airport and had just grabbed my own cup of coffee and a breakfast sandwich and was getting ready to take the shuttle back over to the terminal.

What if I hadn't turned off my cell phone two nights ago? It could have been like one of those scenes in a star-crossed-lovers movie. I'd be in a taxi headed from the conference center to the airport, tears rolling down my face. Then the taxi driver would drop me off at the Austin airport, and between sobs I'd hand him some bills and tell him to keep the change. I'd run through the airport trying to catch the last plane out, and when I took my shoes off at security, a sprig of lemon basil would flutter to the floor. I'd pick it up and stare at it, hold it to my nose and breathe in the dwindling scent, and burst into tears again. I'd board the plane and take my seat. I'd gaze sadly out the window. And then my cell phone would ring. It would be Steve. Whatever he said would make me laugh. I'd get off the plane just in the nick of time. Music would soar and closing titles would roll and we'd live happily ever after.

An electronic buzzer went off. I jumped as if it were the perfectly timed phone call. But it was only the dryer. Because my life was not a movie. I couldn't ask for a retake, a rewrite.

The perfect chiastic quote flitted just out of my reach. Something about how you can't go back and start a new beginning, but you can start today and make a new ending.

As I folded my clothes from the dryer straight into my suitcase, I could almost imagine that new ending. The *Dancing With the Stars* thing would be a fond memory, or at least a distant one. I'd be sitting in my L.A. apartment, which was lovely but not pretentious. I'd have just come back from a jog and finished showering, and as I slid into a silk robe and wrapped a plush towel around my hair, I'd pick up the phone. Because by then I'd know who I was and what I wanted my life to be, and exactly what I wanted to say to Steve Moretti.

But first, I had a long way to go. The *DWTS* shows lived and breathed by the fans online, that much I knew. And Tag was often referred to as a New Age phenomenon, but in many ways he was really a new media phenomenon. And, truth be told, I was responsible for creating him.

I'd once read that everyone in the movie industry had a number assigned to them based on their value. Nobody ever said the number out loud, but everybody in the know could tell at the drop of a name whether that person was a 45 or a 97 or a −3. Whether acting, directing, or costume designing offers came your way, whether your name made the invitation list for A-list premieres, and even whether or not you could get reservations at the right restaurants was based entirely upon this mysterious, fluctuating number.

In a way, the social media revolution was a great equalizer. Now we all had a number. Whether you wanted to buy into it or not, in this day and age our personal power was measured by our Web reach. There was no secret or mystery to this number; it was simple arithmetic. Just add your Facebook friends and fans to your Twitter followers to your blog followers to your website newsletter list. The number you got might trigger flashbacks to high school popularity indexes, but in many ways it was much kinder. In high school, it was almost impossible to increase your cool quotient. Today, you can build your Web reach with steady, hard work.

I knew, because that's what I'd done for Tag. His number was well up in the hundreds of thousands and growing rapidly. And still, almost all the people connected to his online hubs felt a personal connection to him. Fans completely believed they were in Tag's inner circle, that they were really his "friends." And right now they were all checking and rechecking for a message from Tag thanking them for voting his sister onto *Dancing With the Stars* and giving them the inside scoop on what would happen next.

The funny thing was that in social media, waiting can be a good thing. The biggest mistake most people make is to tweet too much, to overpost on Facebook, to send out an e-newsletter weekly or even daily. It doesn't take long till it all becomes noise and your new friends tune you out and ultimately break up with you.

I'd learned to alternate periods of silence with flurries of activity, varying the patterns to break the rhythm and keep everyone on their toes. In a way social networking is like any other relationship: We all want the ones we can't quite predict, the ones we can't control.

But all of that effort had always been for Tag. My own sphere of influence could be listed on the palm of one hand, without writing on any fingers. And most of those people weren't even talking to me anymore.

I knew what I had to do. I wasn't sure who in the family might be watching Tag's Facebook page, so I didn't dare pretend to be Tag and send an e-blast congratulating me yet, but I could at least make a quick, subversive start on my own virtual life.

First I set up my own Twitter account. Then I wrote a new tweet for Tag's account.

Stay tuned to cheer my fav sister Dee on DWTS! All follow @DeeCanDance and spread word to universe. Peace in, peace out. Tag.

But instead of posting it publicly, I instructed my auto-reply app to send the message to Tag's new followers in the form of a DM, or direct message.

Next I instructed my auto-follower app to have Tag follow anyone in the world who'd tweeted anything about *Dancing With the Stars* or *DWTS*. Almost without exception, they'd be thrilled out of their minds to be followed by Tag. So they'd follow him back and get his DM telling them to follow me.

Total genius, if I did say so myself. Maybe I should have felt more guilty, but there was barely a twinge. By the time I got myself settled on the left coast, I'd have thousands of my own Twitter followers. And because the message went out only to new followers, I had virtually no chance of getting caught. I mean, Tag was a narcissist, but even he couldn't follow himself. And the good news was that even though my brother texted and talked on his iPhone all day long, he was basically computer illiterate.

Wendy dropped me off at the water shuttle terminal, while Blythe got both sets of kids off to school. They'd even packed me a breakfast sandwich to eat on the ferry ride across Boston Harbor to the airport. If worse came to worst and I was out of a job when I came back, maybe they'd let me do their marketing after all. We could always change the name of the company from Afterwife to Afterwife and No Life.

I couldn't wait to get on the plane and up in the air. I knew Tag and my parents' flight wasn't due in for hours yet. I'd even double-checked their itinerary to make absolutely sure. But as I surged with the crowd through the maze of corridors at Logan Airport, I couldn't shake the feeling that I was about to run right into them.

I found my gate and took a seat in a faux leather chair. I moved my carry-on in front of my feet to camouflage them. I tapped the toes of one foot and then the other, trying to see if I remembered anything at all from my last dance class, decades ago. I moved on to a kick ball change and then I upped it to a shuffle. Sitting safely in a padded vinyl airport terminal chair, I could shuffle with my right foot, but my left was a bit sluggish. The good news was I could still shuffle. But could I Shuffle Off to Buffalo? That had been the trickiest beginning tap step of them all, the one that I'd practiced over and over on the linoleum kitchen floor so I'd be able to keep up with the big kids.

But the truth was, even if I could somehow manage to Shuffle Off to Buffalo, shuffling off to Hollywood was another thing entirely.

What made me think I could pull this off? Maybe it wouldn't be so horrible after all if Tag and my parents found me before my flight took off. I mean, if you weighed family confrontation against international humiliation, the embarrassment quotient might be slightly lower on the family side. And with luck my family's outburst wouldn't last an entire season.

Plus, I could practically write the script for that one. "How could you?" Tag would say. "How could you destroy everything I've worked my entire life to build?" He'd raise his palms to the heavens, exposing just the right amount of forearm. "Not just for me, but for all of us."

"Easy, tiger," my father would say. He'd stretch himself up to his full height so he could get an arm around Tag's shoulders. "I'm sure your sister didn't mean anything by it, did you, Dee-Dee? Just give her a chance to explain."

My mother would cut in. "Five p.m. Tag's house. We'll all sit down and discuss it like civilized human beings, and then those of us who haven't been disowned will have a nice family dinner."

A voice cut into my reverie, but it was only the announcement that first class was boarding. I stood and stretched and looked over my shoulder for a last-second stay of execution. Then I took a deep breath, found my boarding pass, and yanked the handle on my carry-on to extend it.

I walked the ramp to the plane that would take me to Hollywood as if I were walking the plank on a pirate ship in the middle of a storm-tossed, shark-infested ocean.

16

When in doubt, eat. When in eat, doubt.

I slept most of the way to LAX. First class wasn't what it used to be, but it was still a whole bunch better than coach. The way it worked in our family was that Tag always flew first class. My parents didn't believe in it politically, so they always flew coach. I split the difference, flying first class with Tag and coach alone. This was the first time I'd ever been in first class by myself, so I took a moment to let it register. I knew just enough about sports to realize that today was the first inning of a whole new ball game.

I ignored the man sitting next to me, as well as his briefcase. I'd planned on starving myself today so I'd look a little better when I got to L.A., but the smell of warm first-class chocolate chip cookies reached my nose before the plane even took off. Since I'd already eaten a breakfast sandwich anyway, I decided I might as well go for the cookies and then stop eating for the rest of the day. I washed them down with a glass of milk. What's the point of chocolate chip cookies without a little milk to dunk them in?

I crumpled my napkin and pressed it into the empty cup. When I handed over my trash, the flight attendant gave me a big smile. Flight attendants tended to ignore me unless I was with Tag, so I wondered if this one was just being friendly because I was sitting in first class.

For the first time, it occurred to me that an actual photo of me might be circulating on the Internet. Wait, maybe even on television—the morning shows, and even *Extra* and *Access Hollywood*. I hoped they hadn't gotten their hands on my high school class picture with the frizzy hair and that soulful gaze I'd attempted, which only ended up making me look bug-eyed. I'd spent most of my adult life dodging cameras, so maybe they'd just show a shadowy female figure stamped with a question mark. At least that would buy me some time to seek professional help. I'd heard those Hollywood stylists could make anyone look good.

The endless line of coach passengers was still boarding, so I turned on my cell phone and tapped the Firefox icon. It opened to a news page. The headline was some political scandal.

I scrolled down. Right under the first story was a tiny photo of Tag in one of his white tunics, standing with some floozy. Perfect. Maybe the media would keep using my more photogenic brother's photo and let me dance in peace.

I looked at the photo again. On my cell screen, it was the tiniest of thumbnails. I squinted. Then I opened the link.

I was the floozy. Actually, *floozy* would have been kind. *Frumpy* was more accurate. I was handing Tag his rock star wireless headset, so finely constructed that all you could see from a distance was a tiny flesh-colored foam-padded microphone that photographed like a beauty mark. My arms were up and my blouse had followed them, exposing about three inches of flabby flesh. My jeans were bagging out in all the wrong places, and I appeared to have a slight wedgy. My roots needed a serious touch-up, and it looked like my hair hadn't been brushed in a month.

Just. Shoot. Me. Now.

I smelled coffee, and realized the flight attendant was standing over my shoulder. "I thought that was you," she said. "How exciting."

"That's one way of looking at it." I pressed the Off button on my phone.

The flight attendant lowered her voice and leaned closer. "Just wondering, is Tag seeing anyone right now?"

"Just wondering," I said. "Do you think I could have another cookie?"

Her face hardened, but she took the hint and left to fetch me my second snack.

I ate my new cookie, pretty much without tasting it. And the whole time I was eating it I was wishing that I wasn't. But as soon as I finished it, I wanted another one, because as awful as I felt while I was eating it, I felt even worse when it was gone.

It was the story of my eating life: *When in doubt, eat. When in eat, doubt.* I ate when I was anxious about something. But as soon as the food was in my mouth, I realized I didn't really want it, so I didn't even enjoy it. Or sometimes even taste it. Maybe I should just start carrying a spittoon with me wherever I went.

I curled up with my tiny white pillow and snuggled under my thin blue blanket. When we reached cruising altitude, I reclined my leather seat back as far as it would go and conked out.

I woke up just in time for lunch, a pretty decent chicken Caesar salad wrap and a half-melted mini–hot fudge sundae. I ate all of it, figuring I needed to keep up my strength for whatever awaited me on the other side of this flight. I drank some water, made a quick trip to the bathroom, then dozed off a second time.

When I opened my eyes again, we were landing. I stretched and rooted around in my bag for a piece of gum. As soon as our wheels touched the ground, I turned on my phone again. A fleet of missed calls and messages came in for a landing. I ignored them all.

My phone rang and I jumped. I checked the caller ID to make sure it was safe to answer. It wasn't a number I recognized, so I knew it wasn't Tag or my parents.

"Hello," I said timidly.

"Welcome to Los Angeles," Karen the producer said.

"Wow. You're good. What, did you watch my plane land?"

She made a sound that was almost a laugh. "You've got the rental car confirmation and the directions to your apartment. I'll e-mail you tomorrow's itinerary once I've got everything confirmed. You'll start the day with a seven a.m. physical with the show physician—"

"Oh, that's okay," I said. "I'm—"

"Policy. It's in your contract. I'll meet you in the lobby and go with you to the exam room. Practice studio locations are confidential, so please do not share any details with the general public or with members of the media."

"Ha," I said. "I'll do my best, but those paparazzi are all over me."

I didn't realize that the flight attendant was listening to my end of the conversation until she rolled her eyes.

Karen the producer didn't laugh either. Did they not realize I was joking? "There's also a confidentiality clause in your contract. The contract, by the way, will be on its way to your brother's agent tomorrow, and we're hoping to have it fully executed by midweek."

I'd watched enough of my brother's deals to know how fast that was. These *DWTS* people didn't mess around. Wait a minute. Tag would *never* let his agent help make this deal happen.

"Um," I said. "Actually, why don't you have the contract sent directly to me? It'll be easier all around that way."

As soon as I said it, I wondered if I should have kept my mouth shut. Now I truly understood the meaning of the word *ambivalence*. I was completely in conflict—half of me still wanted to find a way out of this mess, and the other half couldn't wait to start dancing.

The plane door was opening. I stood up, tucked my cell phone in the crook of my neck, and reached for my carry-on.

"Will do," Karen said. "Well, then, rest up and enjoy your first night in Hollywood." Her voice changed pitch and got all warm and fuzzy.

"Oh, and we're hoping Tag will want to come out to support his sister, especially since it was his idea in the first place."

I tried not to gulp.

"So when you talk to him, please do let him know we've got a front-row seat reserved for him at every sho-ow."

I closed my eyes. "I wi-ill," I said. "Just the second I talk to him."

As soon as we hung up, I turned off my phone again so Tag couldn't reach me.

I deplaned and followed the signs to baggage claim, passing all sorts of famous-looking people whose names were right on the tip of my tongue. Or maybe everybody who lived in L.A. simply had that look.

I climbed into the shiny black Land Rover *Dancing With the Stars* had rented for me instead of the compact I would have rented for myself. I could get used to this Hollywood thing.

When I turned the key in the ignition, the seat started rumbling. Then it started moving around—up and down and forward and backward, as if it were weighing and measuring me.

"Cool it," I said. "Like I'm not feeling self-conscious enough as it is."

Once the seat was satisfied, I typed the address of my temporary home sweet home into the GPS.

Los Angeles is so overwhelming it makes Boston seem like a cow field with a few cobblestone paths running through it. But my Land Rover gave me height. And shiny black bulk. It wasn't quite a Hummer, but it had the same going-off-to-war-in-a-tank vibe.

And in a way, that's what it felt like. That I was going off to battle. The battle of my life. Of maybe even for a life.

Tag had done some gigs in L.A., so I'd been here several times before. I managed to circle my way out of LAX and head north on what we would have called Route 1 at home but L.A. people called *The One*. I took a right on La Tijera Boulevard and then a left on South La Cienega Boulevard. As each new direction crackled out from the

GPS, I pretended I was taking a Spanish class. "*Tijera*," I repeated. "*Cienega*." I wondered if people from L.A. felt like they were taking a foreign-language class when they came to Massachusetts. *Worcester. Woburn. Gloucester. Scituate.*

Twenty-five minutes later I managed to pull into the tiny parking lot without taking anybody out. I slid out of the Land Rover and stretched.

And then it hit me: This was my *Mary Tyler Moore Show* moment.

Just like Mary, I'd actually had the courage to move away and start over. I was here. This was it.

It wasn't Minneapolis, but I spun around three times and threw my imaginary hat up in the air anyway.

And right then and there I decided that, whatever it took, I was going to make it after all.

17

A bird in the hand is worth two in the bush,
but a bush in the hand will feed the whole flock.

My temporary apartment was beyond bland; it was lifeless. Not a single thing in it even hinted that a real person might survive here, let alone flourish. It felt like a failure-to-thrive holding tank.

The front door opened directly into a no-nonsense rectangle of kitchen-dining-living room. The walls were white. The appliances were white. The cabinets were white. The dishes and mugs inside the cabinets were white. The wall-to-wall carpeting was beige, as were the ceramic tiles on the bathroom and kitchen floors. The living room side had a beige pullout couch, a matching chair, and a tarnished brass reading lamp. A white hallway was just big enough to hold the doors to two tiny white bedrooms and one tiny white bathroom.

I'd been expecting the equivalent of a five-star hotel, or at least a three or a four, so I hadn't even brought a blow-dryer.

I opened the cabinet under the bathroom sink and pulled out a tiny white blow-dryer.

"What else could I possibly need?" I said. My words actually echoed throughout the apartment.

The whole place smelled like bleach. I pulled up the white plastic miniblind in one of the bedrooms to open the window and let in some air. It didn't open. I tried the window in the living room. Nothing.

My temporary apartment was permanently airless. I wondered if I could buy a carton of fresh air to go somewhere, maybe at one of those oxygen bars, the ones with the big serpentine hookahs. Did they still have those places, or had I missed an entire fad without taking a single airy toke?

I was so not a nester. Even when Mitchell and I were in one of our honeymoon phases, his idea of decorating was to upgrade the flat-screen TV. Mine was to bang another hole in the rough sheep shed walls and hang up the latest beachy watercolor my sister Colleen had painted for my birthday.

Now I had an overwhelming urge to do something, anything, to my temporary home to make it feel like mine.

I cranked up the AC as far as it would go and grabbed the key I'd picked up from the guy who managed the place. The three-hour time difference between coasts had given me some bonus hours, so I figured I might as well get some fresh air and do a little shopping.

I made a mental shopping list: some art for the walls, food, underwear.

Instead I found tchotchkes, and lots of them. Every other store I passed sold T-shirts, postcards, and refrigerator magnets. I was sure walking just a block or so would take me to an entirely different class of shopping, but in which direction?

Tag could always smell a mall a mile away, and for just a second, I realized I missed him. If he were with me, we'd be pawing our way through the T-shirts right now and scooping up tacky finds like they were hidden treasure—a yellowed Spice Girls T-shirt or a Harrison Ford bobblehead doll.

"You know," he'd say, "lots of people are bobblehead fans."

"Don't start," I'd say.

Tag would hold poor bobbly-headed Harrison up to the dim light coming in through the dusty window. "I'm just saying. It's something we should consider. Either that or an action figure. I'd make a good action figure."

I bought a laminated refrigerator magnet of the Hollywood sign and a poster of the *Dancing With the Stars* mirror ball trophy. Plus a candle for ambiance.

"Home sweet home," I said to the guy at the register. He ignored me. It was hard to tell whether it was because I didn't seem important or because he didn't speak English.

I handed him Tag's platinum American Express. "I'm going to be on *Dancing With the Stars*," I said, trying out the sound of it.

He dragged the card through the little machine. "I have two scripts. One of them is basically in development."

"Great," I said. "Good luck."

His tired brown eyes met mine. "Yeah, you, too."

The next item on my list was underwear, which I seriously needed if I had any hope of starting a new life, especially a televised one, but the only underwear store I could find was a Frederick's of Hollywood. I stood outside for a while, casually glancing at the leathery, feathery display in the windows and marveling at the fact that Frederick was actually from Hollywood. Or at least in Hollywood. Eventually I decided I didn't have the guts to go in, so I kept walking.

I found a little corner grocery store, the kind that makes you doubt even the freshest-looking produce because it's so dank and dirty inside. I double-checked the date on the milk. I sniffed some scentless coffee and decided to buy it anyway. I picked up a box of Special K, then put it down and grabbed some peanut butter and English muffins instead. And a single banana.

The banana almost made me cry, right there in the dingy little store. Somehow nothing makes you feel more alone than buying a solitary piece of fruit.

The woman behind the register must have sensed it. Or maybe she just could tell I wasn't from around here. "Hi there," she said. "What brings you to the Land of Oz? Business or pleasure?"

I smiled. "I'm going to be on *Dancing With the Stars*."

She smiled back. "I'm going to be on *Two and a Half Men*. I'm waiting for a callback, but I'm pretty sure I nailed it."

I wandered down the street with my groceries. There were probably some hip restaurants around, but I had no idea where they were, and I also didn't think walking into a restaurant with a half gallon of milk would be a very hip thing to do. I stopped at a Subway and bought a large turkey sub, so I'd have leftovers for breakfast in case I didn't have time to toast the English muffins. Then I walked across the street to another dingy store and bought a package of peanut M&M's for dessert, just in case.

I kept walking. The crowds of T-shirt and fanny pack–wearing tourists seemed to be thinning and the area appeared to be getting sketchier, but it was hard to tell. I decided to go one more block and then turn around.

I stopped in front of a pet store. Three tall, ornate bird stands filled the display window. Their elaborate scrollwork was the first thing I'd seen so far that made me think of Old Hollywood. An assortment of canaries sat on perches behind the metal bars and peered out at freedom.

"I feel ya," I whispered. "That's exactly how things looked to me. Just yesterday, in fact."

A chiasmus, one of Tag's most famous, popped into my head: *A bird in the hand is worth two in the bush, but a bush in the hand will feed the whole flock.*

I had no idea what it actually meant, and I was pretty sure Tag didn't either. But he always managed to hold an entire auditorium of starry-eyed followers right in the palm of his hand with that one. He had this great spiel about how it's not all about strategy or competition. You have to let go of that me-first mentality and focus on nurturing the rest of the world. With. Your. Passion.

I shook my head to dislodge my brother from my brain and opened the door to the pet store.

Growing up, we had a standard poodle named FooFoo that we'd rescued when we found him running around lost and panicked at a massive outdoor Grateful Dead concert on Boston Common one summer.

"I think it's having a bad trip, Eileen," my father said as the dog circled by our family's enclave of blankets and lawn chairs for a third time.

"Don't be ridiculous, Timmy," my mother said. "It's just upset because it can't find its owners."

The dog's wiry black fur was perfectly groomed—shaved close to the body, with longer bursts of fur creating a hat on top of its head and a pom-pom at the tip of its tail. The fur on its legs was longer, too, like go-go boots. I'd been dancing my heart out to "Sugaree," hiding behind my family so they couldn't see me, spinning around and around until I thought I'd become airborne. Now I had a sudden urge to start singing "These Boots Are Made for Walkin'." Fortunately I was old enough to know that something like that could get you kicked out of a Dead concert.

The dog was the kind that would wear a jeweled collar, but it was collarless. It jerked its long pointy nose back and forth frantically as it searched the crowd.

Colleen and Tag jumped up at the same time. Colleen held out a Necco Wafer. "Here, doggy doggy doggy," she yelled, her voice barely making a dent in the blare of "Sugar Magnolia."

"Come to papa," Tag yelled, waving a good-size chunk of Devil Dog in the dog's direction.

The dog stopped, tilted its head back and forth at our family a few times, then trotted over to me. When I bent down to pat it, it lapped my face.

"What?" Colleen said. "I don't get it."

"It's a dog," Tag said. "Ya know, takes one to know one?"

"I know you are, but what am I?" I said.

My mother and Joanie Baloney made their way to the information tent to report it, but the dog, which turned out to be a boy my father had already named FooFoo, stayed with me.

"A dog has lost its people," the concert organizers announced when the band took a break. "Please count your dogs."

When we got home, we tried everything from posters to a pet psychic my parents knew to find FooFoo's rightful owner. Eventually we got to keep him. My parents didn't believe in shearing poodles politically, so they let his fur grow out until it looked almost like dreadlocks. He was so smart that my father used to say he was the brains of the family.

I didn't care how smart he was. I just knew that FooFoo was the one person in the entire world who always picked me first and who loved me just the way I was. He died of old age when I was away at college, and my mother didn't tell me because it was the week of final exams. When I got home, I was devastated to find out that FooFoo was buried behind the garden.

Tag shared custody of his two shelter dogs. Colleen went on to have an assortment of cats and Joanie a series of purebred golden retrievers that wore bandannas around their necks to match the rest of the family. But I'd never given my heart to another pet.

Now, with my new life starting, maybe it was time. Briefly I considered buying a couple of canaries, but I decided they'd probably be even more depressed in my temporary apartment than they were here in the pet store. Plus, I wouldn't be home enough to give them the kind of attention they deserved.

Then I noticed the big fish tanks along the back wall of the store.

I walked over and stood there, watching for the right fish to come along. By the time the guy came out from behind the register and asked if he could help me, we'd found each other.

I waited until he scooped up my two goldfish and poured them into a clear plastic bag filled with water from the tank and handed them to me.

"Fred," I said, "meet Ginger."

*The magic in these soles will bring out
the magic that was in your soul all along.*

I was nervous, really, really nervous, and it didn't help that my first
stop of the day was the 7 a.m. physical with the *Dancing With the
Stars* physician.

I'd barely slept a wink. When I got back from my walk, the temperature in my temporary quarters had dipped so low because of the
air-conditioning that the place could have passed for an igloo. It was
so cold I probably didn't even need to put the milk in the refrigerator,
but I did. Then I turned off the AC and sat on the hallway floor with
the apartment door open, holding the goldfish until I was sure frost-
bite wouldn't be an issue for any of us.

Getting Fred and Ginger out of the plastic bag and into their
goldfish bowl turned out to be a lot more stressful than I'd an-
ticipated. I washed and rinsed the bowl extra carefully, then filled
it halfway with tap water and added a carefully measured capful
of Nutrafin Goldfish Bowl Conditioner. I let the water come to
what was now a more palatable room temperature. Then I lowered
Ginger and Fred, still in their plastic bag, into the bowl. I waited a
couple of hours until the water temperatures merged and I was sure

everything was copasetic. Finally I took out the bag and untied the knot at the top.

I gauged the width of the opening of the goldfish bowl against the opening of the plastic bag. There seemed to be a fair amount of room for error. I pictured Fred and Ginger flopping around on the hard tile floor of my sad little transitory kitchen. I hoped if I accidentally killed anybody, they'd at least both go together.

"One, two, three," I said. Ginger splashed into the bowl right away, but one of Fred's fins kind of doubled back behind him. I held my breath and gave the plastic bag a shake. I flicked it with one finger. Finally Fred plopped into the water. He seemed stunned for a moment, then he wiggled off on a lap around the bowl.

Crisis averted, I gave them an extra-big sprinkle of goldfish food and went to find my turkey sub. I finished the whole thing before I remembered I was going to save half for breakfast. I brushed my teeth and carried Ginger and Fred into my bedroom and put them on top of my tiny white dresser.

I leaned over until my face was close to the tank. "I kept fishing in the deep blue sea until I found the only fish meant for me," I sang.

I was starting to scare myself with all the echoing, so I crawled into bed. I stared up at the ceiling for a long, long time. Then I remembered the M&M's. I turned on the single bedside light and climbed out of bed to get them.

I climbed back in again, pulled the covers up to my chin, and tore open the bag. "If the first one is turquoise, I will call Steve Moretti," I said. Alone in L.A., I was starting to find his motives a little less suspicious. Or maybe my proximity to Hollywood had simply increased my level of denial.

I wiggled one finger around in the bag and slid out a single M&M. It was orange so I just ate it.

"If the next one is turquoise, I will call Steve Moretti." It might have been my imagination, but it seemed like Fred and Ginger were intrigued by my game. Their noses were practically pressed up to my side of the bowl.

The next M&M was yellow, so I ate that one, too. I mean, what would I say to him anyway? *Hey, it's Deirdre. Sorry I ran away like that. Anyway, long story but guess what? I'm going to be on* Dancing With the Stars.

Great, he'd probably say. *I have a script that's basically in development.*

I closed my eyes and ate the rest of the M&M's without even checking their colors. Then I crumpled up the empty wrapper and reached over and turned off the light.

I still wasn't the least bit tired, and now my stomach hurt. I sat up in bed and reached for my laptop. Belatedly, it occurred to me that I'd never actually watched an episode of *Dancing With the Stars.* Who had time to watch TV when you worked for someone like my brother?

I waited for my laptop to power up. It's not like I didn't know the basics: that you had to dance. And that there were celebrity dancers and professional dancers, and the costumes were really cool.

I found hulu.com and searched for *Dancing With the Stars.* Hundreds of episodes popped up. "A journey," an announcer's voice said when I clicked on one randomly, "is the act of traveling from one place to another."

"Ha," I said. "Not a problem. Been there, done that."

Under glittery ballroom lights, a couple was introduced. The male's shirt was unbuttoned three-quarters of the way down, but he looked positively overdressed next to his partner, who was wearing only low-slung black tights and a black sports bra covered in sequins. And five-inch heels.

I choked back a scream. I clicked on episode after episode until I couldn't take it anymore.

Then I typed *The Mary Tyler Moore Show* into the search bar. Half-way through the "Put on a Happy Face" episode, my heart finally stopped thumping enough to go to sleep.

I was still trying to get out of my physical, preferably as a start to get-ting out of *DWTS* altogether, while I peed into a clear plastic cup and twisted the cover on.

I opened the bathroom door. "You know," I said as I handed over my cup, "one of my hips gets kind of stiff when it rains. Oh, and I'm not really sure all my vaccinations are up-to-date."

Karen the producer rolled her eyes. "We'll alert your dance partner."

"And I have this little cough I can't seem to shake." When I coughed, it sounded fake even to me.

The doctor smiled. "You look as healthy as a horse."

"Thanks. But next time you might want to go for a slightly less bulky image. Are you sure I really need a physical? Couldn't I just ask one of my parents to sign a permission slip?"

"It's for insurance purposes," Karen said. "And because we want you to be safe, of course."

At that, Doctor Dance, or whoever he was, pointed to the scale.

"No way," I said.

"Way," he said. Or maybe it was *weigh*.

I climbed up on the scale and closed my eyes. "Just do me a favor and don't say the number out loud, okay?"

He said it out loud anyway. I cringed.

"Before you know it," he said, "you'll be in the best shape of your life."

"Can you put that in writing?"

To my complete surprise, the exam deemed me danceworthy, so our next stop was the costume designer.

"And I was just feeling so good about putting my clothes back on," I said.

"Don't get used to it," Karen said.

"But doesn't it make more sense to get some dancing in first?" I started to say that the first show wasn't until next week, but the words got stuck in my throat as the reality of my situation hit me: I was going to dance publicly. On television. A week from today.

Karen had already started walking. "Fittings for the other celebrities started last week."

"Ha," I said. I took a little hop and a skip to try to catch up with her. "I'm sooooo not a celebrity."

Karen turned her head. Her lips were pursed. "You will be soon. One way or the other."

I finally caught up and matched my steps to hers. I was trying to bond, since I figured I needed at least one ally in Hollywood, but she wasn't making it easy. "Just curious, but how many people watch this show anyway?"

Karen looked up from her phone. She'd been texting nonstop since I'd met her this morning. "Twenty-three . . ."

"Million?"

"But we're hoping for an uptick in numbers this season." With that, Karen and her phone wandered away without saying good-bye, leaving me at my next stop.

A female costume designer would have been embarrassing enough, but wouldn't you know my appointment was with a guy named Anthony and his tape measure.

"Sorry," I said after we introduced ourselves, "but I'm probably not going to fit into Kelly Genelavive's clothes."

Anthony laughed and looked over his shoulder. "Honey, a two-year-old couldn't fit into her clothes," he whispered. "She hasn't had a full meal since 1993, bless her emaciated little heart."

He was making me feel so much better I felt guilty. I made my face look concerned. "How is she doing?" I whispered.

Anthony swung his arms wide. "Drama," he said. "It's all about the drama."

He reached around me with the measuring tape. I cringed.

"Relax, lamb chop. I will make you more beautiful than you have ever been in your life."

"The bar is low."

"Illusion mesh," he whispered. "It's a beautiful thing."

I knew the dance bar, on the other hand, was going to be high. To start, Anthony helped me pick out a pair of dance shoes. Piles and piles of shoe boxes from every dance shoe manufacturer on the planet took over one whole wall of the wardrobe room. The assortment was so overwhelming I just stood there.

"Do any of them come with training wheels?" I finally asked.

Anthony laughed. "What size are you, darlin'?"

I held up the appropriate number of fingers.

Anthony held out a pink box. "Jewel started with these. She loved them."

I crossed my arms over my chest. "Didn't she end up with stress fractures?" I distinctly remembered seeing her sitting in the audience in a walking cast. Or maybe it was two.

Anthony shook his head. "Drama." He reached for another box. "Here, try these. They were Kirstie's favorite."

"Okay," I said. "If they're good enough for Kirstie, they're good enough for me."

The shoes were flesh colored and the heels were nonintimidatingly low. They were amazingly light, lighter than a pair of flip-flops and almost as light as a pair of sneaker socks. I buckled the strap over my instep and walked a few steps. I slid one sole across the floor and then the other. No stick at all. My right foot shuffled perfectly, and my left wasn't far behind. I could almost imagine shuffling all the way to Buffalo in these babies.

"Wow," I said. "I had no idea it was all about the shoes. So anytime I get into trouble I just click my heels together?"

Anthony grinned. "You got it, Dorothy. The magic in these soles will bring out the magic that was in your soul all along."

It wasn't quite a chiasmus, but it was close enough to feel like a good omen.

Anthony winked. "And if that doesn't work, baby cakes, there's always rehab."

19

Live to dance and dance to live.

Sorry," I said. Apparently *sorry* was becoming my mantra. "But I'm probably not going to be as good as Kelly Genelavive."

"Kelly Genelavive," my dance partner said, "was a thug with hair spray."

My partner's name was Ilya. He was elegantly handsome in a kind of chiseled-featured, slicked-backed-hair, narrow-hipped, tight-butt way that they simply didn't breed in Marshbury.

Karen had delivered me to Ilya, then slipped away again as soon as she introduced us. I didn't even really like her, but I still felt completely abandoned every time she left me. Whose idea was this *DWTS* thing anyway? Maybe I could still get out of it with a quick injury and a public-service announcement. *Don't drink and surf the Internet*, I'd say. I'd be propped up on crutches, with a couple of walking casts and maybe even a big white bandage on my forehead. *It's simply not worth the risk.* My sad eyes would find the camera. *Look what happened to me.*

As if I'd summoned it, a real camera appeared. The guy who was holding it started tiptoeing around the room like that might keep me from noticing him. I'd watched enough *DWTS* episodes last night to know that my only hope was to ignore him. If I stamped my foot and asked him to leave or to come back later, if I cried or ran off to brush my hair or to put on some makeup, that would be the footage they'd show to twenty-three million people on international TV right before my first dance. I mean, basically *DWTS* was reality TV with some choreography thrown in.

My dance partner held out his arms.

Every inch of me wanted to turn and run away, as far and as fast as I could go.

He wiggled the fingers on both hands in a come-hither gesture.

When I was a little, little girl, I used to think that if I closed my eyes, it would make me disappear. I closed them now.

No such luck.

I tried to take a step, but my new dance shoes seemed to have sprouted roots. "Oh, please don't make me do this," I said.

Ilya crossed the space between us. He was wearing a white T-shirt and black jeans and a black vest and black sneakers, and even walking across the room, he moved with a wiry feline grace.

He grabbed my right hand and rested the fingers of his other hand gently on my waist. I was so jumpy it tickled. I bit my lower lip to try to stop the giggle that slipped out of my mouth.

Ilya started waltzing me around the practice studio as if he were taking me out for a test drive. The room was long and open, so we had lots of ground to cover. One whole wall was covered with a devastating expanse of mirror. I tried not to look.

I flashed back on that old Felix the Cat cartoon from my childhood and realized that's who Ilya reminded me of: He was a dead ringer for Felix. And then suddenly I couldn't get the stupid theme song out of my head. It was driving me nuts, but I couldn't get the words quite right either, which was driving me even nuttier. Something about Felix the Cat being the wonderful, wonderful cat and how you'll laugh so hard your sides will ache and your something will go whackety whack. Or pitter pat. Or something like that. And that's Felix the somethingful cat.

My dance partner stopped abruptly. Clearly my Felix the Cat flash-back was not helping my waltz. The good news was the camera guy wasn't laughing. At least not out loud.

When I opened the door to our practice studio to make a bathroom run, Karen the producer was standing there. She handed me her phone.

"Hello," I said into the phone for lack of a better idea.

"Just checking in to see if you need anything," Joanie Baloney said in her most adorable voice.

"How did you get this number?"

"Oh, I must have made a copy when I wrote down your messages."

"You must have?"

"I just thought one of us should have an emergency number for you."

Karen's arms were crossed over her chest. If she'd been wearing a watch, she would have been looking at it.

"So," Joanie said, "how's it going?"

"Listen, I can't talk. Mostly because it's not my phone."

"Listen, I'm just trying to help. And if you'd actually answer your own phone, I could call you on that."

"If I actually wanted to, I would," I said sweetly.

I rolled my eyes at Karen, just to let her know this wasn't a volun-tary conversation. She didn't smile.

"Fine," Joanie said, "be a bitch. Do you have plants you want me to water or anything?"

"They're all dead," I said, "but thanks for asking."

Joanie let out a puff of air right into my ear. "I just wanted to make sure you're okay."

I sighed. "Thanks. I'm fine."

"Good. Oh, and Tag wants to know what his schedule looks like for the next few weeks. And he can't remember where he put his password to log onto his computer."

I clicked the End Call button and handed the phone back to Karen.

She shook her head. "And your mother wants you to call your brother."

"Sorry about all this," I said.

"If you're having cell phone issues, let me know and I'll hook you up," she said as she wiped the phone on her sleeve.

Ilya leaned back so he could look me right in the eyes. "I am a world-class teacher. A world-class dancer. I am the best at what I do. The best in the world."

"That's very reassur—"

"Shhh." He started dancing again, turning us to the right and then to the left. "I can mold you, I can shape you. I can tear you down and build you into what I need you to be. I have created champions out of nothing. Out of air."

We looped around the perimeter of the room, spiraling in circles within a larger circle. It was like being on a Ferris wheel, only sideways, or on one of those awful cup-and-saucer rides. I wanted him to stop, but I didn't, because I knew the room would just keep spinning. I wondered if a *DWTS* contestant had ever puked on her partner.

"I was a world champion before I was seventeen. My father was a world champion before he was seventeen. And his father before him. My mother was my father's professional partner. Together they have won sixteen international Latin dance championships."

"Wow," I said, keeping my response to one word. I knew my limits, and it was the best I could do under the circumstances. I was thoroughly amazed at Ilya's ability to dance and talk at the same time.

We were still circling, but now we were crisscrossing the room in a figure-eight pattern. I was trying not to count the number of times

I'd stepped briefly on my partner's toes, but we had to be approaching double digits by now.

"In my house, our entire world was built on one principle: Live to dance and dance to live. Dance was our religion."

"Not that I'm making excuses," I said, "but I was brought up Catholic."

He stopped. I stopped, too, but the room kept spinning just like I knew it would. My mouth went dry and I began salivating the way I always did just before my stomach started heaving. I knew my only hope was to keep breathing, long and slow, in through the nose and out through the mouth.

"Oh, boy," my partner said as he watched me breathe.

"Sorry," I said. In the short time we'd been together it was at least my eighth apology.

"Did your father never dance with you?"

I took another slow breath before I answered. "Of course he did. My whole family danced around the house all the time when I was growing up, but only to the Grateful Dead."

Ilya seemed to think about that, or maybe he was thinking he'd be grateful to be dead himself right about now.

"Show me," he said.

I put my hands over my head and waved them back and forth. Then I swiveled side to side as I played imaginary tambourines with both hands. Or maybe they were imaginary maracas.

Ilya pressed a palm to his forehead, like Homer Simpson, only classier and without the *doh*. "You have no formal dance training at all?"

He looked so sad I just wanted to cheer him up. "Of course I do. Intro to ballet, jazz, and tap. I can even Shuffle Off to Buffalo."

He raised one eyebrow. Most people have to raise them both together; he was that coordinated.

I realized he was waiting for me to show him.

Alone in a hotel room in a strange city, dancing my heart out, I'd fantasized this moment a hundred times before.

I took a deep breath and headed for Buffalo. In my new dance shoes it actually worked pretty well, as long as Buffalo was to my left. But unfortunately, when I tried to shuffle back to the Buffalo on my right, I tripped.

I took a couple of running steps, trying to find my balance. Ilya caught me before I fell.

He pulled me back into dance position. He straddled my legs and started bending me over backward as if I were a reluctant Gumby. "Turn your head. Like this."

I turned my head. "Gee, that's comforta—"

"Shhh." He bent me as far as I could go, then circled me around from the waist. He lifted me up. He started leaning away from me. "Put your weight on me."

"Seriously?"

By way of an answer he dragged me across the shiny hardwood floor. I could feel the toes of my new dance shoes getting scuffmarks.

"Even you I can turn into a dancer," he said.

Up until that moment, I was still under the illusion that I actually had *some* skills, *some* talent, even if my shimmering potential had been cut short as a child.

I waited till he stopped sweeping the floor with me and stood me up again. "I'm *that* bad?" I asked as casually as I could.

"No," he said. "It would be worse if you had no rhythm."

It wasn't much, but it made me ridiculously happy. It was all I could do not to break into a jazzy rendition of "I Got Rhythm."

Ilya held me by one hand and walked me over so he could pick up a tiny remote. He pushed a button and changed the music on the stereo to something sultry and sexy.

"Uh-oh," I said.

"Shhh." He brought me back to the center of the room. He pressed his front side to my back side and grabbed my hands. He started circling both our hips seductively, completely controlling the movement of mine.

Then he started circling our hips in the other direction, around and around and around again.

He stopped suddenly, his front still pressed to my back. I waited to see what would happen next. Maybe he was finished and it was time for a cigarette.

"Aaaaaaaaaand," he said, moving our hips in a slow, teasing circle.

"Give-it-to-me," he said, our hips doing a sudden bump and grind.

"Aaaaaaaaaand," he said again.

I held my breath.

"Give-it-to-me."

I pressed my lips together so my teeth wouldn't rattle while we bumped.

"Aaaaaaaaaand."

I heard a sigh and realized it was coming from me.

"Give-it-to-me."

If Mitchell had danced like this, I might have tried harder to make things work.

Ilya let go of one hand and spun me away from him with the other. He reeled me back in like a yo-yo. Then he put his hands on my shoulders.

He shook his head. "But we have only seven days. Even for the best of the best like me, this is an impossibility."

Wouldn't you know it, just when I was starting to get into this. I wondered if he was going to try to trade me in for a newer model. *Say it's not so, Ilya*, I wanted to plead.

I waited.

He didn't say anything.

I couldn't stand the suspense any longer. "So what does that *mean*?"

"Basically," my *DWTS* partner said, "it means we'll do what we can."

20

Practice what you preach, and remember
that preaching takes practice.

I fell asleep like a ton of bricks, maybe even two tons. When I woke up I was a whole new simile: I felt like I'd been run over by a golf cart.

"That fish bowl is looking pretty good to me," I said to Ginger and Fred.

I inched my way out of bed and hobbled into my little white bathroom. My calves felt as if they'd atrophied overnight and were now pulling my heels and knees in to meet each other. The muscles of my arms and shoulders were actually trembling, and the rest of me wasn't far behind.

Reaching in to turn on the shower was a challenge. So was stepping over the side of the tub. I closed my eyes and waited for the hot water to work its magic.

When the water turned cold, I got out. It was possible that I was a little bit less stiff, but it was also possible that I was imagining it because I wanted it to be true. I wrapped a towel around me and hobbled out to my little white kitchen. I put an English muffin into the little white toaster that I'd discovered toasted only one side of the bread. While it was half toasting, I started a pot of scentless coffee.

I couldn't believe it was morning already. I picked up my cell phone from the counter and thought about turning it on. Not because Joanie Baloney wanted me to, but because it might be a good idea to check messages one of these days. Tag and my parents were settled in at home by now, and basically this was a golf week for Tag. And a bowling week for my parents. Tag would be churning out some new chiasmuses between holes and texting me all day long with them. He'd want to talk strategy. He'd want me to hang out with him. He'd want to yell at me for what I'd done.

Just before I'd climbed into bed last night, I'd thought again about calling Steve Moretti. But who even answers their phone anymore? If only my father had written my e-mail address instead of my phone number on that little piece of paper he gave him. Although e-mail seemed pretty formal these days, too. Maybe I could text Steve instead. But it would be hard to fit whatever it was I had to say in a text message. I mean, *yo, whassup?* didn't quite cover it. So maybe I could text him to ask when he might be available for a phone call, because what if I just called and took him by surprise and he didn't even remember me and I could hear it in his voice. Or worse, what if he didn't want to talk to me anymore and instead of just ignoring the ring until it went to voice mail, he pushed the End Call button, the ultimate blow-off. Somehow not answering my text would be less painful. At least I could pretend it had gotten lost in cyberspace.

I sat on the couch and gazed up at the poster of the *DWTS* mirror ball trophy that I'd adhered to the opposite wall with four chewed pieces of Orbit spearmint gum, since I hadn't thought to buy tape. Back when we were in junior high and mirror balls were called disco balls, Tag was the first person I knew to get one. He hung it from a hook on the ceiling of his room and rigged up a spotlight with interchangeable lenses made out of blue, red, yellow, and green plastic. When you turned on the spotlight and gave the disco ball a spin, hundreds of mirrored facets flashed endless patterns of light all over the room. I used to sneak in there when Tag wasn't home, find a good song on his transistor radio, like Gloria Gaynor's "I Will Survive" or the Bangles' "Walk Like an Egyptian," and dance for as long as I dared.

I closed my eyes and meditated on what it would be like to stun the whole world with my amazing grace and charm and dancing ability. To carry the mirror ball trophy home with me, hell, maybe even buy it its own first-class seat on the plane. To hold the glittering orb in my hands as I assumed my rightful place as the new family star.

The coffeemaker gurgled and sent a final spurt of coffee into the pot, snapping me back to the new day. I put my cell back down on the counter. I had enough going on. As soon as I got the dancing thing under control, I'd reevaluate. But right now it was all about survival.

The English muffin popped up. On the one hand, I knew how much better it would taste if I turned the halves around so the other sides could toast, and on the other hand, I was really, really hungry. And if yesterday's busy schedule and my fear of eating in front of my partner and his rock-hard abs were indications, peanut butter on an English muffin might be the high-calorie point of my day.

I slathered the peanut butter on thick, poured a cup of coffee, and added some milk. Then I grabbed the fish food and brought it into the bedroom so Fred and Ginger and I could have breakfast together.

When I opened the apartment door to leave, the super was standing there with his fist up, ready to knock.

He switched hands and held out his cell phone. "It's your sister."

"Which one?" I said.

The super glared at me. "Listen, lady, this isn't in my job description." He was barefoot and his hair was wet. A trench coat was belted around his waist like a bathrobe, and water was dripping onto the linoleum floor.

"Sorry," I said. "I just remembered. I don't have a sister."

Joanie Baloney's voice squeaked from the super's cell. "She does, too."

I reached for the phone. "What?"

"Listen, I'm just trying to be a good sister. Mom and Dad and Tag are never going to speak to you again if you mess things up. Oh, and Dad says Mom wants you to call Tag, but honestly, I can just give him a message for you."

"Everything's under control," I said. I was pretty sure it was even true, at least if you factored out the dancing part.

"Tag was just thinking how much easier it would be for you if I took a few things off your plate."

The super made circles with his index finger, telling me to wrap it up, Hollywood style. A small puddle was forming between his feet.

"Sure," I said. "That makes total sense."

There was a beat of silence. "Great," Joanie said.

"Okay, well, have a nice day." I couldn't find the hang up button so I just handed the phone to the super.

"Wait," Joanie yelled.

The super shook his head and gave me the phone again.

"What's the password?"

"Guess," I said. As I handed the phone back to the super yet again, I took a moment to imagine everything grinding to a halt without me around to manage things. I had to admit, I was thoroughly enjoying hearing my little sister squirm.

I found my way to the practice studio without a hitch. Ilya was already there. If he noticed that the black yoga pants and baggy T-shirt I was wearing today looked a lot like the black yoga pants and baggy T-shirt I wore yesterday, he didn't let on.

I sat on the edge of the small practice stage, easing out of my flip-flops and strapping on my dance shoes. I'd expected blisters, but I couldn't find a single one. Amazingly, even though my feet hurt, they didn't hurt any more than the rest of me.

Ilya and I had practiced for more than four hours yesterday. The *DWTS* rules said that you could only practice for five hours a day, and you had to take a thirty-minute break every two hours. You also had to take one day off a week, but since I'd already had the first seven days off, I was pretty sure that was not going to happen this week.

Ilya was already dancing around the room with an imaginary partner. I had to admit she was a lot lighter on her feet than I was. If I tiptoed away now, I wondered if he'd even miss me.

I pushed myself up into a standing position.

Ilya stopped. Maybe he heard my muscles scream.

He smiled. "Today the real work begins."

A wave of buyer's remorse hit me with tsunamilike force. What had I gotten myself into? I had a perfectly nice little life back home in Marshbury. I was good at my job and almost never felt like I was in over my head. Now I was so far over my head that I wasn't sure it was still attached to my aching body.

Maybe my best bet would be to tuck my tail between my legs and catch the next plane home and face the inevitable family meeting.

"What," my mother would say while one of Afterwife's dinners heated in Tag's professional-grade oven, "in the world were you thinking, Deirdre?"

"Apparently I wasn't," I'd say.

I'd peer down at my folded hands. The more pitiful I made myself look, the faster this would go and then we could eat. I was pretty sure I smelled Afterwife's famous turkey-asparagus potpie.

"What a loozah thing to do," Tag would say. Over the years, he'd developed just a hint of Madonna's fake British enunciation. His Boston accent came back only when he was really, really mad.

"Give her a chance, son," my father would say. "I think the guiding principle here is that we've all got to practice what you preach and remember that preaching takes practice."

"Not now, Dad," Tag would say.

"I think," Joanie Baloney would say, "what we really need to discuss here is who can best handle Tag's interests from this point forward."

I'd glare at her. "Oh, shut up."

She'd glare back. "You shut up."

Maybe I'd stay in the *DWTS* competition after all. I took a deep, ambition-building breath.

"I'm pretty sore," I said. "Do you think we could take it a little slower, just for today?"

Ilya crossed his arms over his chest. He was wearing jeans and a tight purple short-sleeved shirt unbuttoned one button too low. Possibly two. His resemblance to Felix the Cat had completely disappeared. Today he looked like a dancer. I could only hope this would help my focus.

Ilya did his famous one-eyebrow raise. "No problem. Perhaps we should skip today entirely given that you are *pretty sore*. There's a McDonald's around the corner. Perhaps we could grab a breakfast sandwich and a double order of fries, and hang around and chitchat until the mall opens."

I knew he was kidding, but I had to admit those McDonald's fries sounded pretty good right about now. And I still needed to buy underwear.

"And then, in six days, when our first performance puts us . . ."

Ilya ran a hand through his slick-backed hair and stopped halfway, his fingers still in his hair.

"... At. The. Bottom. Of the. *Leaderboard* ..."

I closed my eyes.

"Perhaps we can celebrate our embarrassment with a double-dip ice-cream cone."

I pictured the huge black *DWTS* leaderboard sign with Ilya's and my names way down at the very bottom. What would our combined scores on the first dance be? 14? 12? 6? How low could that leaderboard go?

21

Whether or not you are good at discipline,
discipline she is always good for you.

I couldn't think of another option, so I opened my eyes.

"Sorry," I said. "I guess I wasn't thinking about your reputation being at stake here."

Ilya took his hand out of his hair and shrugged.

I'd never really thought about it from his point of view. I was the booby prize, the short end of the stick. Even if Kelly Genelavive was a thug with hair spray, at least she was a young, beautiful, famous thug with hair spray. And even though this might be the most embarrassing thing I'd ever do in my entire life, dancing was Ilya's religion. His livelihood.

"Do you get paid the same amount no matter how well we do?" I asked.

He waited a beat, then shook his head.

"So how does it work?"

I watched him try to decide whether to answer. "A hundred and fifty K for the first two weeks."

"But that's good, isn't it? I mean, if they can't vote us off until the end of the second week. Or is it the first week? Never mind, don't tell me. What else?"

"Twenty thousand for each week we stay in it, then fifty K for making it into the finals."

"What do the winners get?"

He grinned. "The mirror ball trophy."

"That's it?"

He nodded.

"Who gets to keep it?"

He shook his head. "The celebrity dancer keeps it. The professionals all have entire rooms full of trophies."

I took a deep breath. "I want that mirror ball trophy. And I want you to know I'll do anything I can do to help you win this thing."

It was my dance partner's turn to close his eyes. When he opened them, he cat-walked the distance between us and grabbed my hands.

"Repeat after me," he said.

I nodded. I threw my shoulders back and pulled my stomach in. I dug down to reach the strength that was deep within me. I steadied myself for the fight of my life.

"We cannot win," my dance partner said.

"What?" I said. "But—"

"Uh-uh-uh." He squeezed my hands between his. Hard.

"I really think if I focus—"

He squeezed my hands harder.

"Ouch."

"We cannot win. Say it."

"Fine." I let out a puff of air. "We. Cannot. Win."

"Say it again."

"We cannot win."

"Louder."

"We cannot win!" I yelled. My voice echoed in our big empty practice studio.

Ilya was still holding my hands. "Now we have faced reality."

"I guess I'm not a huge fan of reality," I said.

"It's the first and most important step," he said, as if it might lead to a chassé or a kick ball change. I tried to slide my hands out from under his, but he held on tight.

I had an itch right in the center of my forehead that I was dying to scratch. I blew some air at it instead. "But I mean, if we can't win, what's the point?"

"The point is that we start where we are. We play to our strengths and keep improving. Americans love to cheer the underdog, so we accept that as our rightful place in this competition and enjoy the ride for as long as it lasts."

"Wow," I said. "You're so mature. Okay, so what do we do now?"

"Now we buckle down and get to work. We find our discipline and we see how far it can take us."

I sighed. "I have to tell you, I've never been all that great at discipline."

Ilya's steely gray eyes held mine. "When I was growing up, my father had a saying: 'Whether or not you are good at discipline, discipline she is always good for you.'"

"Your father would fit right in at my house," I said. "Okay, I'm in. What do I have to do?"

"First of all, you can't dance like a grandma."

"What?"

"You can't. Dance like. A grandma."

"Sorry," I said. It was as if my self-esteem were a balloon and Ilya had just popped it with a pin. I mean, I knew I wasn't Kelly Genelavive, but a *grandma*?

He didn't seem to notice. "You've watched the show?"

I nodded.

"Did you ever see anyone dance like a grandma?"

I bit my lower lip and shook my head.

"Right. Even the real grandmas don't dance like grandmas."

I didn't mean to, but somehow I started to cry.

"Shhh," my dance partner said.

I kept crying. I bent forward and covered my face with my hands.

Ilya started patting my back as if he were burping me. "Let it out. Just let it out."

I let it out. I cried and cried and cried. I cried about dancing like a grandma. Then I worked my way backward from there. I cried about the fact that the only thing people really liked about me was my brother. I cried about Mitchell not caring enough to commit to a life with me, even if I hadn't been sure I wanted to commit to a life with him either. I cried about wasting such a big chunk of my life not having a life. I cried about always feeling second fiddle, or even fourth fiddle, in my family, and then hitching my wagon to the family star anyway. I cried about not having the guts to make it on my own after college, about drifting through high school, about the parties I hadn't been invited to, the friends who'd dumped me, about being such a wimp that I just sat back and let Joanie Baloney take away the things I should have fought for.

I cried because I was sad. I cried because I was embarrassed. And lonely. And scared. I cried because I wanted with all my heart to be a different kind of person, the kind of person who knew who she was, the kind of person who didn't *dance like a grandma*. But I simply didn't know how to get there.

When I ran out of tears, Ilya handed me a tissue.

"I'm sorry," I said. "It's just a lot, that's all."

"I know," he said.

"If only I'd started dieting and working out about six months ago. Or even six weeks. If only—"

"Shhh." Ilya reached for my hand. I started to tuck my damp tissue in the waistband of my yoga pants, then stopped when I realized it was a totally grandmotherly thing to do. Ilya pointed and I lobbed it into a little plastic wastebasket in the corner. With my luck I probably threw like a grandma, too.

"Let's go talk to wardrobe," he said. "I think it might help you get into character if you're wearing a costume."

"Okay," I said. "Just let me run out to my car first. I can't remember if I locked it."

I focused on not walking like a grandma as I blinked my tear-ravaged eyes against the hot Southern California sun. My legs and shoulders screamed as I climbed into the Land Rover. I turned on the engine and cranked up the air-conditioning as high as it would go. I dabbed my eyes with a tissue and blew my nose.

I fired up my cell phone. I had no idea who I thought I was going to call. A massage therapist? A therapist therapist? 911? My mother?

My phone came to life. According to the phone log, my parents had called twice, Joanie had called a million times, and Tag was apparently just sitting there hitting redial over and over again.

Mitchell had called, too. Three times.

I knew better, but I tapped his name on the screen anyway.

He answered on the first ring. Instead of hello, he said, "She lost it."

For a minute I thought he meant his pregnant bride-to-be had lost it the way I had, maybe tried to run him over with a golf cart or even an SUV.

"What?" I said.

"She lost the baby."

I felt an awful jumble of relief and guilt for feeling relief.

"Why are you telling me this?" I finally said.

Mitchell let out a long sigh. "I don't know. I guess I needed someone to talk to . . ."

I leaned forward and propped my forehead on the steering wheel.

"It's just . . ." Mitchell said. "I mean, you're a girl. Do you think she'll still want to get married?"

My neck muscles were so tight I had to use my hands to help me lift my head back up.

"I'm going to hang up now," I said. "I have a lot going on, and none of it has anything to do with you."

Mitchell laughed a sad little laugh. "That's right, I almost forgot about the dance thing. You're all over the Internet, by the way. Are you out there now?"

"Yup."

"What's it like?"

"Scary."

"I bet. You'll do great, though. You always could do anything you set your mind to."

"When did I ever set my mind to anything?"

"Seriously? I mean, holy crap, you run your brother's entire *empire*. He wouldn't have any of that without you. You're smart. You're organized. You can charm the pants off of anyone."

"Yeah, right." I was a little bit surprised by Mitchell's supportive words, and maybe even a tiny bit bolstered by them—at least enough to head back into the studio. "Listen, I have to go. Take care of yourself."

When I got to the wardrobe room, Anthony was pinning up the hem for a former famous gymnast. Or maybe she was a former famous ice-skater. In any case, I'd definitely seen her before. She had long strawberry blond hair, cornflower blue eyes, and the body of an eight-year-old boy.

She turned a dazzling white smile on me. I wondered if her cosmetic dentist knew Tag's cosmetic dentist.

"Hi," I said. Hopefully she'd leave before I had to take off any clothes.

"Hi," she said. "I am so excited to finally meet you."

I resisted the urge to look over my shoulder.

She stuck out her hand. "Who are you again?"

22

Dying to dance is the only diet you need.

That's what I'm talking about," Ilya said when I walked out of the dressing room. Actually, I was pretty sure my top half walked out a full minute before my bottom half did.

"Are you sure?" I said. I was wearing a black push-up bra that had lifted my breasts so high they were practically in my line of vision. Anthony was still working on my costume, but he'd given me a black strapless sheath to wear. It was short, really short, and seemed to consist mostly of fringe and sequins. And two little flesh-colored spaghetti straps to keep me from losing it entirely, for which I was thankful beyond words.

"Now that's a lot of sexy," Anthony said.

That's what I was afraid of. "Does it make me look, you know . . ."

Anthony flung his arms wide. "No, it does not make you look *fat*. This is what a woman should look like. Trust me, if we took you out of la-la land and dropped you and that balance beam who just walked out of here off on a street corner, every red-blooded straight male in Middle America would jump right over her and make a beeline for you."

"Thanks," I said. "I think."

"You're not fat," Ilya said. "You're curvilicious."

"You're a bombshell, dumplin'," Anthony said. "It's all about the Spanx. It's a beautiful thing."

The truth was I was wearing two undergarments, one that started just under my push-up bra and then turned into panty hose and another that wrapped around me and hooked in the front, like a corset. Actually, it probably *was* a corset.

But the best part so far was that Anthony had given me a shopping bag full of underwear samples to keep. There wasn't a pair of cotton grandma panties in the bunch. I'd buried my own graying underwear in the bottom of the bag since I was too embarrassed to leave it in the wastebasket for some hip cleaning service person to find. Or worse, maybe the paparazzi went through the trash looking for intimate details about the celebrity dancers. I could imagine turning on my laptop again only to see my pitiful underpants splashed all over the virtual front page of the *Hollywood Reporter*.

A pretty platinum-haired woman holding a round brush came out from behind a screen that divided the huge room in half.

"Gina," she said.

"Nice to meet you," I said. "I'm Deirdre."

She lifted a section of my hair with the brush. "You'll need highlights and lowlights. And a good cut. Maybe an uplift for the first dance, to give you more height."

Another pretty woman, this one with pitch-black hair with a white streak in the front, came out from behind the same screen. "Lila," she said. As soon as she glanced at my toes, I wished I'd put my dance shoes back on before I came out of the little dressing area. "Yikes, we're talking a major panicure here."

"Sorry," I said.

Lila brushed away my apology and reached for one of my hands. Her fingernails were painted black with white polka dots. I couldn't take my eyes off them.

"Not good," she said. "We'll go with long fake nails, give you a

French manicure, and cover it with lots of clear sparkle. And presto, those short, stubby fingers of yours will be long and elegant, a dancer's dream."

I looked down and faced the new reality of my short, stubby fingers. Who knew?

"And false eyelashes," she said.

"To cover my short, stubby natural ones," I said.

"Your eyelashes are fine," Gina said. "We just need to up the glam factor. And wait till you get your spray tan. You'll look like you haven't eaten in a week."

"Speaking of which," Ilya said, "let's go grab a quick snack from craft services and get back to work. Thanks, team."

I thanked the glam squad profusely. Too bad the winner couldn't take them home along with the mirror ball trophy.

I'd read just enough about the entertainment industry to know that craft services meant the food that was delivered to the set of a television show or film set. As Ilya and I walked down the hall, I promised myself that I wouldn't eat a thing when we got there. I'd just keep Ilya company while he ate.

The door to one of the other studios was open, so we peeked in. A famous football player, at least I was pretty sure it was football, was shuffling his feet slowly in a circle. A beautiful professional dancer had one leg up with her ankle resting on his shoulder. Her arms were extended gracefully, like butterfly wings.

"Whoa," I whispered.

"Yeah," Ilya said, "the male celebrities have it easier. They get to do a lot of holding while their partners dance around them."

"Men," I said.

The woman glanced over and frowned at Ilya. He grabbed my arm and we continued down the hall.

"You know," I said, "I pictured us all practicing in a big room together, cheering each other on."

Ilya stopped and held open the door to a little lounge with a kitch-enette at one end. "We do some of that once we get to the group dances later in the season, but it's better to put on our blinders and keep to ourselves until after the first performance. Too much looking over your shoulder to see what everybody else is doing will only make you more nervous. We need to focus on our own strengths."

"Or lack thereof." My stomach betrayed my lack of resolve by growling fiercely.

I sat down at a long table and used every ounce of discipline I had to pretend I wasn't hungry. I knew you counted sheep to fall asleep, but I wasn't sure what to count to make the hunger go away. Donuts?

Ilya sat down across from me and slid a plate in my direction.

I tried not to look at it. "That's okay—"

"Eat," he said.

"Oh, all right. But don't worry, right after this, I promise I'll start a strict diet. I'm thinking Dukan, but I was just reading about a resur-gence of the apple cider vinegar diet. Did you know it was actually started in the 1820s by Lord Byron? I thought that was so fascinat-ing."

The truth was I had enough experience to write my own diet book. I'd gone on my first diet right after Tag's classmate had called me a porker. Ironically, the Atkins diet involved eating copious quantities of pork rinds, and no carbs, which we called starches back then. My waistbands were loose in no time, but my pee started to smell funny and I got dizzy when I stood up too fast. When my mother found the diet page I'd ripped from one of Colleen's magazines under my bed and threw it out, I was more relieved than disappointed.

Over the years I'd become a diet connoisseur. I'd tried the grape-fruit diet, the cabbage soup diet, the Russian peasant diet, the lem-onade diet, the South Beach Diet, as well as Weight Watchers, Jenny Craig, Slim-Fast, and Nutrisystem. They all worked. And then as soon as I started eating normally again, my weight went right back to where I'd started, plus a few extra pounds. Sometimes I thought that if I'd never started dieting, I'd probably be looking pretty good right now. Other times I was convinced I just hadn't found the right diet yet.

Ilya popped a strawberry into his mouth. He closed his eyes and chewed slowly, a look of pure bliss on his face. *I'll have what he's having* flashed through my head.

"Dying to dance is the only diet you need." Ilya nodded at my plate, then reached for another strawberry. "Eat. But only what will help your dance. Think of your body as a fancy sports car that deserves only the best gasoline."

My plate was piled high with fresh fruit—big slices of cantaloupe and strawberries and kiwi and papaya—plus one piece of string cheese and exactly ten almonds. I ate every bit and washed it all down with a big glass of water with lemon slices floating in it.

Ilya checked his watch. "So now we are ready to dance."

In some ways, the second day was easier because based on the experience of the first day, I knew I would probably live through it. But in terms of the actual dance, it was harder. Mind-blowingly harder.

"Our first performance is the cha-cha," Ilya announced as he reached for the iPod remote. Yesterday I'd been so overwhelmed trying to keep up as we tried out a variety of steps and sequences, I hadn't even thought to ask what our first dance would be.

"Oh, good," I said. "At least I can count to three."

"Actually, it's four."

"Ha. I knew that."

Ilya ignored me and clicked the remote. I don't know what I was expecting, but when "Smooth" by Santana blasted out, I felt like an old friend had just shown up.

"Ohmigod," I said. "You can cha-cha to Santana?"

Ilya winked. "As long as you don't tell them."

One-two-threeandfour became my mantra, my chant, my life.

Front-back-threeandfour, back-front-threeandfour, slide-slide-three-andfour, one-two-turnturnturn, walk-walk-walkwalkwalk, step-step-chachacha. Who knew there were so many ways to count to four?

The costume really did help. The Spanx reminded me to pull in my stomach and the corset helped me stand up straighter. When the long black fringe of my minidress brushed across my thighs, I felt sexy, and when my sequins sparkled in the mirror, I could almost believe, just for a moment, that I was the one who was sparkling.

"Smooth" was the perfect song. Ilya played the first part over and over and over again, and I never got sick of it. When Santana sang the line about hearing my rhythm on the radio, I actually felt Ilya's rhythm, my rhythm, the rhythm we were creating together. And the part about being like the ocean under the moon got to me every single time—it reminded me of home, but also moving beyond home, heading out to sea and on to my next horizon. Ilya got into it, too, and after a while, every time the *forget about it* line came around, we'd both yell it out loud.

Sometimes, when I really needed to lift my spirits, I'd put on a great old song like that and dance all around the sheep shed. I'd play it over and over and over again. I'd forget about how I probably looked and just have fun. I'd work it. I'd own it. And before I knew it I could feel all the bad stuff slipping away and I'd truly believe that my life could only get better.

In some ways, dancing with Ilya was starting to feel a lot like when I danced in secret, only a zillion times better.

23

Step up that pep and put some pep in that step.

A s soon as we'd put in our five hours, Ilya had given me a grocery list and directions to the nearest Whole Foods.

"Don't forget to eat," he said, as if that had ever happened in my entire life. "You need the energy. Just remember, put only the high-test fuel in your tank."

I put my hands on my hips. "Did you just call me a tank?"

"You are a beautiful woman, Deirdre Griffin. The only thing left is for you to start behaving like one."

"Ha," I said. "And to learn how to dance."

He grinned. "Okay, two things. Now go get some rest."

I sat in the Whole Foods parking lot and turned my phone on again just long enough to delete some more messages from my family. There were a whole slew of numbers I didn't recognize, too. I decided to save them until I had more energy.

Mitchell called as I was climbing out of the Land Rover to head into Whole Foods, my thumb poised to power off my phone again.

"What?"

"I just remembered that I forgot to tell you that my leg's fine. I mean, it's still sore, but nothing was broken or anything. I just didn't want you to feel guilty."

I held out the phone so I could roll my eyes at it, then put it back to my ear. "Don't worry. I wasn't."

"Okay, I'm just going to come right out and say this. The whole time everything was going on . . . You know, the whole baby and wedding thing . . . I kept thinking that if I was ever going to get married, it should have been to you, Dee."

"You asked me once, remember?" I heard myself say. It was years ago now, at least five, maybe more. Mitchell had come home from a friend's bachelor party, woken me up from a dead sleep, knelt on the floor by the sheep shed bed. "Marry me," he'd said. "You're the best goddamn thing that ever happened to me. You're the moon and the stars and the goddamn solar system all rolled into one."

"Yeah, I remember. You told me to sober up and ask you again in the morning."

I remembered that, too. And I remembered waiting, not just the next morning but for weeks, maybe months, until I pretended I wasn't waiting anymore. "You never asked me again, Mitchell."

"Maybe you shouldn't have shot me down when I asked you the first time."

I didn't say anything. I threw some organic chocolate double-chunk brownies into my cart, then remembered Ilya's list and put them back on the display stand.

"Okay, you're right," Mitchell said. "I should have asked you again. I don't know, maybe I thought we had a good thing going and I didn't want to ruin it. And maybe sometimes I have a tendency to be kind of selfish."

"Ya think?" I lowered a six-pack of lemon-lime seltzer into my cart.

"Would it be okay if I came out there to see you? You know, just hang out, talk things through. I could really use a break from everything around here, and I don't know, I was thinking maybe you could use some company."

I stopped in the middle of the aisle. I couldn't believe he was going there. And the scary thing was, I could almost picture going there, too.

"Good-bye, Mitchell," I said. I pushed End Call, then closed my eyes and shuddered.

I navigated the crowded aisles, tossing a premade salad with mixed baby greens, walnuts, cranberries, and goat cheese into my cart. And a veggie roll-up on whole grain. Plus a box of Skinny Cow fudge bars.

As I carried everything out to my rental car, thoughts of Mitchell still danced in my head. I pushed them away.

Traffic was a nightmare, but eventually I made it back to the apartment and curled up on the sofa with my dinner. No offense to Afterwife, but it was the best meal I'd had in ages. I savored every bite. When I was finished I felt satisfied but not stuffed.

"Delish," I said. My whipped chocolate dessert was refreshingly cold and lighter than air. I lapped the last of it off the stick and wondered how many of these I'd have to eat to start feeling less like the cow and more like the skinny.

I fed Ginger and Fred. I tracked down the washer and dryer on the floor below and threw in my wardrobe of yoga pants and baggy T-shirts along with all my new underwear. I was exhausted, but it was a good tired.

I waited till the underwear was draped over my shower curtain rod and the rest of my clothes were twirling around in the dryer. Then I found my cell phone and scrolled past some messages from my family and about a gazillion e-mail requests for Tag. There were a few e-mails from friends, too, and a crazy number of requests to interview me. A message from someone at *DWTS* said that the contract would be on its way shortly.

I tapped the Phone icon. I found Steve Moretti's message and listened to it twice. Every time I got to the part where he said, "Hey, this is Steve. The guy you just kissed and ran away from?" I scrunched my eyes shut.

Did he really want to use me to get to Tag, or had I simply jumped to that conclusion because it was the tape that played, over and over in my head, whether it applied to the situation or not? Why was it so hard for me to believe that someone might actually want *me*?

I stared up at the ceiling and tried to remember exactly what had happened in Austin. First I said the Tambourine Twins' boots looked stupid with sundresses, admittedly not my finest moment. Then Tag said something about Steve and a business deal or talking business or something like that. And then Tag went right for the jugular, like he always did, and accused Steve of trying to get more money out of him by hitting on me.

It didn't even make sense.

Okay, so maybe I overreacted. Maybe I got the whole thing a little wrong.

Like a lot wrong.

Actually, totally wrong.

In fact, maybe I needed to call him right now.

Somehow I hit the Call icon before I had time to rethink my re-thinking. Two rings in I remembered it was after 10 p.m. on the West Coast, which would mean it was after 1 a.m. on the East Coast.

I started to hang up and then I remembered caller ID. Whose genius idea was that, anyway? I mean, I grew up in the generation where girls called boys only to chicken out and hang up when they answered. It was a whole new world now.

"Hello," Steve said. He sounded pretty good considering the hour.

"Listen," I said. "I'm really sorry—"

"I can't answer the phone right now, but leave a message and I'll get back to you."

The thing about voice mail beeps is that they always come before you're ready for them.

"Hi," I said after his finished beeping. "Sorry to call so late. Um, you might not remember me anymore, but you asked me to have breakfast with you? In Austin? Anyway, um, I just wanted to say I would have liked to have done it with you. Ha, I meant have breakfast if that came out weird. Anyway, long story, but I'm actually kind of tied up for the next couple of weeks, but I can talk at night. Pacific time. Oh, I forgot to say this is Deirdre. Griffin. Tag's sister? Okay, hope you got that job you pitched at the university. And, well, bye."

After I hung up, I stared at my phone and tried to judge how bad the message I'd just left had been. I mean, on the leaderboard of phone messages I'd left for men over the course of my life, where would it rank? Definitely not at the top. I knew it wasn't a brilliant message. But was it so bad that it didn't deserve a callback? Someone really should invent a voice mail message retriever or even an Undo button.

A jolt of adrenaline hit me like lightning. Who the hell cared whether or not I'd just left an embarrassing phone message? In less than a week I'd be embarrassing myself in a much bigger way, in front of most of the world's television-viewing population.

With that thought, I decided to pack it in early. Dancing five hours a day makes sleep look like the best thing ever. I could feel every muscle in my entire body yelling *sleep, sleep, sleep.* I dragged myself back down to the little laundry room and back, draped my dry clothes over one of the little kitchen chairs, brushed my teeth, and went to bed.

I conked out almost immediately, just as I had the last two nights. But a nonstop series of dreams kept waking me up. I dreamed that Tag was chasing me down the street with a golf club. *You know who you dance like?* he yelled. *Miss Piggy.* Just as I turned around to see where he was, his golf club turned into an umbrella. *Step up that pep and put some pep in that step,* he roared down to me while he floated away like Mary Poppins. Somehow I was holding my own golf club now, but I couldn't get it to turn into an umbrella. I held it up as high as I could and tried my hardest to float away like Tag. I jumped, I kicked, I even twirled the golf club like a baton, but inside I knew I was just too much of a porker to ever become airborne.

I dreamed that Joanie Baloney had mailed me a big box. When I opened it, it contained matching orange-and-yellow cha-cha costumes for her whole family, even the dog. *Where's mine?* I said, over and over. She kept turning her head, and I kept dancing around to her other side to try to get her to look at me. *Come on*, I said. *Where's mine?* She turned and gave me her meanest look. *You should have thought of that*, she hissed.

I dreamed that I had to go into a big computer room and take a test before they'd let me into the *DWTS* ballroom. The test was multiple choice, and every time I clicked on one of the little circles to select it, I'd realize it was the wrong answer. But when I clicked on my new choice, my first answer disappeared, but the computer wouldn't let me input my new answer. I was so panicked my heart started thumping and I thought it might jump right out of my chest. I decided I'd copy the questions onto a piece of paper to prove that I knew the answers, but when I finally found a piece of paper, the words started disappearing faster than I could write them down. *Can I at least keep the underwear?* I sobbed. Karen the producer leaned over my shoulder and turned off the computer. *Sorry*, she said, *policy.*

When I heard the toilet flush, at first I thought I was in a new dream. I opened my eyes. I was definitely awake and I was absolutely positive I'd heard the toilet flush. My heart started beating a mile a minute in real time. My next thought was that if Mitchell were here I could make him deal with it and I could just hide under the covers. The absolute worst part of being single was that there was no one to pass the buck to.

I flashed back on a story I'd once read about a guy who'd broken into a woman's house to take a shower. She wasn't feeling well and came home early from work to discover him in her bathroom. She banged on the door and asked reasonably, "Why are you in my house taking a shower? Who *are* you?"

The guy introduced himself through the closed bathroom door.

"I'm calling the police," she said.

"I already called nine-one-one from my cell phone," he said politely. "I was afraid you might have a gun."

Given my luck with men, the intruder in my shower was probably not that conscientious. And like an idiot, I'd left my cell phone on the kitchen counter. Wait. Maybe it was Steve Moretti. He'd been so excited to get my message, he'd jumped on the first plane. I tried to do the math—length of flight minus time difference plus time to figure out where I was staying and then to break into my apartment—but it was too much for my sleep-addled brain.

As soon as I faced the reality that it probably wasn't Steve, my heart started beating like crazy again. Okay, my only hope was to get out of bed fast, run to the kitchen, grab my cell and keys, and call 911 on my way out the front door.

The apartment walls were so thin I heard the water in the bathroom sink turn on. At least he was a hand washer.

I slid out from under the covers. A tiny bar of light from the hallway guided me to the door. I'd just found the doorknob when I remembered Fred and Ginger. I turned and followed the wall with one hand until I came to the little dresser.

I reached for the fishbowl.

I heard the clunk of the water shutting off next door.

"Shit, shit, shit," I whispered. I wondered if the tiny bedroom closet was big enough to hide the three of us.

Just because he was clean didn't mean the guy in my bathroom wasn't a serial killer. I decided to make a run for it.

I tucked the fishbowl under one arm like a football and opened my bedroom door.

24

If you give a woman a fish, she will eat once,
but if you teach her to fish, she'll open up a pet store.

The bathroom door and the bedroom door opened at the exact same time.

I didn't consciously scream. It was more like I heard a loud scream and realized it was coming from me.

Ginger and Fred started to slip out from under my arm.

Tag dove. Star that he was, he executed a perfect catch and landed on his side holding the fishbowl. Not a single drop sloshed over the edge. It was like a page from our childhood favorite, *The Cat in the Hat.* Tag was Thing One and I was Thing Two.

My brother peered into the bowl. "Mmm, sushi."

I grabbed the fishbowl away from him. At first I thought my heart was pounding right out of my chest, but then I realized someone was banging on the door to the apartment.

I looked at Tag.

"What?" he said. "It's not *my* place."

"Get up," I said. He pushed himself up off the floor, and Ginger and Fred and I followed him to the door.

"Everything okay in there?" the building super asked when Tag opened the door. He was wearing the top half of a pair of old-fashioned pajamas over boxer briefs, and he was carrying a base-ball bat.

"No problem, buddy," Tag said. "I told you it'd be fine. My sister was just jumping for joy to see me. Sorry. I'll make sure she keeps it down."

I peeked around Tag so I could yell at the super. "I can't believe you let him in. He could have been anyone."

The super looked at me like I was dense. "I have every one of his videos."

Tag looked back at me over his shoulder. "I autographed them all, of course."

The super nodded. "And then we had a few beers. And then we got hungry so we sent out for pizza."

"Dirk knows the best pizza place," Tag said. "Thin, thin crust, just the way I like it."

"Who the hell is Dirk?" I said.

The super gave me a hurt look.

"You're Dirk," I said. "Sorry." It was the story of my life. I could live with someone for ten years, and then Tag would breeze in and in ten minutes he'd find out a whole laundry list of things I'd never even thought to ask. Case in point, I actually had lived with Mitchell off and on for ten years, and who did he go running to as soon as he decided to get married? The one and only It Guy.

"I've got an early morning," the super said. "Remember? The call-back on that Animal Planet show I was telling you about? So, as long as everything's okay here . . ."

"Good luck, man." Tag reached out to knuckle-bump him, then he nodded at Fred and Ginger. "And remember, if you give a woman a fish, she will eat once, but if you teach her to fish, she'll open up a pet store."

"Ha," the super said. "That's a good one." He turned and disap-peared down the hallway.

"Write it down," my brother actually said to me.

"In your dreams." I took the three baby steps required to see the little clock on my little stove. "Do you know what time it is?" I said.

Tag shrugged. "I'm still on East Coast time, so it's actually three hours later for me."

"Oh, shut up." I shifted the fishbowl to my other arm. "Listen, if I don't get back to sleep right now, I'll never make it through tomorrow. The extra bedroom's the last door down, if you haven't already taken it over. And if you left the toilet seat up, go put it down right now."

Tag grinned. "What's up with all those girlie-girl undies in there?"

I glared at him.

Tag yawned. "Nice to see you, big bro. Thanks for flying all the way across the country to see me."

I yawned, too. "Make yourself at home. Oh, wait. You already did."

Tag disappeared into the guest room and came back with a red plastic folder.

Just in case he was madder than he was acting and might explode, I took a step back.

He opened the folder to reveal a pile of photocopies. "From Mom. She said to tell you she's keeping the originals to make a scrapbook for you."

"Original what?" I said.

Tag pulled out one of the pages. "First Non-Celebrity Woman Becomes *Dancing With the Stars* Contestant. Thousands cry, 'She's one-of-us!' and pledge their support on the Internet."

I grabbed it away from him. "Seriously?"

Tag smiled. "Seriously. I gotta hand it to you, Dee. This is one genius way to extend my brand."

Bright and early the next morning, I was reminded how much my brother hated to be alone.

"Why don't you call *Dirk*?" I said. "Maybe he can get you a cameo as a hound dog on Animal Planet. Now that would be a great way to *extend your brand*."

Tag stretched and rubbed his eyes. He was wearing jeans but hadn't put on a shirt yet. He'd pigged out on pizza and beer last night and there wasn't an ounce of bloat on him. If I'd done that, I probably would have woken up five pounds heavier.

"I was thinking I'd just tag along with you," Tag said.

Tag tagging along was an old joke, so I didn't even bother to smile. "No, you can't come with me. You can drop me off, you can borrow my rental car, but you absolutely cannot come with me. Rehearsals are private."

I wasn't too sure how Karen the producer would feel about me loaning out the Land Rover, but I was going to have to pick my battles here. And apparently Tag hadn't been able to handle renting his own car all by himself. I was actually surprised he'd managed to book a flight and figure out which one was the taxi. Unless Joanie Baloney had made his travel arrangements for him.

I'd have to think about how to deal with Joanie later.

I handed Tag half a peanut butter English muffin and put another one in the little white toaster.

He took a sip of his coffee. "This coffee sucks. It has no smell."

"So go to Starbucks," I said. I was standing in the kitchen. Since there was only room for one person, Tag was standing in the little dining area off to the side of the kitchen. He put one bare foot up on the seat of the chair, which really pissed me off.

"Somebody has to sit there, you know," I said.

"I think several thousand people already have," he said. "This place is a pit."

It was fine for me to call this place a pit, but where did my pit-crashing brother get off calling it a pit?

I decided to save that question for another time, too, since I didn't want to be late for rehearsal. I grabbed a pair of yoga pants and a T-shirt off the back of the chair and headed for my bedroom.

I fed Ginger and Fred. While they were eating I whispered, "Listen, I know he's a little bit nuts, but underneath he's a good person. And I wouldn't let him near you if I thought you were in any danger."

Tag had managed to find his shirt and sneakers all by himself and was waiting by the front door with the keys to the Land Rover. When I held out my hand for the keys, he actually gave them to me.

Just like us, everybody and their brother were on the road this morning. But even in the heavy traffic it was only a twenty-minute ride to the rehearsal studios. Tag channel-surfed and adjusted the bass on the radio while I focused on driving. I'd been feeling so good yesterday, but now with Tag here, my rhythm was off. The interrupted sleep had left me fuzzy, and I was torn between wanting to put Tag on the next plane home and being relieved that he was here.

Sister Sledge started blasting out "We Are Family." Instead of changing the station, Tag actually turned up the volume.

I reached for the knob and turned it down. "Don't start. It's way too early."

He turned it back up again. "Come on. It's our theme song."

"Are you on drugs?" I said.

He didn't hear me because he was singing at the top of his lungs. He loved that line about how I've got all my sisters with me.

When he got to the "We Are Family" part, I couldn't stop myself from joining in. I didn't even like the song, but I had to admit it was somehow irresistibly singworthy.

"Made you sing," he said when the song finally ended.

"Big whoop," I said.

We were coming up on the tall wrought-iron gate that protected the rehearsal studios. I'd been thinking that I'd just pull into the parking lot around the corner and leave the Land Rover idling while I jumped out and Tag moved into the driver's seat.

But if I let Tag know where the official parking lot was, then he might be just smart enough to figure out where the rehearsal studios were. Security was tight, so I didn't think he'd be able to talk his way in. But given that he'd talked his way into my locked apartment last night, I wouldn't put any money on it.

So, brilliant strategist that I was, I kept driving past the big iron gate. I turned my head so that if the guard out front happened to be looking, he wouldn't wave or anything.

I counted two blocks, then pulled over in a loading space.

Tag looked out his window. "Wow, you practice in a barbeque place? Did they set that up especially for you?"

"Funny," I said. "So funny I forgot to laugh." I hadn't thought of that expression in decades. If Tag kept pushing my regression button, before I knew it all I'd be able to say would be *gaga* and *goo-goo*.

I put the Land Rover in Park and waved my hand vaguely. "No, it's over that way. But it's really hard to find and I don't want you to get lost. Anyway, I'll give you a call when we're getting ready to wrap for the day."

Tag slid his designer sunglasses down his nose and looked over them. "*Wrap* for the day? Sounds like little sis has gone Hollywood."

25

*When pretending to have people,
one may talk in the third person.*

Anthony made me close my eyes while I tried on my costume.
"I want it to be pure, unadulterated perfection when you set your eyes on it, sweet pea," he said. It was a little bit weird to be standing in the middle of the wardrobe room wearing only two sets of undergarments while I scrunched my eyes shut and held my hands up over my head, but I went with it.

"Careful, darlin', careful," he said. "We're really working the illusion mesh on this baby."

I poked my hand through a sleeve that felt lighter than air. "Just promise me it will give the illusion that I can dance."

"You got it, honey bunches of oats." He pulled up a zipper that stretched the length of my back. Other than that brief kiss with Steve, it had been months and months since a man had touched me, and now they couldn't seem to keep their hands off me.

"What's so funny, bunny?" Anthony said.

"Nothing," I said. "I was just imagining how irresistible I must look."

As Anthony poked pins into my hem, I tried not to think about how short my costume felt. Instead I focused on the fact that he'd pinned in a few places on the sides, too. The apartment hadn't come with a little white scale, and I had to admit it was kind of nice not having to wake up every morning and decide whether or not I dared weigh myself. But even after just two days, I felt lighter already. Maybe the *DWTS* diet would finally be The One. I mean, dancing five hours a day had to do something, right?

I raised my arms again while Anthony slipped my first dance costume off and my practice costume on. I felt almost like royalty. Having an official dresser would probably get old fast, but it sure was a nice change of pace.

Karen the producer was standing right outside the wardrobe room. I'd turned off my phone again after I left the message for Steve so that I wouldn't get distracted from my work. Or possibly so I wouldn't notice if he didn't call me back. Or maybe I was just avoiding calls. In any case, Karen handed me her phone.

"What?" I said into the receiver, my new standard greeting.

"Have you heard from Tag?" Joanie Baloney asked.

"Um, not lately."

"I can't find him *anywhere.*" Her voice hit a high note the way it always did when things weren't going her way.

"Gee, that's too bad," I said. "I bet that makes it a lot harder to steal my job, doesn't it?"

I pushed the only red button I could see and handed the phone back to Karen.

"Sorry," I said. "Up to you, but you might want to consider blocking that number."

She was already scrolling through something on her phone. "Hmm," she said.

I had an urge to reach for my own phone so I could stare at it while I said *hmm,* too.

She finally looked up and sort of smiled. "So, we're still waiting to connect with Tag. Does he have any other people I can try?"

I sort of smiled back. I certainly didn't want to let Tag in the *DWTS* door, but I also didn't like the inference that I was incompetent. "His people are her people, too," I stalled randomly. "And they're pretty busy these days." *When pretending to have people, one may talk in the third person* popped into my head. I wasn't sure it was technically a chiasmus, but it was close enough, so I filed it away in case my family ever let me sit at the dinner table with them again. Though Marshbury seemed like a million miles away right now.

"We'd like to get the word out that he'll be sitting in the front row at the premiere," Karen said.

I shook my head to bring myself back to reality, or at least to the general vicinity. I really needed to think this through. Okay, on the one hand, if Tag were in the audience, his fans would know he was cheering for me, and they'd vote for me. But on the other hand, the last thing I needed was Tag showing up and making everything all about him the way he always did.

Besides, I had everything pretty much under control without him. Ilya was a great teacher and my dancing had come a long way already. And I didn't really need Tag to get his fans' votes. I just had to pretend to be him. So I simply had to jump back on Facebook and Twitter and also send out an e-blast to our list, and we'd be good to go. Piece of cake. Or at least a Skinny Cow fudge bar.

"Tell you what," I said to Karen, just to get her off my back. "I'll make a point to track Tag down today and see if I can get him to commit to that front-row seat."

"Beautiful," she said.

"Why, thank you," I said jokingly, but she was already screen-tapping her way down the hall.

As I walked along in my tight black practice costume, the fringe tickling my thighs, I did feel practically beautiful. I'd never really understood the whole costume thing before, but now I got it. It was amazing the way a little piece of shiny black fabric and some sequins could transform me into a far more exotic version of myself. Gone was bland, boring, wallflowery Deirdre Griffin and the safe life I lived. Maybe if masquerade balls came back in vogue, I might actually start dating again.

I could almost believe that along with my shiny black practice sheath, I'd put on a more daring persona. And I needed one. There was a Robert Frost quote hanging on the door of one of the practice studios that read, "Dancing is a vertical expression of a horizontal desire." I understood that now, too. Here's what they don't tell you about ballroom dancing with a professional partner: It's a lot like seduction. With a stranger. Who is lean and fit and handsome, and just happens to be about ten million times better at it than you are. Every bit of insecurity you have—body image, coordination issues—floats right to the surface.

As if *Is he touching my back fat?* and the tricky dance moves aren't tough enough, the other thing they don't warn you about is that basically you and this stranger will spend an inordinate amount of time bumping and grinding away at each other. Wearing really thin clothing that pretty much gives you the lay of the land underneath. It's both creepy and oddly, inappropriately sexy. But you're not allowed to pull away and say, *Whoa, time-out.* You're supposed to get all hot and steamy and into it, and let's not forget, point your toes at the same time. And then, at the end of the dance—*wham, bam, thank you, ma'am*—you're strangers again, like it never even happened.

It was Oscar-worthy acting with killer choreography thrown in. When it came to the amount of transformation I needed to get into character, a costume barely covered it.

The sun was just starting to peek into the windows on the far side of our studio. Another beautiful day in Southern California, and if I was lucky enough to survive the next five-plus hours, maybe I'd even get to spend a little bit of time outside in it. Hopefully I'd have enough energy to find a sidewalk café near a beach somewhere with

Tag. At some point, I knew I was going to have to get him out of here, but it might be nice to have someone to hang out with for a little while.

When I walked into the studio, Ilya was leaning back against the wall, wearing black jeans and a tight black T-shirt and scrolling through messages on his phone.

He looked up. "Good morning, sunshine."

"Ha," I said.

As soon as I sat down on a folding chair and started buckling my dance shoes, he put his cell away and reached for the iPod remote.

The muscles that connected my shoulders to the back of my neck tightened at the first notes of "Smooth." I had an overwhelming urge to whine. Or to beg for a nap. Or even to eat something huge and decadent and *smooth*, like a hot fudge sundae with extra whipped cream.

When Ilya held out his arms, I made myself let go of everything but the music. We went through the sequences over and over and over again, separately and then all linked together. Ilya had broken the dance down into four parts to make it easier for me to learn. On the one hand, I was starting to feel optimistic that I sort of knew the steps now. On the other hand, I couldn't imagine that my overloaded brain could possibly remember all this come D-day.

"That's it," Ilya said as he circled me around from the waist. "You got it, baby. Now give me some more."

I gave him some more. I gave him more than I even thought I had.

Side by side, we went into a series of kicks. Flick-flick-chachacha starting with the right foot. Flick-flick-chachacha starting with the left. More of the same facing all four walls. Then some slide-slide-turnturnturns, walk-walk-runrunruns, reach-reach-bumpbumpbumps, straddle-straddle-chugchugchugs. We finished the sequence, and then Ilya scooped me into his arms again and danced me around the room.

Our flirty finale involved my partner miming *hey, you, come here,* and me spinning around three times by myself—on three-inch heels, no less—and right into his waiting arms. Ilya didn't wear a catcher's mitt, but I'd noticed that he gauged my trajectory like a baseball player and somehow managed to casually and gracefully position himself just where he needed to be to catch me. For which I was seriously grateful.

"Outstanding," he said after the third full run-through.

"Really?" I said.

He raised his eyebrow. "It's an expression. But we're getting there."

I took a deep breath in through my nose and let it out through my mouth. "It would be a lot easier if this stupid room would stop spinning." Ilya was still holding me, which was probably the only reason I was still on my feet.

He let go and ran a hand through his hair. I was starting to know all his gestures now—hand through hair, one eyebrow up, twirl of the iPod remote, automatic reach for his cell anytime we took a break. We were already like an old married couple in some ways.

He raised an eyebrow. "Did you work on your spotting last night like I told you to?"

"Right. In my two-foot-by-two-foot apartment. Where the biggest open space is the bathtub."

"Okay, five times, all the way down to that wall and back, no stopping, tight turns the whole way."

"You're such a slave driver," I said, but I did it anyway. If you've never tried spotting, what you do is focus on a nonmoving point in the distance. When you turn, you let everything else become a blur, and then when you come around again you find that same point as soon as you can. Theoretically, the dizzy stuff that makes the room appear to be spinning instead of you slips away because your focus is on that nonmoving point. It actually worked pretty well when I was doing it in a drill. But I knew that once I started dancing again, spotting and remembering the steps would seem a lot like patting my head and rubbing my stomach at the same time. While running on a treadmill.

When I turned in one direction, I focused on a rectangle of blue paint between two white-trimmed windows. When I turned in the other direction, I focused on the center of the closed door. Five big step-turn-steps would take me across the length of the room if I stretched out my legs, six or seven if I made the circles tighter.

"Crisper, sharper," Ilya said after the first pass. "Looooook-turn-looooook.

"Better," he added after the second.

After the fifth set, I dropped my head and rested my hands on my thighs. "I think I'm getting the hang of it," I said between breaths. "I hardly feel like puking at all anymore. Okay, your turn."

Ilya laughed. I didn't think he'd really do it, but he stepped into the center of the room, turned his head toward the far wall, and extended his arms. Then, *boom*, it was like an explosion of grace as he spun the length of the room and back so quickly I couldn't even count the turns.

When he stopped, I heard clapping behind me.

I turned. Tag was leaning back against my spotting spot on the door, his legs crossed at the ankles, the Land Rover keys dangling from one hand.

"Wow," Tag said. "Impressive."

"What—" I said.

"Not you. Him." My brother flashed his million-dollar smile at my dance partner.

Ilya cat-walked over and held out his hand.

"Ilya," I said politely. "This is my brother, Tag. He was just leaving."

26

Dancers are the athletes of God,
but is God the athlete of dancers?

I'm a big fan," my dance partner said to my brother.

"Yeah, who isn't," I said.

"Ditto," Tag said. "It's like watching poetry in motion. I'm humbled."

"That's a first," I said.

Tag ignored me. "You know, Einstein said that dancers are the athletes of God."

"But is God the athlete of dancers?" I said. Nobody laughed.

"So what do you do in the off-season?" Tag asked, as if Ilya really was an athlete, maybe a hockey or football player. I rolled my eyes at his cluelessness.

"My brother and I run a small chain of dance studios," Ilya said. "And my three kids are all competing now, so that keeps my wife and me pretty busy."

"All dancers?" Tag asked.

Ilya grinned. "Two dancers and one fencer. Whatever floats their boats, you know?"

Tag nodded. "One of my four is talking culinary school. One wants to be a firefighter and one the president. The one in preschool is un-committed."

I was still looking at Ilya. Even though I'd been spending most of my waking hours with him, I had no idea he was married, let alone that he had three kids. I'd never even once thought about him having a life outside of *Dancing With the Stars*. It was like being in kinder-garten and running into your teacher at the grocery store and being totally blown away that *Mrs. Forest eats*.

"Basically, then," Tag said, "you're a brand. So, what, you have a website and some dance videos?"

Ilya nodded. "Yeah. Nothing too fancy yet, but we're working on it."

Tag nodded. "Make sure you strike while the iron is hot. I have to tell you, my videos are our bread and butter. And once you make them, they're the gift that keeps on giving. You just mail them out and put the money in the bank."

I swiveled my aching neck so Tag couldn't miss the astonished look on my face. I mean, like my brother had mailed a package in the last decade. Or set foot in a bank, for that matter. He probably couldn't identify an ATM.

"And no need to hire a big production company." Tag raised his palms to the heavens, a sure sign that he was getting into this. "Just buy your own camera and have at it. People want *you*, not all the bells and whistles."

Ilya was nodding away.

"What about social media?" Tag asked. "Facebook, Twitter—"

I couldn't believe it. Like my brother would know Facebook from a library book, Twitter from glitter.

"Oh, we're tweetin' fools around here," Ilya said. "All the profes-sional dancers have Twitter accounts, plus most of the celebs. Great way to get the vote out, plus it really helps raise our own visibility. Everybody's starting to amp things up right about now—some of the teams have even brought in social media gurus."

I swiveled my achy neck around to Ilya. "Seriously?" I asked.

He shrugged. "The stakes are high."

Okay, so I'd just have to up my game, too. Tag was my piece of celebrity, so maybe I'd have to plant him in the audience after all. But the thought of needing Tag made me absolutely crazy. Like the old saying goes, I couldn't live with him, but I couldn't live without him either.

"Well, let me know if you need any tips on strategy," Tag said.

Just when I thought the day couldn't go downhill any faster, a guy poked his head in. "Props," he said. "I'm checking in to see if you need anything for Monday night."

Tag grinned at Ilya, then held his arms out in front of him and took a few doddering steps. "Just a walker for my sister."

My face burned while everybody yukked it up. It was like we were kids again, and Tag was telling all his friends what a porker I was.

Still laughing, the prop guy finally turned and left.

"Leave," I said to Tag.

"What? We were just starting to have some fun."

"Now."

"I mean, face it, you're a bit outclassed in the dance department, but come on, you know I was only kidding." Tag turned to Ilya. "The only problem with my sister is that she can't take a joke."

I turned to Ilya, too. "And the only problem with my brother is that he's a self-absorbed . . . self-centered . . . egotistical . . . insensitive . . . vain . . . narcissistic . . ."—I took a deep breath—". . . jerkface."

Tag shook his head. "That's more than one problem."

"No shit, Sherlock," I said.

Then I stomped out the door.

"Half an hour," Ilya called after me.

The tears I'd been fighting won out.

* * *

I knew better. But I found an empty practice studio and called Mitchell anyway.

He answered on the fourth ring. "Hey," he whispered. "I can't really talk right now. Can I call you back later?"

I closed my eyes. "You're still with her."

"Well, I mean, it all kind of just happened. She's still pretty upset, so I'm not really sure what's going on right now."

My mouth filled with the taste of disgust. It was grainy and metallic. Mitchell was an idiot, but what was my excuse?

"Hey," Mitchell whispered, "I was just thinking. Maybe you can get me the contact info for the bandleader on the show. You know, just in case they happen to need a backup drummer? That *Dancing With the Stars* band kicks some serious butt."

I heard a woman's voice say, "*Who* are you talking to?"

"No one," Mitchell said. And then he hung up.

My first thought was to get out of Dodge. I'd push open the heavy wooden door to the practice studios, then make my way through the tall iron gate and past the security guard. I'd walk the two blocks to that barbeque place Tag had pointed out, and I'd sit in a dark corner at the back of the restaurant, preferably in a booth for even more camouflage. Then I'd order up every disgustingly fattening thing on the menu. A heaping pile of barbequed pork on a big fat white roll. Coleslaw dripping with mayo. Chips, chips, and more chips.

But unfortunately I was wearing a skintight black minidress, which probably wouldn't stand out all that much in this neck of the woods, but I knew I'd feel funny eating barbeque in it, and I'd probably have to ask for a bib. And then there was the shoe issue. Nancy Sinatra's boots might have been made for walkin' back in the '70s, but my thin-soled dance shoes weren't meant to encounter the rough surface of a sidewalk.

I could change back into my baggy T-shirt and yoga pants and flip-flops, but then I'd have to face Anthony again, and maybe even

Gina and Lila from hair and makeup. One *Are you okay?* and I was afraid I'd burst into tears again. Even a kind look might put me over the edge. I was hurt and angry and humiliated, and I couldn't tell how much was about Tag and how much was about Mitchell and how much was simply about how it sucked being me.

So I headed for craft services. I pushed the door open carefully. If someone was in there, I'd just grab a bottle of water from the fridge and keep moving.

The room was empty. A refrigerator stood guard on the far wall and long counters edged the adjacent walls. I scanned past a coffeemaker, a microwave, napkins, and plastic utensils to a platter of fresh fruit covered with plastic wrap, a bowl of raw almonds, a box of reduced-fat, reduced-salt crackers. A package of dry-roasted wasabi peas.

I crossed the space and opened the refrigerator. A big Tupperware container of baby carrots. String cheese. A tray of portobello mushrooms stuffed with fresh spinach and tomatoes and topped with a minuscule sprinkle of mozzarella. Carrot juice, iced green tea, bottled water.

I opened the freezer. Ice cubes. Lemon-flavored Italian ice. A stack of Lean Cuisine single-serving entrees. A stack of Healthy Choice single-serving entrees.

I slid the two stacks apart and reached behind them, my fingers grazing the icy back wall of the freezer.

I'd almost given up hope when I found it: an entire unopened package of Lindor dark chocolate truffles. I wanted to sink right down to the floor with it, maybe even crawl under the table, the way I used to when I was a kid and needed to protect my stash of chocolate chip cookies from my siblings.

Instead I made myself fill a plate with carrot sticks and fruit slices. I put the plate on the table and sat down in a chair. I unfolded a paper napkin on my lap, with the Lindor package tucked under it. If anyone happened to come in, they'd never know I wasn't eating rabbit food.

One by one, I unwrapped the little truffle balls and popped them into my mouth, then tucked the crinkly cellophane wrapper back into the package. I ate with speed, with precision, with focus. I knew I should slow down and at least try to taste the rich dark chocolate, the fluffy truffle filling, but taste felt somehow beside the point.

It was like I had a hollow leg, or an empty hole in the pit of my stomach. And all I wanted to do was fill it up so it didn't hurt so much.

I finished every single truffle, then I stuck my hand into the empty package and rooted around carefully to make sure I hadn't missed anything. I felt sick to my stomach and completely disgusted with myself, but if another package of truffles had magically appeared, I would have eaten those, too.

I crossed my arms over my bloated stomach and rocked back and forth in the chair. There had to be a way out of this mess. I wondered if Ilya would get paid if I managed to trip and fall and injure myself enough to get sent home before Monday.

It was probably too late to find him a second replacement, so maybe *DWTS* would have to go ahead with ten couples instead of eleven.

Then I pictured Ilya's three kids, two in ballet slippers and one holding a sword, having to miss their own competitions because I'd taken money out of their dad's pocket.

All I had to do was get through the first two weeks.

Then I could figure out what to do with the rest of my life.

27

If fat can be your biggest fear,
can fear also make you fat?

I walked down the hall to the women's restroom feeling like I was going to throw up at any moment.

When I got there, someone had beaten me to it and was actually vomiting in one of the stalls. My stomach turned over at the sound. I wondered if I'd lost my admittedly tenuous grip on reality and was just hallucinating.

My second thought was that a violent stomach bug might be going around. Maybe I'd be lucky enough to catch it. If I were legitimately sick, the ball would be in *DWTS*'s court. Maybe they could pull in a last-minute ringer after all. Everything would work out for the best. At least with a new partner, Ilya might have a chance to make it into the finals.

I waited. Nothing. No more vomiting, no groaning. Maybe I really was losing it, and I'd imagined the whole thing.

"Are you okay in there?" I finally asked.

I heard a flush. The stall door opened and the gymnast/ice-skater came out and headed for the sink. She leaned over it and splashed water on her face. Or maybe she was rinsing out her mouth. I didn't really see because I was too busy noticing how narrow her hips were.

Did they make sizes smaller than 0, or did she have to shop in the toddler section?

It was like we weren't quite the same gender, or maybe the same species. I mean, I didn't even fantasize about squeezing into single digits again. Size 10 was about as low as my imagination would go. Unless it was a really expensive store, in which case I could dream about fitting into an 8. The logic was twisted but the marketing brilliant: The more you paid, the smaller the size you got for your money.

I seemed to be frozen in place, one hand on a stall door.

The gymnast/ice-skater turned around and flashed me a big smile. "I'm so happy to finally meet you," she said.

"Deirdre Griffin," I said, to spare her the next line.

She said it anyway. "Who are you again?"

"Just a last-minute replacement," I said. "Who are *you* again?"

She smiled. "Ashley Jane Dobbs." She said it like it was one word, Ashleyjanedobbs.

In the nick of time, I remembered seeing her in a leotard on a Wheaties box a long time ago. "Gymnast, right?"

The look she gave me clearly said *duh*. "Six golds, nine silvers. I don't even count the bronzes."

"Of course you don't. Anyway, I'm sorry you're not feeling well. Stomach bug?"

She sighed dramatically. "Blueberry muffin."

"Blueberry muffin," I repeated.

She sighed again. "Not even half. The whole thing. Normally I'd jump on the treadmill, but who's got time with all these rehearsal hours, you know what I mean? So I just cut to the chase." She opened her mouth and made that old gag-me-with-a-spoon gesture from the '80s.

"Wouldn't you burn it off in rehearsals?" I was horrified. But I was also kind of intrigued. I'd always thought bulimia had a cutoff age, like maybe a few years after you finished college.

She opened her cornflower blue eyes wide. "OMG. Have you ever been five foot one?"

"I think when I was born," I said, "but I'd have to check my baby book."

"Two extra pounds and I look like a horse."

"Probably just a pony," I said. I was having a hard time gauging just how insulted I should be. I mean, here was this little person whose thigh was probably the size of my wrist on a good day talking to me about looking like a horse. What did that make me? A hippopotamus?

Her eyes teared up. "Fat is my biggest fear."

I said what she was waiting for me to say. "You don't look like you have an ounce of fat on you."

"Are you sure?" She turned around so she could see her butt in the mirror and pointed. "Even right here?"

"I don't see a thing," I said.

She twisted around to get a look at the other side of her hindquarters.

I shook my head. "Not there either."

Ashleyjanedobbs turned around and adjusted her long strawberry blond hair. Then she met my eyes in the mirror. "Okay, thanks. You look good, too."

After she left, I peed. I flushed the toilet. I stared at myself in the mirror as I washed my hands. My overstuffed stomach hurt. I deserved it. I'd completely ignored my dance partner's instructions to put only high-test fuel in my body, and I'd filled it to the brim with food that shouldn't be in there.

I closed my eyes. For the rest of the day I'd move like an old jalopy. I'd be sluggish and sloppy, and if I stepped on Ilya's toes I'd probably break them all. I flashed on Mitchell and his recently pregnant girlfriend. I wondered if she shopped in the toddler section, too.

I dried my hands and pushed the stall door open again. I leaned over the toilet and reached my index finger toward the back of my throat. I gagged. I reached in a little farther and touched the back of my tongue. I gagged again and my stomach heaved a little.

The white porcelain toilet was clean. The travertine floor tiles were pretty clean, too, and they were cold when I knelt down on them. I lifted up the toilet seat and rested one hand on the edge of the bowl.

When I bowed my head, I flashed back to the confessional of my Catholic childhood. "Bless me, Father, for I have sinned," I whispered. "I ate a whole package of Lindor dark chocolate truffles and I really don't want to be fat. If you let me throw up this one time, I promise I'll never do it again. I'll start eating healthy, and I'll become someone we can both be proud of."

I put my elbow on the toilet bowl and rested my forehead on my hand. I was suddenly just so, so tired. How could I have lived so long and learned so little? How did other people manage to cobble together lives that weren't built on a foundation of self-destruction and self-sabotage?

I mean, I'd been doing so well. I'd peeled back Tag and the rest of my family's grip. I'd been eating better and I was starting to learn my dance to the point that I wasn't just doing the steps. I was actually *dancing* them. I'd settled into my apartment. I had pets. I'd done my laundry. I'd even managed to call Steve Moretti, and whether he called me back or not, just having the guts to do it seemed like a step in the right direction.

How many hundreds of times had I been here over the course of my life? A week or two, even a month or two or three, of moving in a positive direction. And then something would happen, like Tag picking at one of my insecurities, and the downward slide would begin. Because just underneath all the sunshine and blue skies lurked the same old disgusting mess of a person who couldn't resist screwing up everything in her entire life.

Tears were streaming down my cheeks and my nose was running.

At least the toilet paper was conveniently located. I pulled a long piece off the roll next to me and blew my nose.

"Fat is my biggest fear," Ashleyjanedobbs had said. Not sickness or death or war or even being the first one kicked off *DWTS*.

Clearly it wasn't mine. But if fat can be your biggest fear, can fear also make you fat?

I'd read enough self-help books and logged enough time watching Oprah to know that it wasn't about the food at all. It was about being afraid, and the fastest way to calm the fear, the one I'd learned as a child, was to distract myself with food. To soothe myself the way a baby might suck her thumb. And once I was past the immediate crisis, I'd turn my focus to a diet plan instead of a live-it plan. And then a new fear would come along, and I'd go through the cycle all over again.

I pictured my walk-in closet at home, my clothes arranged in order of decreasing size, a daily reminder of how I didn't measure up.

And yet, why did I think Ashleyjanedobbs wasn't much happier than I was? And how many times had I seen a woman heavier than me looking happy and vibrant and sexy. Clearly, starving yourself didn't necessarily get you more in life.

Maybe it was exhaustion, or being out of my element and in over my head, but it suddenly hit me like a ton of tap shoes. I had a choice here. I could spend the rest of my life worrying about how I didn't measure up. Or I could get in the game and dance my ass off.

Right then and there, kneeling on the cold tiles of the women's restroom, I decided I was over it. No more coveting a former gymnast's size 0. The lens I used to look at myself was so twisted that I'd probably never even know what I really looked like anyway. What mattered was that I didn't let it get in my way anymore.

I turned on my phone, ready to face my life in real time.

I was just coming out of the bathroom when Mitchell called back.

I answered on the first ring. "It's over," I said. "Permanently. Don't ever call me again. For anything."

28

Ask not what your professional dancer can do for you,
ask what you can do for your professional dancer.

Our practice studio was empty, but I tracked Ilya down in the craft services room.

Karen the producer looked up when I opened the door. She actually smiled at me. "Wow, you work fast. Thanks for getting your brother here for us."

"That's how I roll," I said. I felt so bloated that if I were a comedian, I might have held my stomach for a cheap, self-deprecating laugh. I brushed the thought aside to make room for something more positive.

A whole group of professional dancers and their celebrity partners, plus wardrobe and hair and makeup, were sitting around a long rectangular table. Tag was clearly holding court. He munched the end off a huge strawberry, then turned his palms up. "So, basically I think it comes down to this: Ask not what your professional dancer can do for you, ask what you can do for your professional dancer."

"And your celebrity gymnast, of course." Ashleyjanedobbs blinked her cornflower blue eyes up at my brother. I'd seen that look a million times before, so I knew exactly what Ashleyjanedobbs was hoping Tag would do for her.

Tag smiled down at her as if she'd just said the most adorable thing in the world. "The point is that by taking the focus away from *me-me-me*, you not only help the other person but also take the pressure off yourself."

"Does that mean you're buying us all dinner?" slipped out of my mouth before I thought it through.

"Absolutely," Tag said. "Name the place."

"There's a great barbeque joint a few blocks down the street," Ilya said.

Ashleyjanedobbs's eyes were still fixed on my brother. "Mmm, barbeque," she said. "My fav."

The portobello mushroom things on the table were in fact minipizzas and somebody had cooked the whole tray. I didn't really feel like eating, but I knew that a stomach full of chocolate would only mean plummeting blood sugar and the urge to pig out again an hour or two from now. The portobello pizzas looked really healthy, so I put one on a plate and added some fresh fruit and a handful of baby carrots.

There was one seat left at the table, so I took it. The people I hadn't met yet introduced themselves: a former wrestler, an actress, a singer, and their respective professional dance partners. So far I'd spent the week almost entirely with Ilya, but I wasn't the least bit surprised that the minute Tag showed up, it turned into a party. He had that magic.

"Back to work," Ilya said as soon as I finished my last bite of food.

I gave Tag my please-go-away look.

He laughed. "Don't worry. Karen wants me to record a promo, and then I promised Ashley I'd peek in on her rehearsal."

"Great," I said.

Tag looked right past me. "So, Ilya. Just give me a call when you guys wrap and we'll all meet up at the barbeque place, okay?"

I turned to Ilya. "I'll give you the number."

Ilya grinned. "It's already on my speed dial."

Taking things one step at a time seemed like the way to go, so when we got back to the studio I put all my focus on our cha-cha. We did it over and over and over again, so many times I lost count. I gave it everything I had and tried my hardest not to worry about whether that was enough.

"Break time," Ilya said two hours later.

"Already?" I couldn't believe it.

This time we had the craft services room all to ourselves. I grabbed bottles of water for both of us and placed them on the table. I counted out ten almonds and added a few slices of cantaloupe and a piece of string cheese to my plate.

Ilya piled his plate high and sat down across from me. I turned my head away from the smell of peanut butter cookie.

"Men," I said.

"We got the metabolism. Women got the brains."

"Good point," I said.

He grinned. "So, your brother tells me you're a whiz at social networking."

"Really?"

"Yeah, he couldn't stop bragging about his genius little sister."

"Right." I took a bite of cantaloupe and tried to focus on how it was not only good but good for me, and how I'd much rather have this than a bite of disgusting peanut butter cookie. "Well, I have to tell you being a social-networking whiz has its downside. That's kind of how you got stuck with me."

Ilya popped the rest of the cookie into his mouth and reached for a strawberry. If I were him, right now I'd be feeling completely disgusted with myself that I'd given in to temptation. He just looked happy to have gotten to the strawberry.

"For the record," my partner said, "I am not feeling the least bit stuck with you. You're a hard worker and you don't take phone calls during practice—"

"That's because I have no life."

Ilya shook his head. "That's the only thing that really gets to me.

I can't tell you what it feels like to be standing there tapping my toes while some celebrity whines to her manager on her cell phone like I'm not even there. Like my time has no value."

"That's awful," I said. I ate another almond. They weren't cashews, but they were pretty tasty in the scheme of things. "Okay, so what was that thing my brother said—ask not what your professional dancer can do for you—"

"—ask what you can do for your professional dancer." Ilya grinned. "I gotta tell you, most celebrities I've met don't live up to the hype, but that brother of yours is the real deal."

"Whatever," I said. "Okay, so my question is what do we need to make happen here, and how can my genius and I help?"

We finished our last hour of rehearsal for the day, and then Ilya pulled his laptop out of his backpack. We folded one of the mats in half for extra cushioning and sat side by side with me holding the laptop.

First I logged onto Tag's Facebook account. "Whoa," I said. "His fan count has almost doubled."

"*Dancing With the Stars* will do that for you," Ilya said.

I wrote a note from Tag and Ilya helped me tweak it. Five minutes later, it was posted on the virtual playground of Facebook, where over 51 percent of Americans hung out, many of them already connected to my guru brother.

> *Galactic greetings and the sunniest of salutations, my friends.*
> *My deepest thanks to you for making my worthy and*
> *wonderful sister Deirdre's lifelong* Dancing With the Stars
> *dream come true. And now together we have the pleasure*
> *of supporting her journey. The season premiere will be on*
> *Monday at 8 p.m. EST. As your humble servant, I will be*
> *sitting in the front row cheering her on and sending winning*

*energy her way, and I want you to know that you will all be
in that seat with me. And most important, each of us will have
the honor of casting our votes for her via a toll-free number,
on the official website, and with text messages. The maximum
number of votes per voter per medium is equal to the number
of couples performing that night, or five votes, whichever is
larger. Between now and then we can also pre-approve up to
eleven e-mail accounts per person for voting, so our message to
ourselves and to all of our friends will be:* Vote early and vote
often.

Peace in, peace out,
Tag

Twitter was our next step, where we managed to keep Tag's message well under the allotted 140 characters and spaces. This is an important part of Twitter strategy since many people won't bother to spread your message, or retweet, if adding their twitter handle puts the message over the character limit. So our Twitter-friendly version was this:

Watch DWTS on Monday and vote x11 by phone & email 4 my
sister Deirdre. Pls RT. ☮ in/out, Tag

"Wow," Ilya said. "I can't believe Tag has that many Twitter followers. This is some serious clout. And here I thought my own Twitter following was respectable."

"Don't compare yourself to anyone else," I said. "Just do the best Twitter dance you can do."

Ilya laughed. "Now where have I heard that one before?"

My fingers were too busy dancing across the keyboard to answer.

"Okay," I said. "Tag has asked all his followers to follow you. And I just remembered that I opened an @DeeCanDance account just before I came here."

I clicked on it. "Whoa. Not too shabby."

Ilya leaned over my shoulder. "You got all those followers in a week?"

I shrugged. "Every once in a while my big bro comes in handy."

The next step was a Facebook page. I didn't have my own personal Facebook account, so I set it up quickly and then built the page. We went through a few names for it and finally agreed that the best page name for a tidal wave of quick support was TAG TEAM. In the info box I wrote: *Vote for Tag's sister Deirdre and her partner Ilya on* DWTS!

"Wow," Ilya said as I downloaded a photo of the mirror ball trophy to use as our profile picture. "You're amazing."

"Stick with me, baby," I said. "Before my fifteen minutes of fame are over, you won't be able to churn out those dance videos fast enough."

29

I yam what I yam, and that's all that I yam.

By the time we got to the barbeque place, Ilya had a Facebook page for his business. I'd gone to his website to find a photo to use for his profile picture and made a few changes there as well. I wanted to do more, so my plan was that I'd pick away at it during our breaks.

Half the *DWTS* cast was already seated at two big red-checked, oilcloth-covered tables that had been pulled together. Tag was at the head, of course, holding court once again. Even the stars appeared to be starstruck as Tag flashed his pearly whites and gestured eloquently while he told one of his favorite stories. I wondered, as I had a gazillion times before, what it would be like to always be so *on*. It was as if my brother didn't even exist unless he had an audience.

Ilya held out a chair for me.

"Thanks," I said as I practically collapsed into it. Every muscle in my body was tired. It felt like a good tired, a tired that I'd earned. Until I looked around the table and saw how much peppier everybody else looked. Even the octogenarian former soap opera star was sitting up straight with her eyes wide open. Except for the fact that her face didn't move anymore, she probably looked younger than I did.

Ilya caught me looking. He leaned toward me. "Repeat after me," he whispered. "I yam what I yam, and that's all that I yam."

"Popeye?" I whispered.

He did his eyebrow thing. "I believe Olive Oyl gave him the line."

"I'm sure she did. By the way, I can't get over those dance pictures of you on your website. Do you have more? We should do a whole slide show of them, and maybe another slide show of your trophies. And I want to post some on your Facebook page as well. Facebook people love photos."

"Hey, hey, hey," my brother said from the other end of the table. "Is your *wife* coming, too, Ilya?" He gestured at me with one hand. "Maybe my sister should go help out in the kitchen."

It wasn't Tag's biggest laugh, but Ilya waited until it was over. "My wife's home with the kids," he said. "We don't mix our business and personal lives."

"Good to know," Tag said.

A waiter came over. "Two margaritas, please," Ilya said. "On the rocks. No salt."

"Are you sure?" I said.

He smiled at me. "Absolutely. You've earned one."

The margarita was frosty and delicious. I drank it slowly and tried to taste each sip, to savor it. I scanned the menu and finally decided on the barbequed chicken sandwich on a whole wheat roll with steamed broccoli on the side. It seemed like a smarter choice than ordering a salad only to go back to the apartment and dream of barbeque all night.

Tag snapped out of overprotective brother mode and turned back into his charming self. The former wrestler told a story about a famous fight I'd never heard of. The singer talked about her most recent European tour. I noticed that the professional dancers stayed in the background and let their celebrity partners shine. If we'd all been asked to line up on opposite sides of the restaurant, queen bees on one side and worker bees on the other, I had no doubt that I'd head over to stand with the dancers. Except that I couldn't really dance. So maybe I'd be left in the center of the room, all by myself, like Little Sally Water from the playground game of my childhood.

Our food came and I ate mine slowly, paying attention to each bite. It was really good, but after about half of it, I wasn't even tasting it anymore, so I finished the broccoli and drank my entire glass of water. When the waiter collected our plates, I asked him to wrap it up. If I didn't eat it for breakfast, I knew Tag would.

Out of the corner of my eye, I caught Ilya peeking at his watch.

"I agree," I said. "Time for me to get some sleep."

We pushed back our chairs.

"Come on," Tag said from the other end of the table. "The night's still young."

"Some of us have to try to dance in the morning," I said.

"I don't need much sleep," Ashleyjanedobbs said.

I walked the length of the table and held out my hand. "Keys," I said.

For a minute I thought he might fight me.

Ashleyjanedobbs smiled up at my brother. "I have a car," she said.

Tag took the keys out of his pocket and tossed them to me.

Ilya walked me out to the parking lot and helped me find the Land Rover. He waited till I was safely inside the car.

I lowered my window.

"Good job today," he said.

I tried to raise one eyebrow but had to settle for two. "But was it outstanding?"

He grinned. "You're getting there."

If I'd been heading home at this hour on a weeknight in Marshbury, everything would be closed by now. The only hope for any action would have been Marshbury Tavern. But here in Los Angeles, lights sparkled and glowed from almost every building, and the streets teemed with people—tourists and stars and wannabes mingling as they decided whether their next stop might be more shopping or a bar or even a tattoo parlor.

For more years than I cared to count, I'd thought that if I could only get out of Marshbury, get out of the sheep shed, get out of my brother's life, then I'd finally be happy. But it turned out the place I'd really needed to get out of was inside my head, a much harder task. I remembered that old quote: *Wherever you go, there you are.*

When I let myself into my little white apartment, Ginger and Fred were circling their bowl, waiting to be fed.

I sprinkled their dinner into the bowl and watched them nibble it off the surface of the water. Then I carried them into the little living room.

I sat on the little couch and watched Fred and Ginger meander around their bowl for a while. It was incredibly relaxing. I wondered what it would be like to get to swim around all day without a care in the world. Probably really boring. But maybe it was all perspective. At this very moment, my fish friends could be staring out through their wall of glass wondering how bored they'd be if they had to spend all their time just sitting like a lump on the sofa.

"Life," I said, "is so damn complicated."

My cell phone began to play its tinny instrumental version of "She Works Hard for the Money."

I didn't even check the caller ID first. I just said hello.

"Hey, it's Steve. Moretti. Remember? We'll always have Austin?"

I had an almost overwhelming urge to say, "Hi, I can't come to the phone right now, but if you leave a message I'll get back to you."

And maybe I would get back to him. Someday. Or maybe not.

I was trying to learn to dance. I was trying to get my act together. I was trying to get my brother to go away. I had a lot on my metaphorical plate and I was trying not to put so much on my actual plate. All at the same time. I was exhausted. I was emotionally overloaded. I couldn't handle one more thing right now. I was really bad at relation-ships, and I'd already messed this one up, not that it was technically a relationship. It was only a kiss. A kiss-and-run. Which was basically nothing. And now I couldn't even remember how many first kisses I still had left. What was Dentyne thinking with that stupid commer-cial? Like life wasn't tough enough without that to worry about.

I opened the Styrofoam take-out container that I hadn't gotten around to putting in the little refrigerator. I reached for the rest of my sandwich, my truffles bloat a distant memory. What I really wanted was chocolate. Not Skinny Cow chocolate but something rich and decadent. A dessert menu of possibilities flashed before me in an in-stant: Ben & Jerry's Phish Food ice cream, peanut butter cookies still warm from the oven, Dove bars, fresh-baked gingerbread topped with homemade whipped cream, Ring Dings. I really wanted a Ring Ding. Did they still make Ring Dings?

A drop of barbeque sauce landed on the coffee table. Bits of congealed fat dotted the leftover sandwich in my hand. I didn't even want it.

"Hello?" Steve said.

I looked at my phone. The man inside it would probably break my heart. Or he'd turn out to be a loser. Or he'd have unresolved issues with his ex-wife, or his ex-girlfriend. Or maybe we'd just be incom-patible. I didn't even know where he actually lived. Or anything about him. And I mean, face it, anyone who was still kicking around single at his age probably had some serious baggage by now. Wait, maybe he wasn't even single. His unresolved issues could be with his current wife. He could be a polygamist for all I knew. The chances of this working out were a gazillion to one. But so was the chance of winning the mirror ball trophy.

I put my leftover sandwich back in the take-out container and closed the cover.

"Hello," I said.

30

Learn to fail or fail to learn.

S o where were we?" Steve Moretti said.

"Ha," I said. "Maybe we shouldn't go there. Maybe I should just apologize for being a total idiot and then we could talk about current events or something."

"Your call."

I was actually blushing. Who still blushed at my age, especially when the other person wasn't even there to see it? I took a deep breath. "Sorry. And how about those Red Sox?"

I'd half forgotten what a great laugh he had, rich and unselfconscious.

I took a slow, calming breath, in through my nose and out through my mouth. "I probably should add that my brother has a tendency to push my buttons. In case you didn't notice."

"When I was growing up, my older sister had me completely convinced that I was adopted."

"Really?"

"Yeah. 'Why aren't there any baby pictures of you?' she kept asking. My parents denied it, but my sister had planted that seed. And she was right, there weren't many baby pictures of me, and believe me, I counted. Repeatedly. It turned out to be part second-child photo syndrome and part the fact that my sister had hidden most of the ones we did have. Anyway, I finally smartened up and tracked down my birth certificate."

"That's awful," I said. "Although I used to fantasize I was adopted. Or that they'd given my mother the wrong baby at the hospital. Or that I'd been dropped from an alien spaceship in the middle of the night because my real people's planet was being invaded. It just seemed like there had to be another set of siblings I'd fit in with better."

"To this day, my sister and I can spend about two hours together before we revert to our childhood selves and start going at each other again. It's not pretty."

"Oh, that's so good to hear."

Steve laughed again.

"Sorry," I said. "I meant that it's good to be reminded that my siblings and I aren't the only ones who do that."

Steve took a sip of something before he spoke. "Maybe siblings were created to make the rest of the cold, cruel world seem manageable."

I tried to picture him. Sitting in a leather recliner with a glass of wine in his hand. Or curled up in bed with a mug of chamomile tea.

"Where do you live?" I asked.

"Good question. I have a place way out on Cape Cod, in Truro. It's pretty rustic, really just a shack, but it's a beautiful spot. And I have a small condo in Boston. I'm traveling all the time, so it works out since they're both pretty much lock and leave. And I have a son in western Mass so I spend as much time as I can out that way."

"How old is he?" I asked. It came out like a whisper.

"Twenty-three. His name is Ben. He's in grad school. Political science of all things."

"Wow," I said. It was the best I could do. I switched my phone to the other ear and watched my hand reach for the sandwich as if it was connected to someone else's body. I stood up and walked over to the refrigerator to put the Styrofoam container away.

"His mother and I were high school sweethearts. We broke up freshman year in college. Then my parents died the week before I graduated and, well, we shouldn't have ended up together again, but I guess it was just one of those things. We tried to make it work for Ben's sake, but it never really did."

"What happened to your parents?"

"Drunk driver. Middle of a Saturday afternoon, a mile and a half from home. They were on their way back from grocery shopping."

"I am so, so sorry."

"Thank you. It's a long time ago now, but not a day goes by that something doesn't remind me of them. They were good people. They never got to meet Ben."

I wiped my eyes with the sleeve of my T-shirt, vowing to call my parents back.

"So where do *you* live?" Steve asked.

"I have a little place on Tag's property. Pretty much my whole family does."

I listened to Steve take another sip.

"How's that working out for you?" he finally said.

"Ha. Not too well, I don't think. But give me another decade or two to make sure."

He laughed again. I could get used to that laugh.

"Well, it's actually a converted sheep shed, so I have to admit it's a pretty cool place. And I don't pay anything to live there, so that's a plus. But Tag won't let me buy it. And living there means that basically I'm on call around the clock. And the guy I lived with off and on for ten years who didn't want kids decided to marry someone else because she was pregnant. And he asked Tag to marry them."

I stood up, took two steps toward the refrigerator, then sat back down again.

"So that's my life," I said. "Or lack thereof."

"Sounds like that must have been pretty painful."

"Which part?" I said. "Oh, Mitchell. I don't know. Yes and no, I guess. I mean, we weren't together at the time or anything. And I think we'd probably been over each other for years. We just kept sliding into it again because it was the easiest thing to do." It felt good to talk about Mitchell in the past tense. "Anyway, I hit him with Tag's golf cart the last time I saw him. And that's the end of that story."

"Do me a favor and remind me of that right before our first fight."

I could feel myself grinning. "Deal. And just so you know, I didn't hit him that hard. He's kind of a whiner."

Steve cleared his throat. "You know, at first I didn't get the whole *Dancing With the Stars* thing, but now I sort of do, or at least I think I do."

"Wait. You know about *Dancing With the Stars*?"

Steve let out another laugh. "Uh, I think I'd have to be living under a rock to miss it. It's all over the news. And the Internet. You've become the celebrity alternative—an Everywoman hero."

I closed my eyes. "Please tell me they're not using my high school yearbook picture. No, don't tell me. I can't even think about it. It's enough trying to survive the dancing part."

"Well, I have to hand it to you. It's a really creative way to put some space between you and your family."

I started to tell Steve about Tag showing up, that in my family the concept of space was nonexistent. But then I just didn't. Maybe I thought it might sound too strange. Maybe I was still hoping Tag would go away. But I think mostly I was afraid it might scare Steve off.

Ginger and Fred were watching me. I ran my finger around the lip of the fishbowl. "Yeah, well, now I just have to survive embarrassing myself in front of twenty-three million people."

"I have to admit I haven't actually watched it, but it's like a dance contest, right?"

"Yeah, pretty much."

"I'm sure you'll take the whole thing."

"That's very sweet, but that's like me telling you I'm sure they're going to let you redesign the gardens at Buckingham Palace."

"Got it. So what's the best-case scenario?"

"I don't know. That once I get voted off, the rest of the cold, cruel world will seem more manageable? I mean, I'm hanging in there and learning a lot, but it's the toughest thing I've ever done in my life. And winning is simply not an option."

"Learn to fail or fail to learn," Steve said.

"Did you really just say that?"

"I most certainly did. I've been trying to find a way to fit it into the conversation since we got on the phone. I want you to know it took a lot of Googling to come up with that baby. I also found a good one by Kermit the Frog about how time's fun when you're having flies."

"You have the heart of a landscaper."

"This is true. Anyway, it was a close runner-up, but I was pretty sure it didn't qualify as a chiasmus."

"Impressive," I said. "Really impressive."

"Why, thank you, ma'am. For the record, I think what you're doing is pretty impressive, too. However it goes, it'll make a great story one day."

I yawned. "And with luck I'll live to tell it."

He yawned back. "I'm sure you will. Listen, you sound like you're falling asleep, and I should get going, too. I have an early morning."

I stood up to get a look at the little clock on the little stove. "Oh, I'm so sorry. I completely forgot how late it is for you."

"That's okay. I enjoyed it. Is there a good time for me to call you again?"

Fred and Ginger were watching my every move. I made a fish face at them.

Relationships were so much work. You had to say all the right things and put yourself out there. And even then it still probably wouldn't work out. By the time I left Hollywood and got back to the real world, Steve Moretti would probably have met someone else. Or he'd make the mistake of tuning in to watch me on *DWTS* and be completely horrified. Maybe he'd go to a pitch meeting the next day and his client would say, "Oh, did you see that awful woman on *Dancing With the Stars* last night? What was she thinking?"

I took a quick breath and scrunched my eyes shut.

"Anytime you call will be a good time," I said.

31

Beauty is in the eye of the beholder, but we are never more beholden than to the person who enhances our beauty.

Seven days is a lifetime. Seven days is the blink of an eye. I went back and forth between the two. One minute I'd be thinking, *Will today ever be over?* And the next minute my heart would start racing as it hit me that today was Thursday already. Long before I was even close to being ready for it, Monday at 8 p.m. Eastern and Pacific time (7 p.m. Central and Mountain) would be here.

It didn't help that I was sleep deprived. Tag hadn't come back to my apartment last night. He was a big boy so it's not like I'd been worried about him or anything. I'd been pretty sure he'd gone home with Ashleyjanedobbs and at that very moment was oohing and aahing over how flexible she was. I just didn't know whether to lock the door and risk having him wake me up in the middle of the night, or to leave the door unlocked and risk being woken up in the middle of the night by an axe murderer.

Eventually I decided that if my brother could get the building super to let him into my apartment once, he could do it again. So I locked the door and carried Ginger and Fred into my bedroom.

But a part of me kept expecting Tag to wake me up from a sound sleep. And I'd finally let him have it, about trying to hog my fifteen minutes of *DWTS* fame, about how he'd acted with Steve at Lake Austin Spa Resort. So I kept going over what I'd say when I told him off, and as a result I couldn't seem to fall into that sound sleep. After I got bored with my imaginary yelling at Tag, I replayed every line of my conversation with Steve at least twice. After that, I went over the steps of my cha-cha a few times.

Just when I'd finally drifted into a deep, exhausted sleep, my alarm went off.

"Focus," Ilya said, bringing me back to the practice studio.

"Sorry," I said. "I don't seem to have it in me today."

We finished yet another run-through of our dance. Ilya ran his hand through his hair. "You're tired, that's all. You need a rest day, but we don't have one. So we'll do the best we can and not sweat it. If we hang in there today, tomorrow will be better."

"Can I call you every day for the rest of my life so you can tell me that?"

Ilya reached for the remote. "I'll make you a video. I'll even sell it to you wholesale."

"Gee, thanks."

We did our cha-cha again. And again. And again. I knew the words to "Smooth" forward and backward, upside down and inside out. I was practically ready to go on tour with Santana. If only I could sing or play an instrument. Or dance, for that matter.

We took a break. I counted out almonds and piled my plate with fruit and baby carrots. I sipped my bottled water. Ilya opened his laptop and I wrote a message from Tag asking his Facebook fans to "like" our TAG TEAM Facebook page. I wrote a shorter version asking his Twitter followers to follow both Ilya and me. Then we posted our own messages, telling everyone how hard we were working and thanking them for their support and asking them to spread the word.

"Wow," Ilya said as he reached for another strawberry. "You need a road map to keep up with all this stuff."

"Now you know how I feel about your choreography," I said.

The next session went a little bit better, but not much. Ilya singled out a few of the steps and had me do them over and over again, and then I worked on my spotting some more.

When our five hours were up, I went right to a hair appointment with Gina. She did what she called a three-step process: warm medium brown to brighten up my overall hair, plus the addition of highlights and lowlights. I didn't quite follow her, but whatever it was she was doing, it took a lot of time. I was hoping I could doze in the chair while my color cooked, but Lila came over and experimented on me with some makeup.

I tried to avoid looking at the mirror in front of me, but at one point I glanced up. I had vampire eyes and ruby lips, and my head was covered with folded-over strips of aluminum foil. Maybe an alien spaceship really had dropped me off in my parents' backyard. After all this time, I could finally call my real people and ask them to beam me back up. Fast.

Lila wiped one of my eyes clean and started again. "That spray tan is going to make all the difference on you, hon. Just you wait and see. Once we get that on, we'll add primer and layer on a mixture of liquid and cream foundations, and then I'll press it all in with loose powder."

Lila kept experimenting until she got a makeup look she liked. Teal shadow made my brown eyes sparkle, big and bright, and the false eyelashes actually changed the shape of my eyes like a mini–eye lift. Lila had brushed a pearlescent shimmer over my brow bones and over the dark spots between the bridge of my nose and my eyes. And she'd contoured my face with darker shades to make my cheekbones stand out and the peaks and valleys of my face more pronounced.

Once Gina had finished blowing it out, I had to admit my hair was amazing, too. The changes were subtle, but the effect was dramatic.

My boring brown medium-length hair suddenly had volume, shine, dimension, *drama*.

If I were sitting around the dinner table with my family I might have said, *Beauty is in the eye of the beholder, but we are never more beholden than to the person who enhances our beauty.*

My glam squad stood behind my chair looking proudly at their handiwork.

"Thank you so much," I said. "I don't know how you did it, but even I think I look good."

Gina lifted up a handful of hair and pinned it into place with bobby pins. My neck looked longer instantly.

Lila made me smile so she could check my teeth for lipstick smudges. "We'll do a camera check to make sure it reads well on television, but I think this is it."

"Thank you again," I said. "You're both incredibly talented. It must be amazing to be this good at something. Do you have your own Facebook business pages?"

Less than half an hour later they did.

Next up was my first media event for the show. I'd been trying to avoid thinking about it, but when Ilya showed up, I knew it was time. I used the wardrobe changing room to upgrade my yoga pants and baggy T-shirt to black pants and a black jacket over a black tank.

Anthony shook his head. "What is this, casual funeral?"

"Sorry," I said. "I didn't bring much with me."

He knotted a long coral scarf around my neck and handed me a pair of big silver hoop earrings. My face brightened instantly.

"Thank you."

"My pleasure, treasure." He scanned the racks of shoes until he found a pair of shiny silver pumps with what had to be five-inch heels.

My feet cramped just looking at them. "Do you think I can carry those and put them on when I get there?"

"We'll stop right outside the door," Ilya said. "Hurry."

I looked at Anthony. "Maybe I can just make you a quick Facebook page first? I mean, it's not really fair—"

"Go," Gina said.

"I'll take a rain check, sugar plum," Anthony said. "Break a leg."

"I know this isn't very original," I said. "But that's what I'm afraid of."

We stopped right outside the open door to one of the dance studios so I could put on my shoes. I'd been to plenty of media junkets with Tag, but being on the other side of the cameras made it a completely new experience. A large curved leather sectional sofa had been placed at one end of the long room. The rest of the room was absolutely packed with cameras and microphones and reporters.

The celebrities were seated and the professionals stood behind their dance partners. Karen and a couple of other producers were milling around, getting everything organized. The judges weren't there, but the two *DWTS* hosts were standing behind a podium going over some notes.

I looked at Ilya. "I don't think I can do this."

"You can and you will." He reached for my hand, which was a good thing since I was tottering on those heels. I managed to sit down without humiliating myself. Ilya walked around behind the sectional and put his hands on my shoulders. Ashleyjanedobbs came running in and squeezed in between me and the wrestler. I would have looked a lot better next to the wrestler, I thought, but I wiggled over to make room for her. Then I sat up straight, crossed my legs at the ankles, and turned my knees sideways to create what I hoped was a more flattering angle.

I took a deep breath in through my nose and let it out through my mouth. I tried to act relaxed and casual, like this was no big deal, like I did this all the time.

All eleven dancing couples were present and accounted for. With luck I wouldn't have to answer a single question.

32

To dance is to live, if you live through the dance.

The impending season premiere of *DWTS* must have qualified as news, since the whole thing was set up like a news conference. Reporters were seated on folding chairs going over their notes.

"Welcome," the male host said. "We've got a truly electrifying season lined up for you, perhaps the most thrilling season in the illustrious history of *Dancing With the Stars*."

The female host introduced us couple by couple, checking her notes as she went. Then she opened it up for questions.

"If you both weighed in and suited up, which of the other celebrity dancers do you think would have the best chance of taking you in a fight?" one of the reporters asked the former wrestler.

He laughed nervously. "Uh, none of them?"

He got a big laugh and I relaxed a little.

"What's the biggest difference between performing a song and performing a dance?" another reporter asked the singer.

The singer cleared her throat. "You use your mouth for one—"

"And you keep your mouth closed for the other," her professional dancer said.

This got an even bigger laugh.

I swiveled my head and smiled at the celebrity dancers on either side of me. We were holding our own, and for the first time I felt like I was a part of the group. I mean, how cool to be sitting up here with people who'd actually been famous, or at least sort of famous. How brave we were to take on this challenge. What an incredible shared experience. And how amazing it would be to have earned the right to tell the story for the rest of our lives.

Maybe we'd be so good the producers would call us all back to do a reunion show in ten years, maybe even five if our season turned out to be truly spectacular. I'd be older, of course, but better. I'd be in killer shape and I'd have a glow that went beyond my spray tan. I'd have kept up with my dancing and maybe I'd even be competing across the country in semiprofessional dance competitions, or at least amateur ones. Steve would have agreed to take some lessons because I gave him a gift certificate for our anniversary. After the first lesson he'd have been hooked, and now we spent almost as much time dancing as my parents did bowling.

Ilya squeezed my shoulders. Hard. I tuned back in just in time to realize that a reporter was asking me a question.

"Excuse me," I said, "but can you repeat that?"

A skinny blond reporter spoke slowly, as if perhaps English was a second language for me. "How. Grateful. Are you. To your brother. Tag. For this experience?"

"Pretty grateful," I said.

In front of me, about a zillion hands shot up. One of the hosts called on another reporter.

"Will Tag be in the audience?"

"So I hear," I said.

"At every show? Or just for the premiere?"

"Um, I think you'd have to ask Tag that."

"Is there any truth to the rumor that Tag will be dancing in one of the numbers?"

"Only if Ilya wants to dance with him," slipped out of my mouth. As soon as I said it, I realized it was the kind of thing you say *to* your brother, not about him in front of a roomful of reporters.

I was right. Silence filled the room. It was dark and heavy, like sludge.

It didn't seem fair. I mean, the wrestler's comment wasn't that funny and the reporters laughed for him.

"Are you saying that after all Tag has done for you, you're refusing to dance with him?" a reporter shouted out.

I looked at the two *DWTS* hosts, hoping one of them would help me out, or at least tell the reporter to wait until he was called on. Neither of them said anything.

My first impulse was to say, *Have you ever seen my brother dance?* But given the way my first joke attempt had gone over, I ruled that one out. Then I thought about pleading the fifth, but somehow I didn't think that would fly either.

I took in the blur of faces in front of me. If they were lions, I'd be dinner.

I lowered my head and looked up humbly. "I am forever grateful to my amazing brother. I was just worried about infringing on his important work. But I'd do anything for him, of course. And if Tag wants to dance, I'd be delighted to."

"I'd dance with him," Ashleyjanedobbs said.

Somehow even this got a big laugh.

Another reporter's voice cut through the crowd. "What's the biggest piece of advice your brother gave you for being on *Dancing With the Stars*?"

Everybody stopped yelling. It was so quiet you could hear a dance shoe drop.

Ilya squeezed my shoulders again.

"To dance is to live," I said, "if you live through the dance."

The entire room erupted in laughter. Not just the reporters, but the hosts, too, as well as the dancers around me and their partners behind us.

I sat up straighter and smiled. I was so proud of myself for hanging in there and winning the room over.

"Is your brother always that funny?" a reporter yelled. "I mean, does he just wake up in the morning and start spouting out killer lines like that?"

"But . . ." I said. I couldn't believe I wasn't even getting credit for my own chiasmus.

"Did he give you any more gems like that for us?" a reporter yelled.

"What dance will you and Tag be doing?" another reporter shouted.

"Is it true they chose Tag first, but he gave his slot to you?"

I just sat there like a lump, mostly because I didn't have the energy to pick up my jaw from the floor. Vaguely I heard one of the hosts jump in and say something about having to save some surprises, and then the other host said to tune in to find out what they'd be. And then it was over.

"That went well," I said to Ilya as he held me up while I slipped off my silver high heels. Holding back my tears was even more challenging than walking in those stupid skyscraper shoes had been.

"You did fine," he said. "It'll get easier."

"Ha. I'm not falling for that one again. That's exactly what you said about the dancing."

I was so demoralized I could have eaten the contents of an entire McDonald's. Not just two tons of french fries and a towering mountain of Big Macs, but an orchard's worth of fried apple pie sticks and a cow's worth of chocolate milk shakes. Maybe even the golden arches outside, too.

I tried to swallow my anger instead, but it caught in my throat like a kernel of popcorn without any butter. I was jealous. Or envious. I always got the two mixed up. One of them meant you wanted what the other person had, and the other meant you wanted to take it away from the person. I wanted both. I wanted to be Tag, and I didn't want him to get to be Tag anymore. I wanted him to have to be me. I wanted him to know how awful it felt to be his sister.

I hated my brother. I hated those stupid reporters. But I wasn't going to let them make me eat a box of chocolates.

I didn't have the energy to hit Whole Foods on the way home, so I swung by craft services after I returned my shoes and accessories to wardrobe. Ilya waited for me while I put a hummus and tabbouleh roll-up in the center of a paper plate and surrounded it with salad greens and slices of roasted veggies.

"Thank you for being my bodyguard," I said as we walked out to the parking lot together. "I don't think I could handle being ambushed by another reporter right now."

"You got it," Ilya said. "Whatever you need, just say the word."

"Thanks. You, too. See you tomorrow. I think."

He leaned over and kissed me on my forehead. "Get some sleep."

I knew the way back to my temporary apartment so well now that I was tempted to try another route just so I'd have something to distract me. Maybe I'd even get lost. By the time I found my way home, another hour or so would have gone by and it would be late enough to go to bed and get that sleep Ilya had prescribed.

Then I could finally stop thinking about the fact that wherever I went and whatever I did for the rest of my life, people would only want to know about the It Guy, my stupid guru brother, Tag.

33

Don't sweat the petty things,
and don't pet the sweaty things.

When I opened the door to my apartment, there was a man on my couch.

As soon as I opened my mouth to scream I realized it was Tag, but part of the scream slipped out anyway. And my heart was already beating like crazy.

"Calm down, why don't you," Tag said. His bare feet were hanging off one arm of the couch, and he was eating what was left of my barbeque chicken sandwich.

"Help yourself, why don't you," I said.

He took another bite.

I shoved his feet off the couch as I walked by him. "What were you, born in a barn?"

"You're the one who lives in a sheep shed," my brother said through a mouthful of my sandwich.

"Who put me there? And don't you dare get any of that on my couch."

Tag held out his hand like he was going to wipe it on the dingy upholstery. "Don't sweat the petty things," he said.

"And don't pet the sweaty things." I shivered. "You're a mess. Didn't your little gymnast let you take a shower?"

He really was a mess. His hair was sticking up all over the place, and he looked like he hadn't shaved in a week. If he thought I was going to wash that stupid white tunic of his with my laundry, he had another think coming.

Tag's cell rang. He reached for it on the coffee table.

"Calm down," he said as he picked up the call. "She's right here."

He tossed the phone to me.

"What?" I said into the receiver.

"I can't believe you lied to me," Joanie Baloney said. "You did too know where Tag was."

"Not now," I said. I threw the phone back to Tag. Or maybe at him.

I put my dinner on the kitchen counter and headed for my bedroom to feed Ginger and Fred.

"I know," I whispered as I sprinkled their food flakes. "I hate them, too."

I changed out of my casual funeral outfit and back into my yoga pants and T-shirt. I took another look at the fishbowl. I'd thought the water was starting to look a little bit cloudy this morning, but now there was no doubt about it—it definitely needed changing. I reviewed the instructions from the guy at the pet store. Every three to five days bring a bowl of tap water to room temperature and add a capful of Nutrafin Goldfish Bowl Conditioner, then pour out half the old water from the bowl and add the new water.

When I came out again, my guru brother was off the phone and had arisen from the couch. He was standing at the kitchen counter eating half of my hummus and tabbouleh roll-up.

I put the fishbowl down on the little dining table. "Get your filthy mitts off my roll-up."

My brother popped the rest of it into his mouth, chewed, then opened his mouth so I could see.

"Gross," I said. "Grow up."

"You grow up," he mumbled.

"I can't believe you just ate that," I said. "That was supposed to be my dinner."

"Finders keepers." He turned on my faucet and stuck his head under it for a drink.

"Drop dead," I said. It was like my entire childhood vocabulary was coming back to me.

"What, and look like you?" Tag said.

"Drop dead twice," I said.

Tag turned off the faucet and wiped his mouth with the back of his hand. "Ooh, the old D.D.T. You're really scarin' me now."

I searched my memory banks for something worse.

"Get bent," I said. I still wasn't quite sure what it meant, but I knew it was bad.

"You're cruisin' for a bruisin'," he said. "Take a chill pill."

I glared at him as hard as I could. If I'd thought I could take him, I would have asked if he wanted a knuckle sandwich.

"Don't you dare give me the hairy eyeball," he said. "I bought that sandwich."

"Get over yourself," I said. "You did not."

"Did too," he said.

He crossed his arms over his chest. "In point of fact, I bought you everything you have."

In every relationship there are lines you just don't cross.

Even with families.

Even with brothers who think they're God's gift to the world.

I put my hands on my hips. "Get the hell out of my life. Now. Permanently. I mean it."

Tag narrowed his eyes. "Who's gonna make me?"

"I'm not kidding. You've ruined my entire life from the second I was born."

"What?"

"You heard me."

"You ungrateful little piece of shit."

"Ooh," I said. "Nice guru talk. Whatever happened to being the change you want to see in the world?"

"That wasn't me, that was Gandhi."

"Whatever."

Tag leaned back against the kitchen counter and shook his head. "I can't believe you said that to me. After everything I've done for you."

I leaned over one of the dinette chairs like it was a walker. "Yeah, right. Everything you've done for me. Treating me like your personal slave. Making me feel like shit. Keeping me from ever having my own life."

My brother's blue eyes glittered like ice. "I give you your life. And you feed off me like the rest of the leeches in this family."

I heard a little gasp and realized it was coming from me. "What did you say?"

Tag glared at me with full force.

"You heard me," he said. "Poor little you. You've got it so bad. All you're after is sympathy. Well, you can find it in the dictionary between *shit* and *syphilis*, and it'll do you about as much good."

"Eww," I said. "Don't you dare ask me to write that down."

"Try being me. Try having to support everybody you've ever met. Try waking up every day and feeling like all you want to do is just pack it in and hit the road. Do something new. Anything. But you can't because you've got to feed the whole world. You're the official fuckin' family meal ticket, and if you bail, the whole house of cards collapses."

I shook my head. "Oh, puh-lease, who created it? Who always had to be the family star? Who made sure everything was always about you? It's like you think you're freakin' Tinker Bell and the whole world is just waiting to clap."

Tag turned his palms to the heavens. "Nothing wrong with that."

"Who is so freakin' controlling that you won't let any of us have our own lives? Who won't let me buy my own sheep shed?" I choked back a sob. "Who called me fat in front of his friends?"

Tag shook his head as if he had water in his ears. "What the hell are you talking about? When did I call you fat?"

"Remember when all four of us used to walk downtown to spend our allowance on Saturdays? That time you told all those boys you were going to put fatso on a diet?"

Tag looked at me blankly.

"I never walked downtown with you and Colleen and Joanie after that," I said. "I was devastated. You scarred me for life."

Tag was still looking at me blankly.

I shook my head. "Great, you ruined my life and you don't even remember it."

"That's just how brothers talk," Tag said. "How about that time when you and your friends all pulled nylon stockings over your heads to make fun of me?"

I'd completely forgotten about that one. "That was different."

Tag smoothed his hair with both hands. The parts that were sticking out bounced back up again. "How was that different? I was really sensitive about my hair. The way I straightened it was a family matter."

"You take over everything, Tag. You're taking over *Dancing With the Stars.* You even took over Mitchell. I think he only stayed around so he could hang out with you."

"Mitchell is an asshole. I only hung out with him to be nice. Because of you."

We looked at each other.

"Are you going to marry him?" I said.

"Not if you don't want me to."

I shrugged. "His girlfriend lost the baby."

Tag shook his head. "Then my guess is no one will have to marry him."

"I know. I just wanted to see if you would have. I hit him with your golf cart. Right before I left."

"That better be a joke," Tag said. "You know the golf cart's off-limits."

"See what I mean. You're a total control freak."

"Takes one to know one."

He turned and opened my refrigerator and pulled out a beer and a box of Devil Dogs. Apparently my brother did know how to shop after all.

He held the beer out in my direction. I shook my head.

He opened it and threw the bottle cap up in the air. It landed right in the wastebasket. Of course it did.

"You're better off without Mitchell," he said.

"I know that," I said. "But he was a lot of years of my life."

"He wasn't good enough for you. You should have dumped him a long time ago."

I reached for Tag's beer and took a small sip. "Well, it's not like there was a long line of suitors following me around or anything."

Tag took his beer back. "That was your choice."

"How was that my choice? I mean, easy for you to say, girls have been throwing themselves at you since you were in preschool."

Tag grinned. "Actually, it started before that."

I rolled my eyes.

Tag guzzled some beer. "Remember when Colleen got asked to her prom by like ten different guys?"

"Thanks for reminding me," I said. "I think that was the same year I got *wallflower* tattooed on my butt."

"You know why they all asked her, right?"

"Because she was pretty and popular and I wasn't?"

Tag let out a distinctly non-guru-like burp. "Coll was always the first one to introduce herself, or say hello, and she was nice to everyone—the art geeks, the band geeks, the geek geeks, the cool dudes like me."

I rolled my eyes again.

"It wasn't that you weren't pretty, Dee. You were just so closed off you weren't available. You weren't *open*."

I let that sink in. "So, what's the scoop with Ashleyjanedobbs? Is she going to be my next sister-in-law?"

"Do not. I repeat, do not, let me go there." Tag took a long swallow of beer.

"There's probably room for one more house on the property," I said.

"Don't even joke about it. Do you have any idea what those living arrangements are like for me? My ex-wives enjoy each other's company far more than either of them ever enjoyed mine. The kids are great and I love them all, but sometimes it feels like they're one big happy family and I'm not even in it. I just show up once in a while and everybody humors me, and then when I leave their real life begins again."

I looked at my brother, really looked at him, for the first time in a long time. Maybe ever. It was simply amazing that two people could live in each other's back pockets their whole lives and have completely different perspectives on their shared experiences.

For a minute I was starting to feel what could only be described as empathy.

And then my cell phone rang.

34

At the end of the day, love is all that's real,
and all that matters is that you really loved.

My cell was on the kitchen counter, so Tag was closer. He reached for it.

"I got it," I said. I took the three steps to my phone in one long leap.

Tag was faster. He scooped it up and flipped it over so he could see the display screen.

"Don't you dare," I said.

Tag grinned. I thought he might hesitate for a second just to tease me. I mean, old habits die hard and all that. But then he'd toss it to me, maybe a little bit higher than necessary so I'd have to dive for it, but at least he'd give it to me.

"Hello," he said.

I opened my mouth and drew in a sharp breath. The sound it made was like a gust of wind.

"Deirdre Griffin's Hollywood residence," Tag said in Madonna's fake British accent.

"Give it to me," I yelled as I tried to grab the phone out of his hand.

Tag put his hand on my head and straightened out his arm so I couldn't reach it.

I circled my arms like a windmill, but I couldn't get any closer. Tag had perfected this hold during our childhood. It was no less humiliating now.

"Give it to me right now," I screamed.

Tag took my phone away from his ear. "Well, what do you know?" he said. "It's our old pal, Steve Moretti."

I lost it. I totally lost it. If his golf cart had been around I would have run him over, then put it into reverse and done it again. And again. And again. And again.

But the only weapon I had was my knee.

So I used it. And for once in my life, my aim was dead on.

I kneed my brother as hard as I could, right in the family jewels.

Tag let out a moan like a wild animal, like the howl of a coyote crossed with the *moo* of a cow. He shoved me with one hand at the same time I twisted away from him and tried to lunge for my phone.

He threw it with his other hand, then doubled over with pain.

I jumped for the phone. My heel hit the dining room chair.

I heard a splash as the cell phone landed in the fishbowl.

The chair tipped over and I landed on the cheap little dining room table.

The table went over and I went with it.

My T-shirt absorbed the fishbowl's water like a wick, and as soon as I felt the dampness I knew.

I rolled over and pushed myself to an upright position as fast as I could.

The fishbowl had turned completely over. My phone was still inside it, but Fred and Ginger had been thrown free and were flopping around in a puddle on the floor.

I screamed. I grabbed the fishbowl and ran to the sink. I turned on the water full blast. I reached my hand into the bowl as it was filling and pulled out my phone.

I grabbed a soupspoon from a kitchen drawer and ran back to Fred and Ginger. Water sloshed over the lip of the fishbowl and drenched my yoga pants.

Ginger looked worse so I scooped her up first. I slid the spoon under her gently like a stretcher, then nudged her all the way on with my finger. I lowered her into the bowl as quickly as I could, then I went for Fred.

Neither one of them was moving much, but they weren't floating on the surface either. The water probably wasn't the right temperature, but at least it was wet. Their little gills were working hard as if they were gasping for air. My hands shook as I poured in a capful of Nutrafin Goldfish Bowl Conditioner.

I hugged the fishbowl to my chest and prayed.

Tag pushed himself slowly to his feet. "What the fu—"

I hugged the fishbowl tighter. "Get out," I whispered. "Now. And if you killed my fish, I'll never speak to you again for the rest of my life."

I carried Ginger and Fred into my bedroom and shut the door.

I slid down to the floor with my back resting against the bed. I held Fred and Ginger in my lap.

"You're going to be fine," I whispered. "I'm right here. Just try to relax and swim through it."

Surprisingly, I heard Tag leave.

Ginger was barely moving. Fred was still swimming, but he was on his side and only seemed to be able to circle in one direction.

Tears streamed down my face. "Don't leave me," I whispered. "Please don't leave me."

Easy for Tag to say that I should have been more available, more open. Huge risks or tiny ones, boyfriends or goldfish, this is what open got you: pain and suffering and a chance to get your heart ripped right out of your chest.

I started to sing. The first song that popped into my head was "Row, Row, Row Your Boat," so I went with it. I sang it over and over and over again. After a while I almost convinced myself that as long as I kept singing, I could keep them alive.

My voice started to go, so I reached for the water bottle on my tiny bedside table and took a quick sip. I lit the little candle and placed it on the floor in front of us. I said another prayer.

Then I went back to singing. This time I sang "Smooth" over and over again. I didn't even think about the dance steps, but whenever I got to the line about being just like the ocean under the moon I pictured Fred and Ginger back to normal and swimming away happily in their miniature sea, waiting to see me again.

If anybody ever tells you fish don't have feelings, don't believe them for a second. Ginger wiggled back and forth slowly as one eye held mine. Fred circled as close to Ginger as he could on every pass. At one point, their fins brushed and they stayed almost touching for a while, their gills opening and closing in time to each other.

I don't think I consciously decided to start singing "We Are Family," I just gradually became aware that I was singing it and that, as stupid as it might sound, it fit.

I thought it would be Ginger, but Fred was the first one to go. His one-way circles started getting smaller and slower and closer to the surface. I wanted to look away or to close my eyes, but I made myself keep watching, keep singing, be there for him. His gills struggled. Then they stopped moving. His round eyes fixed and he floated to the surface, still on his side.

"I am so, so sorry," I whispered to Ginger. "This just sucks."

Ginger didn't last much longer. I guess she didn't see the point. She let go and drifted to the surface, and before I knew it they were both floating on top of the water, their little orange bodies bumping into each other and drifting away, then bumping into each other again.

I cried until I couldn't cry anymore, until I couldn't even remember what I was crying about. Then I closed my eyes and drifted off, the fishbowl still in my lap.

I hadn't closed the blind in my little bedroom window, so the first shreds of daylight woke me up. I brought the fishbowl into the bathroom with me. I took a quick shower and brushed my teeth.

I threw on some yoga pants and a T-shirt. I checked my phone to see if it would turn on, not that I expected it to. Its screen stayed dark, but I didn't even care. I didn't think I'd ever feel like talking to anyone again anyway.

I carried Ginger and Fred out to the Land Rover. I guess it didn't really matter, but I was afraid their fishbowl would tip over on the floor, so I poured out some of the water carefully and buckled them into the passenger seat.

I turned on the GPS and screen-tapped BEACH. Then I sang "Row, Row, Row Your Boat" the whole way there. My voice was raspy and my throat hurt and my head pounded from lack of caffeine, but it seemed like the least I could do.

Even in Los Angeles, there wasn't much traffic at the crack of dawn, so I followed Highland Avenue till I got on the I-10 heading west, and we were at Santa Monica Beach before I knew it. I pulled into one of the empty lots and carried Fred and Ginger across a ramp that led to the pier. We descended the steps to the beach. We passed some volleyball courts and kept walking until I found the most beautiful part of the beach.

I sat down on the sand and crossed my legs. I held Ginger and Fred in my lap.

"At the end of the day, love is all that's real," I whispered, "and all that matters is that you really loved."

I dug them a hole in the wet sand close to the water, as deep as I could make it using my hands. Then I poured them in carefully and filled the hole with sand, one slow scoop at a time.

I marked their grave with a single heart made of tiny beach stones, even though I knew that as soon as the next tide came in it would wash them all away.

35

A spirited dance is fueled by your spirit.

Dance is about feeling, not thinking. To dance well, you have to check your brain at the door along with your street shoes. In the early stages, of course, you have to learn the individual steps just like the words of a new language. You have to analyze each one and figure out how best to give each step its due.

After that you have to learn to string the words of your steps into phrases, and then into sentences, to determine where to break them up and how to punctuate them. And then you have to figure out how to group your dance sentences to make paragraphs that pull you through and lead you by the hand into the next one.

But by the time you're ready to tell the whole story, you transcend all the building blocks that got you there. You get out of your head, and you dance with your body. And you have to dig deep, then open up and let go. A spirited dance is fueled by your spirit.

After I left the beach, I forced myself to go to rehearsal. I stopped fighting myself. I got out of my own way. I did what my dance partner told me to do. I ate and drank what my body needed. I closed my eyes and held my hands high while Anthony pulled my costume over my head for a final fitting.

When our five hours were up, I went back to my little temporary apartment. I carried the empty fishbowl in with me. Someday I'd use it for a vase and fill it with flowers, and it would have a lot more meaning than Afterwife's empty soy milk bottle.

But first I needed sleep. Tag's bedroom door was open and both he and his stuff were long gone. Maybe he'd already been moved out when I woke up this morning. I hadn't even noticed. The dining area table and the chair I'd knocked over were upright again. I knew I didn't do it, so it must have been Tag. The floor was dry and even the empty beer bottle and the paper plate that had held my hummus and tabbouleh roll-up had been thrown away.

The apartment seemed eerily quiet, as if I'd gotten used to coming home to the sound of an apartment full of cats meowing or birds chattering, not two tiny goldfish named Ginger and Fred.

I ate the single-serving Healthy Choice lemon chicken I'd brought home from the craft services refrigerator so I didn't have to stop at the store, and then I went to bed. I fell asleep right away, a deep, dreamless sleep.

I got up the next day, rinsed and repeated. Ilya and I had a scheduled hour to practice dancing on the actual ballroom stage. I tried to take it in, to imagine what the huge empty room would be like with the orchestra playing and cheering people filling every seat, but I was numb.

"Don't think about it," Ilya said. "Just dance." And of course he'd choreographed our number so well that our steps filled the stage and we finished directly in front of the now empty judges' table.

"Look right at them and smile," Ilya said.

I smiled carefully at the three empty seats.

"Bigger."

I smiled bigger.

When we were finished for the day, I drove back to my apartment, then took off on foot to track down a temporary phone with prepaid minutes, just enough for an emergency phone call.

I pushed open the door to the little corner store. The woman behind the counter was the same one who'd been there my first night in L.A.

"Hi," I said. "How did it go with *Two and a Half Men*?"

"Don't ask," she said. "But I've got three auditions this week. One of them is practically a shoo-in."

I wished her luck and she helped me pick out a temporary cell phone.

As she rang up my purchase, I glanced over at a stand filled with newspapers, the cheap supermarket tabloid kind. A familiar face on the front page caught my eye, so I picked it up. It took me a moment to realize the face was mine.

"I'll take this, too," I said. I folded the paper in half and tucked it under my arm.

As soon as I was outside, I opened it up again. In the photo, a coral scarf was looped around my neck and I was seated in a row of people on a leather couch. Ashleyjanedobbs was sitting next to me looking like a tiny porcelain doll.

"TAG'S SISTER SCARED ITLESS," the headline screamed.

I took another look at the picture. My eyebrows were up and my mouth was open like I was about to scream, so wide open that even on newsprint I could almost count the old silver fillings in my back molars. My hands were holding on to each other in my lap, as if for dear life. My knees were flopped over to one side at such a strange angle that it looked like I might be *Dancing With the Stars'* first wheelchair contestant. The silver skyscraper heels attached to my feet looked like they belonged to a completely different person, like someone had built me with a Mrs. Potato Head game and thought it would be really funny to put those shoes with those legs.

I looked at it some more. Then I started to laugh. I laughed and I laughed, and as soon as I began to settle down, I'd look at the picture again and start laughing some more. I wiped my eyes with the back of my hand. A couple of tourists wearing fanny packs crossed the street so they wouldn't have to walk past a crazy person.

Standing on the sidewalk between two souvenir shops, I read the whole thing, about the odds-on favorites for winning and who would probably be the first ones kicked off, about who had talent and who didn't, about who had great chemistry, and who was probably sleeping with whom. There was a whole paragraph about Tag, and I was referred to once simply as his sister and once as his Itless sister.

Okay, so I was Itless. Big freakin' deal.

I tore the article out of the newspaper. Maybe I'd add it to my mother's scrapbook, and one day I'd flip through to this clipping again. And I'd look it right in the eye, and I'd laugh and I'd laugh and I'd laugh about how crazy I'd been to take this on. Rash. Impulsive. Foolhardy.

But brave, too, really, really brave.

The truth was I'd been scared Itless my whole life. I'd kept everything I did safe and small. I'd hidden behind not just Tag, but my whole family, and even Mitchell, so I wouldn't get hurt.

But living a little life hadn't kept the hurt away. Life hurt sometimes. It just did. Maybe it seemed silly to be so heartbroken about losing a couple of goldfish, but you know what, I was. Fred and Ginger were mine, and mine alone, and it hurt like hell that they were gone. But the sadness didn't take away from the joy they'd brought me when they were alive.

So maybe it made sense to go for the biggest life you could handle, the one that had the highest highs to balance the lowest lows. Jump on. Buckle up. And when it was over, at least you'd be able to say, *Oh, well, that was fun.*

I was climbing aboard the roller coaster. I was putting myself out there. I'd take my dancing as far as it would go. I'd build my social-networking empire. I'd become a truly amazing social media maven. A genius. A freakin' guru.

Sure, I was scared. Shaking in my go-go boots scared. There were big risks, *huge* risks, but there was also the potential for some pretty huge personal satisfaction.

I was going to be on *Dancing With the Stars* on Monday night. This Monday night. As in the day after tomorrow. And I was going big or going home. Or maybe going big *and* going home. It didn't really matter what the rest of the world thought or did or how soon they kicked me off the show. What mattered was that for the first time in my life I was open. Available. I'd had the guts to reach out and grab that proverbial brass ring when it circled by. And I was going to do my best to enjoy the ride.

As soon as I got back to my apartment, I phoned home.

My father answered on the first ring. "Hey, Dad," I said.

"Honey," he said.

I heard a click and then my mother said, "Deirdre?"

"Hi, Mom."

"Your mother and I have been worried about you," my father said.

I took a deep breath. "For how long? I mean, did you guys ever worry about me when I was a kid, or was I just, you know, the family wallflower?"

"Where did *that* come from?" my mother said.

"Of course we worried about you, Dee-Dee," my father said. "We worried about all four of you kiddos. We still do."

"See," I said. "You always lump me in with everybody else. I've spent my whole life feeling like I didn't measure up."

"Deirdre," my mother said, "your father and I may not have been perfect parents, but we love you very much. And if it makes you feel any better, we've had similar conversations with each of your sisters as well as with your brother."

"Seriously?" I said. "Even Tag?" I mean, how dare any of my siblings think they didn't get enough attention, but *Tag*?

My mother laughed. "Sweetie, you've got the power to be as special as you choose to be."

"And your mother's got the scrapbook to prove it," my father said. "But you've only got one family, honey, so sort things out with your brother, okay?"

After we hung up, I headed into the bathroom to do my homework. Lila had given me a whole kit. I started with the loofah mitt and some exfoliating cream. I slathered on the cream and scrubbed my entire body until I'd taken off a layer of skin, maybe even two. Then I lathered gobs of rich foam shaving gel on my legs and underarms and bikini line, shaved, then rinsed off and did it again. Finally, I covered my entire body with a rich moisturizer.

I walked around the little apartment naked while my skin absorbed the moisturizer. I never walked around without clothes, but maybe I'd start. I mean, there was no one here but me, so who was I actually hiding from? And maybe it was only my imagination, but things felt a lot less jiggly than they had a week ago.

When all that was left of the moisturizer was a soft glow to my skin, I put clean sheets on the bed. I found my laptop. I plugged it in, climbed into bed, pulled the sheets over my legs, and fired it up.

I stopped by Ilya's and my TAG TEAM Facebook page. Hundreds of messages had been posted on the wall. There were some crazy ones and a few nasty ones, but most were messages of support and encouragement.

I skimmed past the crazy/nasty messages, but I read all the rest, one by one. I took the time to acknowledge them with a quick thank-you or a click of the Like button.

Dance, Deirdre, Dance! one of the messages said.

You give hope to midlife women everywhere! another one said.

Midlife. I took a moment to think about that one. How could I possibly have reached midlife already? You'd think I should be able to get some sort of rebate for wasting so many years not really having a life. But if midlife was the middle point, then even though there was a lot of water under the bridge, there was still plenty up ahead. And I had to admit midlife was a helluva lot better than endlife. I had a lot of living left to do.

Midlife Rocks! still another message said. I liked it. Maybe when things slowed down I'd get a bumper sticker made out of that one. Or even a tattoo.

I kept reading.

I am so sick of this celebrity culture where you're either famous or you're nothing, you're either 22 or you're old.

Seeing you out there is almost as good as seeing me.

You're dancing for all of us, Deirdre!

I finished reading and thanking everyone for their support. I put the laptop away and turned out the light.

And then I stared into the darkness until I figured it out.

I was okay with dancing for all of us.

But first and foremost I had to dance for me.

36

Once you get past the rocky parts,
midlife really can rock.

I had to admit I was a little bit nervous about losing my spray tan
virginity.

"Relax," Lila said.

"Easy for you to say," I said. "It's not your first time."

She fired up the air compressor. "You won't feel a thing."

I closed my eyes. "Why do people always say that right before they
hurt you?"

I was standing in a corner of the makeup room that had been
covered with clear plastic shower curtain liners. I was wearing only a
strapless bra and a pair of itsy-bitsy teeny-weeny bikini underpants
from my *DWTS* stash. Even though I'd had to goop it on thick last
night, I'd been told not to use moisturizer today because it might
block the absorption of DHA, the active ingredient in spray tan. Lila
had helped me apply a barrier cream, a heavy petroleum jelly–based
cream, just a little bit to extradry parts like my elbows and knees, and
a thick layer on all the parts she didn't want to tan. Who knew that
tanning the palms of your hands or the soles of your feet, or even the
webs of your fingers or toes, or your cuticles, is a sure giveaway that
you've been spray-tanned by an amateur?

She tucked my hair into a hairnet and gave me a plastic eye cover.

"Wow," I said when she started spraying me. "Now I know what a houseplant feels like when it gets misted." The compressor had a tube that connected it to a little sprayer that Lila was sweeping back and forth in front of my body in long, even passes. It was cool and refreshing, and it smelled a little bit like a vanilla milk shake.

"Just wait," Lila said. "The tan will help you get into character. As soon as the color deepens, you'll feel all sexy and exotic."

"Any chance you can put the leftovers in a take-out container for me?"

Lila laughed. "St. Tropez created a special signature shade for us that's actually called DWTS. It's the darkest one they make, and you can't get it anywhere else. But their other shades are probably better for real life anyway, and you can buy them on the St. Tropez website."

"Wow," I said. "It's a whole new world out there."

"Okay, hon, turn around and face the wall. Do you want a tan line or not?"

"Excuse me?"

"Some people like a tan line across their back so that the tan looks more natural."

I thought about it. "No thanks. I think I'd like to look like I had the nerve to go topless."

"Do you want a full-frontal tan then?" Lila asked, as if she were asking if I wanted cream with my coffee.

"I don't think so," I said. "I think I just want to look brave from the back."

Lila undid the rear hooks for me. I held the bra over my breasts.

Then I thought it through while she sprayed my back.

I threw my bra across the room like a Frisbee and turned around.

"What the hell?" I said. "You only go around once, so you might as well go around tan."

Next came the panicure that Lila had promised—long fake

fingernails and a French manicure on my fingers, and bright coral polish on my toes. My fingers looked long and elegant, and my toes looked positively sexy, even to me.

From that point on, it was all a blur. Time sped up, like one of those clocks in an old movie with the big hands that start spinning around and around, faster and faster, to show the hours passing.

Ilya and I danced, careful not to sweat off our spray tans before they finished curing. We ate healthy food. We posted on Facebook and Twitter. I worked on one of the slide shows for Ilya's website.

"Really," he said, "you don't have to do it now. This can wait."

"I want to. And anyway, it relaxes me." I added another picture of Ilya, in classic ballroom hold with his wife, Kateryna, his unbuttoned shirt matching her glittery champagne-colored costume. She was gorgeous. They both were.

"How did you two meet?" I asked.

Ilya ran a hand through his hair. "Our families were friends in Ukraine. When we met again at a competition in the U.S., there was an immediate connection. We both knew what it was like to try to fit into a strange new world."

"How old were you when you came over here?"

"Thirteen. With almost no English."

"Wow. I can't even imagine. Kids are so mean at that age."

Ilya picked up the iPod remote and twirled it between two fingers. "You can't get bogged down in what happened. You have to move past it and learn to be thankful for it."

"Huh?" I said. "I mean, I get the first part, but what do you mean, learn to be thankful for it?"

He shrugged. "Whatever comes at you, it's all energy. You have to take it and make it work for you. My best dances come from that place."

Maybe my best dances could come from that place, too.

We headed over to the *DWTS* ballroom for another practice run.

This time we took our steps right out to the very edges of the stage, and when I finished my final three spins and landed in Ilya's arms, the judges' table hardly appeared to be moving at all.

I flashed the three empty judges' chairs my biggest smile.

"That's it," Ilya said. "Give it to 'em. Knock 'em dead."

We jumped in the Land Rover and headed back to the practice studio. We went over the trickiest steps again. And again. We drank some more water and ate another snack.

I went to my wardrobe appointment. Finally, Anthony let me see my costume.

It was amazing. Truly amazing. It was a tight sheath like my practice costume, but the color was a deep, rich purple, almost an eggplant. The whole thing was covered with tiny black beads threaded through clear translucent sequins, with ultralong black fringe layered over that. Anthony held the hanger up high and swished it around. The fringe danced back and forth elegantly, gracefully. Even if I froze, at least my dress would keep dancing.

But most amazing of all, the dress part was attached to what looked like a see-through long-sleeved flesh-colored T-shirt dotted randomly with the tiniest semitransparent glittery sequins.

Anthony slipped it over my head and helped me work my arms gently through the sleeves.

"Illusion mesh," he said. "It's a beautiful thing."

It really was a beautiful thing. There was almost nothing to it. It was lighter than air. But it had stretch, heavy-duty stretch, and plenty of it. It was like being naked but with reinforcement.

The teardrop cutout in the front showed some serious cleavage through an almost-invisible illusion mesh safety net. I turned around and looked over my shoulder in the mirror. The dress dipped low and looked almost completely backless, but I was fully locked in without a trace of back fat. I turned around again and lifted my arms out to my sides. I watched my upper arms while I shimmied. Not even a hint of a wiggle.

"Ohmigod," I said. "This stuff is amazing. If you could make me a full-body suit, I'd probably walk around naked for the rest of my life."

Gina and Lila came out of the other side of the room.

"Hot," Gina said. "Totally hot." She pinned my hair up off my neck to get the full effect.

"Smokin'," Lila said. "And guess what? I have forty-two new likes on my Facebook page."

"I'm right behind you," Gina said.

I'd forgotten all about Anthony's Facebook page, so I put one together quickly and promised to give him a tutorial later. Then he let me take my costume to the practice studio for a test drive.

"You're a beautiful woman, Deirdre Griffin," Ilya said when he saw me.

I checked myself out again in the wall of mirrors. "Thank you," I said. "Who knew."

A chiasmus appeared like a rainbow: *Once you get past the rocky parts, midlife really can rock.*

Suddenly, as if we'd been transported by magic, we were standing in the parking lot and Ilya was saying, "Get some sleep. Tomorrow's the big day."

I bit my lower lip. "But, I don't think—"

Ilya put his hands on my shoulders. "Exactly," he said. "From now on you don't think. Get out of your head. Your legs are our money-makers now."

"Ha," I said. "If that's the case, I'm thinking we'd both better keep our day jobs."

37

Success is getting what you want,
but happiness is wanting what you get.

Liiiiive from Hollywood," the male host said. "This is the season premiere of *Dancing With the Stars*."

The ballroom was big. The state-of-the-art entrance staircase that moved on a rising platform was steep. The camera lights were hot and bright. Lights, lights, and more lights—one enormous glowing chandelier and a series of smaller ones, strands of twinkling lights, waterfalls of undulating lights, crisscrossing trippy strobe lights—made everything feel like a mirage.

I'd made it down the stairs in one piece during this morning's dress rehearsal. Our cha-cha had gone well, too, and we'd even hit all the marks we'd worked out during our camera-blocking session. But could lightning strike twice, and if so, could it happen for me?

When Ilya and I came out of the makeup trailer, Karen the producer led us to a little bench set into a nook of midnight blue satin curtains for our preshow interview. The female host sat in the center with a microphone and a guy holding a camera stood across from her surrounded by camera lights. Karen wanted us to sit on either side of the female host, so I had to let go of Ilya's hand.

When the camera started rolling, the female host turned to me.

"So, Tag's sister Deirdre, just moments before twenty-three million people will watch you dance live for the first time, how are you feeling?"

"Can't complain," I said.

Under the hot glare of the camera lights, her teeth sparkled against her spray tan. I was mesmerized. I wondered if mine were doing the same thing. I took a quick peek at my arms through the illusion mesh. I'd spent decades slathered in sunscreen. Now I had some serious tan going on. I liked it.

The female host cleared her throat. "Word is out that your famous brother Tag is in the audience. What will you say to him when you see him?"

"Hello?" I said.

Her teeth disappeared behind pouty lips and about three tons of lipstick. She leaned a little bit closer. "How successful do you think you'll be in this competition?"

"It depends on your definition of success," I said. I turned and faced the camera. I gave it my most sparkly smile. "Success is getting what you want, but happiness is wanting what you get."

The female host let out a little gasp. "Did Tag give you that line?" she whispered.

I kept looking at the camera. "Actually, it's mine. Or I should say I found it on the Internet. That's what I do—I'm a social-networking guru. Tag is one of my clients, but I also raise visibility for a whole range of other clients via Facebook and Twitter and a variety of Internet strategies." I leaned forward to look over at Ilya. "My dance partner, Ilya, is one of my newest clients. In case you don't know it, he owns a renowned and fast-growing chain of ballroom dance studios that offer training for amateurs of all ages as well as those with professional aspirations."

Ilya smiled at the camera, his white teeth sparkling against his spray tan. "Just go to Facebook and search for Dance With Ilya."

"So, getting back to your question," I said when he finished, "the truth is we're in it to win it, but however it goes, we're planning to enjoy the ride for as long as it lasts, and also to take advantage of every opportunity *Dancing With the Stars* brings our way."

The female host didn't seem to have heard me. "Are you dedicating tonight's dance to Tag?" she asked.

My eyes filled. "Actually, we're dedicating it to Fred and Ginger."

Ilya and I high-fived each other after the interview. "Whoa, baby," he said, his Ukrainian accent slipping in the way it always did when he used American slang. "You just bought yourself about twenty-three million new clients."

"Me?" I said. "How about you? You and your brother aren't going to be able to build those dance studios fast enough."

I leaned against a wall while Ilya roughed up the soles of my dance shoes with a sheet of fine-grade sandpaper to keep me from slipping. Before we knew it we were lined up with the other ten couples behind a wall that traversed the space behind the staircase.

The male and female hosts took turns introducing each couple and waited while they descended the staircase together to thunderous applause.

The staircase had a steep scary pitch. The steps flashed distractingly with strobe lights that changed color and reminded me of my brother's disco ball spotlight of long ago. They spilled each couple out onto the ballroom dance floor facing the judges and the audience. Right now my entire focus was on not landing on my butt on the way down.

Ilya held my hand as we faced the staircase. My heart did a funny little hip-hop thing, threatening to dance right out of my chest. Hopefully, illusion mesh held hearts in place as well as flesh. I took a deep breath in through my nose and let it out through my mouth.

"Tag's sister, Deirdre Griffin, and her professional partner, Ilya Balanchuk," the male host boomed.

I didn't sashay or strut or glide or wiggle my way seductively down the stairs, but I didn't fall either. It was enough.

Ilya and I joined the other couples standing in a semicircle on the ballroom floor, bouncing either awkwardly or rhythmically to the *DWTS* theme song. Ilya put his hands on my shoulders and I matched my movements to his. I smiled at the big black blur of the audience. Then they cut to commercial and we were herded back to the camera-studded greenroom like so many glittery, spray-tanned sheep.

Ashleyjanedobbs patted the chair beside her as if we were in elementary school and she'd saved me a seat in the cafeteria. I sat down and waited for my legs to stop shaking.

She leaned over to whisper, "Guess what? Some Broadway producers are here to see me. I've been trying to get a show for like *ever*."

"That's great," I whispered. "Good for you."

She leaned closer. "Just don't tell Tag, okay? It's not like I'm dumping him—I just need to focus on my career." She closed her cornflower blue eyes and then opened them again. "Actually, I *am* dumping him, but I'm really good at it so he won't even notice."

"Be gentle with him," I whispered. "He's pretty fragile."

I clapped and smiled while the first few couples performed and got their scores from the judges, but I didn't hear or see a thing. Ilya came over and stood behind me and rubbed my shoulders. I took deep breaths.

A guy dressed all in black led Ilya and me to opposite wings of the stage, and we stood there waiting for a while, maybe seconds, maybe centuries. I was too numb to tell. The male host introduced us again and we inched forward to our respective edges of the stage. It was like a bad board game. I just wanted one good throw of the dice, maybe double sixes, so I could get all the way home.

A tape began to play on huge flat-screen monitors scattered around the ballroom.

A close-up of me filled them all—messy hair, no makeup, a ter-rified look on my face. The camera pulled away to reveal my baggy T-shirt, which made my upper body look like a square box on top of the black legs of my yoga pants. I took a tottering step on my flesh-colored dancing shoes, as if I were learning to walk for the first time.

Ilya crossed the space between us with a wiry feline grace. He still looked like Felix the Cat with his white T-shirt, black jeans, vest, and sneakers, but mostly he looked like my friend Ilya.

Video Ilya held out his arms.

"Oh, please don't make me do this," Video Me said. I'd forgotten all about the audience until they burst into laughter.

The camera cut to Ilya putting his hand on my waist and me gig-gling, to the two of us attempting to waltz around and around our practice studio as I stepped on his toes repeatedly. Then it showed me with my arms up over my head, playing air tambourine and rocking out to an imaginary Grateful Dead song, and finally my last-ditch ef-fort to dig into my intro to tap repertoire and Shuffle Off to Buffalo.

While everybody applauded, I made eye contact with Ilya across the vast expanse of stage between us. He raised one eyebrow. You could look at it that twenty-three million people had just watched a clip of me at my lowest point, on one of the most embarrassing, over-whelming days of my life. Or you could look at it that I'd come a long way, baby.

The *Dancing With the Stars* orchestra filled the room with a big, bouncy rendition of "Smooth."

The real Ilya and I crossed the space between us.

And we danced. We did our front-back-chachachas, our turn-turn-chachachas, then we circled around and around the stage, covering every inch of it. We did our bumps and our grinds and we launched into our series of kicks. I hit every beat, sometimes a little bit too hard, sometimes not quite hard enough, but hey, I hit 'em. My adrenaline was pumping so intensely that I almost forgot and started singing along at the top of my lungs, just so all that energy had somewhere to go. Instead, I sent it back out into the universe through my arms and my legs and my hips.

There was a Martha Graham quote taped to our practice studio door. The famous one about how there is a life force that is translated through you into action, and because you're the only you in all time, this expression is unique. I got it now. I really, really got it. There was only one Deirdre Griffin and she was pretty spectacular. Maybe I'd spent most of my life as the family wallflower, but now I was a wallflower in *bloom*.

I'd never felt so alive.

Ilya scooped me up again and cha-cha-chaed me around the stage. He let go and danced away and before I knew it he was miming, *Hey, you, come here*. I launched into my three turns, and Ilya caught me without even having to dive for me.

"Outstanding," he whispered as the audience burst into applause.

38

You can spend all your time fishing,
or you can put it all into one big fish.

I saw my parents first. They were standing in front of their first-row seats wearing matching tie-dyed T-shirts that proclaimed DEIRDRE! "That's my daughter," my father boomed, his voice breaking through the applause.

"Way to go, sweetie!" my mother yelled.

When Tag took a step forward, I knew without even looking up at the huge flat-screen monitors that every camera was on him. He held out a big bouquet of flowers.

Ilya gave me a little push. "Go," he whispered.

I crossed the stage as gracefully as I could. Tag met me halfway. He handed me the flowers and then pulled me in for a hug.

"I'm sorry," he whispered. The applause had started up again, thunderous this time, and everyone in the audience was on their feet.

"You'd better be," I whispered.

"I got you a new fish to make it up to you."

My eyes teared up. "I don't want new fish. Even if you bought me the New England Aquarium, I want you to return it right now."

"You can spend all your time fishing," Tag whispered, "or you can put it all into one big fish."

He turned his head. I followed his gaze to the audience.

And then I saw Steve Moretti sitting next to my parents, smiling at me.

"Don't forget to write that one down, okay?" Tag whispered. "I can definitely use it."

Everybody waited while Ilya and I changed out of our costumes and into our street clothes after the show. I was starving, but it was a good hungry, a hungry that I'd earned.

We walked down the street together, stopping to talk to the line of reporters and paparazzi. Most of the questions were for Tag, but Ilya and I got a few good plugs in, too.

"Do you think your mother and I got on camera?" my father said as we continued down the street. "Not that I care, but it would mean a lot to our bowling team. They took the night off to watch."

"We'll have a family meeting as soon as we get back," my mother said. "To figure out who gets to come to the show next week."

"Your sisters," my father said, "are champing at the bit."

"For the record," Steve whispered as he held out my chair at the barbeque place, "those were my flowers."

"Hey, hey, hey," Tag said. "Who went to all that trouble to track you down? Who got you a front-row seat at the season premiere of *Dancing With the Stars*?"

I smiled at Steve. "Thank you. They're beautiful."

I unwrapped the florist paper and Steve asked the waiter to bring a pitcher of water.

He pointed. "That's blue star; it's actually an *Amsonia*. And that's an anemone called Pink Star. And these flashy ones are stargazer lilies. There's a bit of a theme, in case you didn't notice."

I smiled at him. "You're pretty amazing, Azalea Guy."

"You're pretty amazing yourself, Twinkle Toes. I had no idea you could dance like that."

"Ha," I said. "I couldn't. My dance partner gets all the credit."

Ilya beamed and looked up from checking his Facebook page on his laptop.

Across from us, my father hit the table with the palm of his hand. He shook his head. "A six? Give me a break. You were robbed. That judge needs to get his eyes examined."

My mother put her hand on his. "That's enough, Timmy. Let's focus on her two sevens."

"Those are solid numbers for the first week," Ilya said.

Tag leaned forward. "What will it take to get them up to eights?"

My mother pulled a piece of paper out of her pocket and held it out to Ilya. "I hope you don't mind, honey, but we've put together a little song list for you."

My father nodded. "I mean, nothing wrong with Santana, but they're not the Grateful Dead."

I saw my mother elbow Tag.

He stood up and walked over to me. "Can I talk to you outside for a minute?"

"What?" I said as I followed him out of the restaurant.

"Listen," Tag said when we got outside, "I need to apologize."

I rolled my eyes. "Yeah, right. You're only apologizing because Mom is making you."

Tag shook his head. "No way. Hey, for your information, not only did I track down Steve all by myself to make it up to you, but I flew him out here and brought him to the show."

"Really?"

"Really. And I not only apologized to *him*, but I gave him my blessing to date you."

"You *what*?" I buried my face in my hands. "Please, please tell me you didn't."

When I finally looked up, my brother was smiling, his fake white teeth lighting up the night.

"Kidding," he said.

"Jerk," I said.

"I know you are, but what am I?"

We shook our heads at each other.

"Anyway," Tag said, "I guess I never thought about how much you needed something that was all your own. Steve. The dance thing. And look, I really am sorry about your fish."

My eyes teared up. "Thank you."

We gave each other a hug and walked back into the restaurant together. My parents beamed their approval.

I slid into the seat beside Steve. He had a great big grin on his face.

"Be careful," I whispered. "Once my family gets its hooks into you, there's no escaping them."

"I'll take my chances," he whispered.

"Just one thing. Remember, back in Austin? What was that business proposal you had for Tag?"

Steve took a sip of wine before he answered. "Let's see, Tag asked me if I'd design a big hometown meditation garden so his fans had somewhere to commune when they came to pay tribute to him . . ."

He leaned a little closer. "You want the truth?"

I nodded.

"I figured he'd be a pain in the neck to work with, but I said yes anyway." Steve smiled. "Just so I could get to you."

"Hey, hey, hey," Tag said from the other end of the table. "You guys aren't talking about me over there, are you?"

I rolled my eyes. "I know you think the whole world revolves around you, Tag, but believe it or not, some things have absolutely nothing to do with you."

Tag reached for his beer. "Don't be ridiculous," he said.

Steve's phone rang. He pulled it out of his pocket and looked at the number.

"Hi," he said. "Sure, she's right here."

He grinned and mouthed *Joanie Baloney.*

I grabbed the phone from him. "How did you get this number?"

"I guess I must have made a copy when I wrote it down for you," Joanie Baloney said.

I shook my head. "I guess you must have."

"Well, it's a good thing I did. You don't think Tag could have gotten Steve there on his own, do you? Like he knows how to book a flight by himself. Oh, and good job tonight."

"Thanks," I said. "Okay, you can take over the event bookings. With all my new social-networking clients, including this new urban landscape designer I'm planning to reel in . . ."

I smiled at Steve. He smiled back.

". . . it's not like I'm going to have time for all of it anyway."

"Great," Joanie Baloney said. "When do I start?"

"I'll call you," I said. I found the Off button and handed Steve's phone back to him.

His fingers touched mine.

Our eyes met, and just for a moment I could almost picture not needing the rest of my twenty-eight first kisses.

Acknowledgments

A huge thank-you to my amazing readers for hanging out with me on Facebook and Twitter and helping me find my way into this book. Your kind words, never-ending encouragement, and great ideas make all the difference, and I truly can't thank you all enough—especially if I want to get my next-*next* novel written!

Sally Kim, editor-in-chief at Touchstone, had a million fans before she became my editor, and now she has a million and one. Many, many thanks to Sally for her sharp eye and even keel—working together has been a truly joyful experience. Another big thank-you to Touchstone's brilliantly creative marketing manager, Meredith Vilarello, to my wonderful publicist, Ashley Hewlett, to Allegra Ben-Amotz, Sally's terrific editorial assistant, and to Stacy Creamer, David Falk, Marcia Burch, Cherlynne Li, Linda Sawicki, and the rest of Team Touchstone, for getting behind *Wallflower* and me. I'm honored and oh-so-grateful to have your support.

Lisa Bankoff is simply the best literary agent in the world, and my gratitude knows no bounds. Thank you, thank you, and thank you again. Another big thank-you to the fabulous Dan Kirchen, Lisa's right-hand man, and to ICM's Josie Freedman and Liz Farrell, as well as to Helen Manders and Sheila Crowley at Curtis Brown, UK. I never forget for a moment how lucky I am to have you all in my literary life.

Thanks so much to all my friends at the incomparable Lake Austin

Spa Resort, especially to Robbie Hudson for being such a gift to authors and readers and to Trisha Shirey for answering a New Englander's questions about Austin gardening.

When Hurricane Irene knocked out the power for four crucial days during revisions on this novel, my friends at the South Shore YMCA kindly charged my laptop while I took a few much-needed spins on the Cybex Arc Trainer. Thank you!

Many thanks to my fiction co-op for creating a virtual watercooler. Your honesty and generosity have made a big difference in my life.

A great big thank-you to the booksellers, librarians, bloggers, and members of the media who continue to support this midlife career of mine. Being a novelist is the best gig ever, and I wouldn't have it without you.

Finally and forever, thanks to my incredible family—especially Jake, Garet, and Kaden—for always being there.

ABOUT THE AUTHOR

CLAIRE COOK wrote her first novel in her minivan when she was forty-five. At fifty, she walked the red carpet at the Hollywood premiere of the adaptation of her second novel, *Must Love Dogs*, starring Diane Lane and John Cusack. She is now the critically acclaimed and best-selling author of nine novels, and divides her time between the suburbs of Atlanta and Boston. She shares writing and reinvention tips at Facebook.com/ClaireCookauthorpage and Twitter (@ClaireCookwrite), and at www.ClaireCook.com.